W9-BWO-304

WITHDRAWN

SILO
AND THE
REBEL
RAIDERS

SILO
AND THE
REBEL
RAIDERS

V. PEYTON

DELACORTE PRESS

Text copyright © 2015 by V. Peyton
Jacket art copyright © 2015 by Iacopo Bruno

Visit us on the Web! randomhousekids.com

Educators and librarians, for a variety of teaching tools, visit us at RHTeachersLibrarians.com

Library of Congress Cataloging-in-Publication Data
Names: Peyton, V. (Veronica), author.
Title: Silo and the Rebel Raiders / V. Peyton.
Other titles: Silo the seer
Description: First U.S. edition. | New York : Delacorte Press [2016] |
Originally published in the United Kingdom by Corgi Books in 2015 under title:
Silo the seer. | Summary: A ten-year-old boy who can see the future is recruited by the Capitol to help keep the people safe.
Identifiers: LCCN 2015043617 (print) | LCCN 2016019671 (ebook) |
ISBN 978-0-399-55241-0 (hc) | ISBN 978-0-399-55242-7 (ebk)
Subjects: | CYAC: Extrasensory perception—Fiction. | Science fiction.
Classification: LCC PZ7.1.P515 Si 2016 (print) | LCC PZ7.1.P515 (ebook) |
DDC [Fic]—dc23

The text of this book is set in 11.5-point Goudy.

Printed in the United States of America
10 9 8 7 6 5 4 3 2 1
First U.S. Edition

To Colin Murray

SILO
AND THE
REBEL
RAIDERS

THE ISLAND

Silo Zyco, Thirteenth Chronicle Keeper for the Islanders, took pen in hand and prepared to make his last-but-one entry. The Chronicles were 350 years old and Silo was ten. But although he often distrusted old things—most adults and the Ancients, to name but two—he was proud to be Chronicle Keeper. They were the only books he had, and he knew them by heart. The first entry of the first volume was written on 1 April 113 and read:

> *On this day we four families—Beans, Mudfords, Pattles, and Zycos—arrived here at this lonely island in the marsh in the hope that we might live here in peace and security, and that by our honest labor build here a community that ages to come shall marvel at.*

Well, they had certainly achieved that, thought Silo,

although perhaps not in the way they had hoped. The peace and security had been a bit optimistic too. He skimmed through years 113 to 213, reading random entries:

Fires on the western horizon. The Uplands are burning.

A great flood. Many houses destroyed.

Died today, Brian Bean, aged thirty-two. Killed by Elmo Zyco over Eel Rights.

The mud fever has returned.

Today the lookout tower was struck by lightning.

And so on for 250 years: the story of lives lived on the margins, of years of hardship when fish and eels were scarce, of floods and drownings and mysterious diseases, violent deaths, family feuds, and the treachery of Uplanders. These were the contents of the Chronicles. The very books themselves told a story, for the first Chronicle was a handsome volume with smooth white pages, while the most recent book was made of ragged gray sheets roughly stitched together. Silo drew it toward him, dipped his quill, and wrote a new entry in small neat writing, as clear as print. Previous Chronicle Keepers had sometimes been chatty or long-winded, and one had included some bad poems about geese, but there were only a dozen pages left, so Silo kept it short:

20 April 366: Today the government inspector arrived.

Of course, it was early morning still, and it hadn't happened yet. The inspectors turned up about once every five years, and Silo dearly hoped that they would come today, because if they did, it would prove beyond a shadow of a doubt that he was a seer.

To be a seer was to have a rare and precious gift. Seers could see into the future, and a good one would have a glorious career in the Capital. There had been many famous and successful seers in the past, legendary figures whose achievements were still talked about. Elmore Davis had saved hundreds of lives when he predicted raging fires in the Western Wilds. Emma Aberdeen's seeings had kept the whole north coast warned of storms and tidal waves for almost thirty years. Chelsea Payne had seen the Great Crab Pox Epidemic of 308, and the whole Capital was evacuated in time to prevent a terrible disaster. Silo wished to be counted among their number, but the problem was, he wasn't sure if he was a very good seer, let alone a great one. He often saw pictures in his mind that didn't seem to belong there, but he had to admit that his mind could be a messy place at times. But last night he had seen, as clear as day, two horsemen approaching from the Uplands. It was a seeing—not a very impressive one, perhaps, but he was sure his gift would improve with time. Silo stared moodily at the entry in the Chronicles for a moment, then stood up with sudden determination. The inspector would come today, and Silo would be ready for him.

Silo's hut was the same one that had always belonged to the Chronicle Keepers. It was a modest two-story building, with the ground floor used for smoking eels, and the whole place smelled strongly of them, as indeed did Silo himself. The top floor was his home, where he lived alone, an oblong room without much in it. He wrote the Chronicles on a table that stood against one of the short walls beneath the only window. A hammock was slung from the beams at the other end, and there was a bucket to catch drips from a leak in the roof, which doubled as a useful fresh water supply. It had rained in the night and the bucket was nearly full. Silo stared glumly at his reflection for a moment—black hair, white face, blue eyes—then plunged his head in, and from there progressed to other parts of his body until he had had a thorough wash. He wanted to look his best. Clothes were a problem, though, as Islanders dressed differently from Uplanders. Islanders had a great deal of wet and muddy work—eel trapping, duck hunting, reed cutting, fishing, and so forth—and they found it convenient to dress with extreme simplicity, and occasionally not at all. They went barefoot, and both men and women wore a sleeveless knee-length garment resembling a sack. Silo possessed two of these, and both were actually made of sacks, roughly taken in to fit his small body and with holes cut for his head and arms.

He chose the one without *cabbage* written on it and pulled it on. He tied a belt of knotted cord around his waist and hung his knife on one side and his slingshot on the other. This morning he would be leaving the safety of the marsh and wanted to be prepared in case he met a zoo animal. Silo put on his cloak and slung his bow and a quiver of arrows over his shoulder, then hesitated for a moment over his boots. He had inherited the characteristic webbed feet of the Zyco family, long-toed and rather large for the rest of him, but his boots were larger still. He decided to stuff the toes with rags and carry them. He would put them on just before he met the inspector. Uplanders noticed things like boots, or the lack of them.

Silo stepped out into the damp morning air and walked along the alley running steeply downhill to the dock. It was early and not many people were stirring yet, but Boris Bean yelled from an upstairs window, "Zyco the psycho, going for a hike-o!" Silo decided to ignore him, for this morning he had more important things on his mind. He reached the quay and the lonely expanse of the marsh spread out before him, stretching flat and bleak beneath a leaden sky. At high tide all this would be awash but now, at low water, little islands were surrounded by mud with only bright threads of water trickling through the wider channels. Between the marsh and the open sea lay the great sweep of the Causeway, a huge seawall that dated back hundreds of years to the time of the Ancients. Once it must have led all the way to the Island, but it had broken many years ago, before the first entry to the Chronicles was written, and now the muddy brown waters of Goose Creek lay between them.

Hitched to the foot of the jetty was Silo's prize possession, a tiny raft made of driftwood. Like all the Island children he was at home on the water, and he sent it skimming over the ruffled waters of Goose Creek with sure strokes of his paddle, balanced as delicately as a cat. The salt wind tugged at his tattered clothing and then the first drops of rain, big as coins, pitted the surface of the creek. He secured his raft to the end of the Causeway and squelched and scrambled his way to the top and onto the broad track that curved away to the Uplands four miles distant. Silo pulled his cloak over his head and padded forth, with only the slop of the waves and the cry of the marsh birds for company. There was a solitary tree at the end of the Causeway, the only one in all the marsh, but it was long dead, killed by a lightning strike, and had been lopped for firewood so that its stunted branches reached to the sky like the fingers of a mangled hand. It marked the end of the marsh and the beginning of the Uplands and stood all alone in the bleak landscape. When Silo finally reached it he wormed his back into a deep scar in its trunk, and there, partially protected from the rain, he put on his boots and settled down to wait.

They came a few hours later from the low hills to the south. The first in sight was a small hairy brown man on a small hairy brown horse. Silo dimly remembered him from their last visit five years ago. He was followed by a man he didn't recognize but who must surely be the inspector himself, a lean and miserable-looking man, splendidly dressed and riding a much larger horse. Following up behind was an enormous white horse that was hairy of leg, mighty of belly, and loaded with baggage. The horses impressed Silo. The Islanders kept no animals because the damp climate of the marsh was disagreeable to them (*4 September 114: Left today, Mill Mudford's dog, Lucky. Swam to the Uplands*), and Silo thought horses awesome creatures.

The inspector was complaining to the hairy brown man: "Are you sure this is the right road, Ruddle? It leads straight into a swamp."

"Yes, sir. There's a swamp right enough, but the Island is actually in the swamp."

Silo thought it was time to make his presence known.

"It's not a swamp, it's a marsh," he said, then added, "I came to meet you."

The inspector eyed Silo. He saw an undersized bony boy with black hair and a white face. With his pointed chin and ears he looked a little like an elf, a moody one, and he had bright, very blue eyes of an unnatural intensity. The inspector had the uneasy feeling that the boy was looking not just at him, but also at the contents of his head and something several miles behind him. He shifted his gaze and noticed that Silo was wearing a sack, bristled with weaponry, and had unusually large feet for his size. He smelled of something the inspector could not quite place but made him wonder how long it would be until dinner.

"Hello, son." The man called Ruddle reined in his horse and smiled, revealing a mouthful of rotten teeth. "And who might you be?"

"My name is Silo Zyco. I'm a seer, Thirteenth Chronicle Keeper for the Islanders, and I know how to make coffee out of seaweed." Silo wanted to make a good impression and he mentioned this last because it was an unusual accomplishment for a ten-year-old—or anyone, for that matter.

"You're very young to be Chronicle Keeper, aren't you?" said the inspector coolly.

"I'm ten."

"But surely that's a job for an adult?"

Silo hesitated before replying. He suspected that the inspector held the usual Uplander's view of the Islanders—that they were a backward and uneducated race—and it was rather difficult to explain things without proving him right.

"The adults on the Island mostly don't read and write too well. The old teacher was Miss Mudford and . . . well, they say she was good once, but she got the mud fever and it settled on her brain. After that the things she taught were"—Silo struggled to find the exact word for the nature of Miss Mudford's teachings—"unusual."

"And so who taught you?"

"Ryker. He was an Uplander. He was good. That's why the young ones can read and write better than the old ones."

"An Uplander?" The inspector made a sweeping gesture that took in mile upon mile of mud and marsh. "Why would an Uplander come to live in a place like this?"

Silo shrugged. They'd all wondered about that.

"And why did you come to meet us?"

Silo stated the obvious. "To prove I'm a seer. If I'd waited until you got to the Island and then said I knew you were coming, you'd think I was lying."

The inspector nodded and nudged his horse forward. The interview was at an end and had not gone as well as Silo had hoped. Ruddle gave him a friendly wink as they moved off down the Causeway, and when he thought they were out of earshot the inspector spoke, but his words blew back on the wind:

"These Islanders, Ruddle—who appoints a ten-year-old as Chronicle Keeper? And what kind of person teaches a child to make coffee out of seaweed?"

As he plodded after them Silo thought fondly of Ryker, who had taught him to make coffee out of seaweed, and blessed whatever quirk of fate had led him to the Island.

Ryker had arrived one day about five years ago. Ben Mudford was manning the lookout tower and rang the signal bell to warn of visitors, so when Ryker arrived there was quite a crowd waiting for him. His little boat was full of water and he was bailing furiously. He nearly made it but not quite. A few yards from the quay the boat lurched and he stood up, revealing himself to be a long lean man of unusual height dressed in Uplander clothes. As he stood the boat sank beneath him and he descended smoothly into the waters of Goose Creek, finally coming to rest with it up to his chin. His long dark hair and beard swirled about his head and he fixed the assembled crowd with shining brown eyes.

"Good morning, Marshlanders. Any chance of breakfast?"

And that evening a new entry appeared in the Chronicles, written in the uncertain hand of one of Miss Mudford's students:

2 November 361: Today arrived RykR, UplandR and strangR on a 6-weak vizit.

The six-week visit had been touch and go to begin with. The Islanders were naturally curious to know what he was doing there. But he wouldn't exactly say. When he mentioned, over a breakfast of eels, that it just seemed a nice place to visit they felt doubtful; when he went on to speak of the joys of the fresh sea air, the beauty of the marsh, and the pleasures of solitude they became downright suspicious, fearing they were harboring a Raider or a tax evader or something worse. Allman Bean, the village headman, told him he must leave by nightfall. Ryker made no immediate objection but presently he mentioned, in a casual way, that he knew how to make coffee out of seaweed. Headman Bean thought intently. It came hard to him as he was not a clever man, but he was one who enjoyed a spot of coffee, and coffee-making was a lost art on the Island (*21 March 350: Died today, coffee-maker Morris Mudford aged 70, of mud fever*).

"Seaweed, hmm? Who would have thought it possible?" A long pause. "And so how long does it take to make, this coffee of yours?"

"If this mild weather continues, and given a plentiful supply of bladder wrack, and peat for roasting, I could have it ready in six weeks."

Six weeks it was, then, and next morning Ryker was gathering seaweed at the tide line.

He used his six weeks wisely. He made himself an expert on Eel Rights. He took over the Chronicle keeping and village accounts, discovering that the Uplanders were overcharging the Islanders for almost everything. He made a new flood-warning system, a magnificent wooden horn powered by bellows that could be heard all over the marsh, and fixed it on top of the lookout tower. Ben Mudford was delighted and caused widespread panic when he tested it unexpectedly one night.

Finally the coffee was ready for Headman Bean and a couple of his brothers to test. They drank; they clutched their throats. Their eyes bulged, then streamed with tears, and they uttered small cries of distress. But then, puzzlingly, the Beans recovered themselves and called for a second cup, and then a third and even a fourth. It seemed that the taste was unpleasant but the results satisfactory, and from that day on Ryker stayed on the Island.

Now he turned his attention to the school, or rather lack of it, for Miss Mudford (she of the unusual teachings) had taken to spending long hours on the dock peering into the murky waters below, and occasionally shouting abusive words at the mudfish that gathered there. Ryker tactfully suggested that, as she was a busy woman, he could help her by teaching the occasional class. The proposal pleased her, and from then on Ryker spent his mornings teaching while she spent hers insulting fish, an arrangement that seemed to give pleasure to both.

Silo had been neglecting his education, but with Ryker teaching he drifted back to school and found it a better experience than he remembered, for Ryker had the gift of making classes interesting, especially when he told them about the Uplands and beyond. The Islanders always spoke of the Island as if it were the only one in the world, but now Silo learned that it was but one of many in the Kingdom Isles. There were islands inhabited by savage zoo animals, islands where Raiders lurked, but biggest of them all was Mainland. Ryker sketched it in mud on the classroom wall, and the Island itself, which had previously seemed like the whole world to Silo, turned out to be the merest dot on its eastern coastline.

He told them about the Capital, home to the Government and its inspectors. The Capital was the hub of Mainland and all its satellite islands, and once it had been a great city of the Ancients and then, at the dawn of their own age, in Year One, it had become the center of government for all the Kingdom Isles. The buildings of the Ancients still stood there in all their glory, including the great Lion and Unicorn Towers, set on a hilltop, encircled by city walls and bordered by the mighty river Rampage on its long run to the sea.

Whereas once Silo's future had seemed bleak and predictable, after lessons with Ryker, he now sensed his destiny. He would go to the Capital and use his powers as a seer to save it from dangers yet unknown, earning the gratitude of its people and the Government. He would become a great man and live his days in comfort, forever free of floods and famine, and he would never eat another eel as long as he lived. Silo Zyco, Seer and Savior, Hero of the People, Eel-Spurner.

Silo mentioned his plans to Ryker, but Ryker wasn't as enthusiastic as he had hoped. He just looked thoughtful.

"Well, I always assumed you'd end up at the Capital one day," he had said. "You're the restless, ambitious type, and restless ambition and marshes don't mix. But wait a while. You've a lot to learn still. The Capital can be a dangerous place for strangers."

As he trailed the inspector and Ruddle down the Causeway he heard the great horn on the lookout tower bellowing out across the marsh, jerking him out of his thoughts. *Moooo-OOH, moooo-OOH, moooo-OOH.* It sounded like a cow, albeit a large and furious one. Ben Mudford had spotted the visitors approaching and was blasting out the news. By now the Islanders would be out fishing, and Silo imagined the quick flurry of activity as they upped oars and cast loose rafts and the whole fleet hastened back, converging on the Island from all points of the compass. He quickened his own pace and presently the familiar mound of the Island loomed through the rain.

He knew, however, that the Government was always on the lookout for seers who could warn the nation of impending disaster. If only he could convince the inspector that he was a genuine seer, he could hitch a ride to the Capital with him. If all went to plan, Silo wouldn't be seeing the Island again for a long time and he felt a sudden affection for it, for it was no ordinary island. In the time of the Ancients a huge building had stood here and the houses of the Islanders clustered upon the ruins like barnacles on a rock. Most were tumbledown two-story huts made of mud and driftwood, topped with a reed thatch and jostling each other in the steep maze of narrow alleyways that made up the village. The Island was encircled by a clutter of jetties and huts perched out over the water on stilts. The biggest of these structures was the communal toilets. Silo hoped that the inspector would be impressed, but he thought it a little doubtful somehow. He untied his raft and paddled across to the Island, struggling to make way against the incoming tide.

When Silo docked, the village was deserted, and he headed to the meeting hall. It stood at the top of the alley and was the largest building on the Island, perched on its highest point and dwarfing the little rain-sodden huts around it. It was topped by a steeply pitched roof, then the lookout tower and a big weather vane shaped like a mudfish. Silo passed beneath its shadow and crept onto the porch. He wanted to enter unobserved, if possible, so he peered through a knothole in the door to judge what stage the meeting had arrived at.

The whole village was gathered. Everyone looked a little

cleaner and tidier than usual, and those who had boots were wearing them. The inspector sat at a table at the end of the hall with the current volume of the Chronicles open before him amid a litter of papers. Headman Bean paced the floor in front of the table. He was an unfortunate choice for headman, but he was oldest of the Beans, the largest by far of the Island families, and Beans always voted for Beans. They took up the whole right-hand side of the hut, a blondish family with doughy faces and eyes set a little too far apart. The Pattles and the Mudfords sat to the left. They would have liked Ben Mudford as headman, but he always came in a few votes too short.

Headman Bean was speaking. ". . . So now that we've finished the tax stuff, let's get on to seers. We know the Government's always on the lookout for them, and we happen to have one on the Island." Silo paused with his hand on the door. It was sometimes useful to know what people said about you when they thought you weren't there. But Headman Bean's next words were: "Step forward, Boris, where the inspector can see you. Boris has predicted all kinds of things. He's a first-rate seer."

This was news to Silo. Boris was Headman Bean's son, he of this morning's "Zyco the psycho" taunt. He was many things—Silo's least favorite person, his parents' pride and joy, and the worst student Ryker had ever taught—but Silo was positive he wasn't a seer. The inspector looked doubtful too. He gave Boris a hard stare and then addressed the Islanders. "Is this true?"

The Bean family nodded, but the Mudfords and Pattles

sat in pointed silence. The inspector sighed and drew a weary hand across his face. "So you're a seer. I suppose you'd better tell us what you've seen."

Boris glanced around to make sure he had their undivided attention, then raised his eyes to the roof beam and spoke in a high, unnatural voice. "I see a vision from the future. I see a beautiful walled city on a hill. In the middle are two tall towers. One has a lion on top and the other has a unicorn."

"That would be the Capital, I suppose," said the inspector, "but it can't be the future. The Unicorn Tower burned down last autumn."

"They have rebuilt it, more beautiful than ever," said Boris, showing an unexpected quickness of wit.

"What else?"

Boris frowned, and a look of horror passed over his face. "The Capital is in danger! I see thousands of ships—Raiders' ships—sailing in from the west—"

The inspector cut him off. "The west is mostly turnip fields. You do know that the Capital is thirty miles inland, don't you?"

Boris was silenced. Apparently not. Behind the door Silo allowed himself a rare smile of satisfaction.

The inspector gave Boris a dirty look and waved him back to his seat. "On the subject of seers—you have a Chronicle Keeper called Silo Zyco. He knew we were coming this morning. He wrote it in the Chronicles and he met us at the end of the Causeway. Did you have news here that we were coming?"

The Islanders muttered and shook their heads.

"Interesting. And has Silo predicted anything else? Something that actually happened?"—this with a dark glance at Boris.

There followed what seemed to Silo a long, long silence, and then finally Lula Pattle said, "He knows when the geese are coming. Every year."

Her mother, Emma, backed her up. "Most of us here think Silo's a seer." Crouching behind the door, Silo felt a glow of pride. "It's not just the geese. He knows when the eels are going to spawn and when the seals will arrive at the point. He's predicted storms a few times . . ." Emma paused. "And then there's that thing that happened at the Hump."

The thing that happened at the Hump: the day Silo knew for certain that he was a seer. It was the day his life changed forever: 11 June 362.

WHAT HAPPENED
AT THE HUMP

Silo had been six in 362. His history, as recorded in the Chronicles, was not only short but tragic. The first entry read:

> *29 February 356: Born today a boy, Silo. Mother Zenda*
> *Zyco. Father a mystery.*

Five years later an epidemic of marsh sickness swept the Island and his mother's name was listed among the victims, so the rest of the Zycos had taken on his upkeep and, in Silo's opinion, were making a wretched job of it. He found himself hustled from hut to hut, a month here, six weeks there, and never made to feel welcome anywhere. Over the years his family had acquired a reputation for being a shifty, antisocial crew: violent, rude, argumentative, and much inclined to borrow things without asking—or steal, as the other Islanders more simply called it. Having studied the Chronicles, Silo was privy to 350 years of history in which the Zycos were recorded doing all that and worse:

> *25 May 299: Died today, Ray Bean, aged 11. Pushed into a whirlpool by Otto Zyco.*

(Although in this case justice had been swift for the next day's entry read: *Died today: Otto Zyco, aged 13. Struck on head with spade by Ollie Bean.*)

However, in the winter of 361/362 things had come to a head and the whole Zyco family had moved to the Hump. The Hump was about a half mile distant from the Island, a soggy mound that protruded from the marsh like a half-submerged whale, and the Chronicle was vague as to the reasons—*Today the whole Zyco family moved to the Hump after a big row*—but Silo found it a change for the worse. The reed huts the Zycos built on the Hump were damp and uncomfortable, and to avoid it, he now started spending his evenings at the dock where, weather permitting, groups of Islanders would gather to discuss the events of the day. Ryker often produced small packets of fish or smoked eels, neatly wrapped in seaweed, from one of his many pockets and passed them absently to Silo, for food was often short in the Zyco family.

On the morning of 11 June he left the Hump early—much too early for school, but he had his reasons. Just then he was staying with a particularly ill-tempered uncle who had neglected to feed him the night before. Silo had found a fried eel the uncle was saving for breakfast and, in the time-honored tradition of the Zyco family, he had borrowed it without asking—eaten it, in fact—and he wanted to be clear of the Hump before it was noticed. Ben waved to him from the lookout tower as he nosed his raft into the waters of Goose Creek. Half a dozen Mudfords were digging for bait worms, and a little fleet of rafts was setting off for the reed beds. And then Silo saw something impossible. A huge gray wall of water rose up in his mind and smashed down on the peaceful marsh like a fist, shattering rafts and whirling away Mudfords like matchsticks.

He blinked and the world settled slowly into place again like grains of sand in a swirled glass. But it had been a seeing and the birds knew what he knew, for the marsh behind him suddenly exploded in a flurry of wings as thousands of ducks and waders took to the sky, crying and wheeling aimlessly across the marsh in great ragged flocks. Something dreadful was going to happen, and soon. Silo dug his paddle into the water and shot out into Goose Creek, screaming at the distant figure in the lookout tower, "Ben! Sound the flood warning! The FLOOD WARNING!" But his voice was lost in the wind. He saw Ben standing stock-still on the tower watching him and the wheeling birds, and in desperation he threw down his paddle and mimed the vigorous pumping of bellows. Ben understood. Within a moment the great horn was bellowing out over the marsh. The rafts stopped, spun in midstream, and started back to the Island. Silo stabbed at the water with his paddle and powered the raft forward with all his strength, for he felt an overwhelming sense of danger. The very air seemed to crackle with it despite the still waters of the creek and the peace of the morning. Silo looked westward to the open sea and saw nothing but calm waters to the horizon, serene under a clear sky. But then the horizon seemed to ripple. It was no longer flat but bulging here and there, and then suddenly there was no horizon at all but just a single great wave higher than any wave had a right to be, a wall of gray water topped with flying spray that came surging inland at terrifying speed.

The raft men had reached the Island and were joining the mass of people running uphill to the surest place of safety— the great meeting hall on the highest point of dry land. Silo put in a last desperate effort to reach the dock and run up the hill. Looking behind him, Silo saw the great wave thunder over the Causeway and surge up Goose Creek; then it struck the Island with a deep boom and he saw, in an explosion of white water, whole rows of houses shiver and shatter under the impact and then be swept away with a grinding roar. It came boiling up the Island, its surface churning with shattered timbers, uprooted jetties, and great swaths of seaweed ripped from the ocean floor. The little houses on either side of the alley shuddered as it swept higher and higher and then, finally, it drew back with a long hissing roar, leaving a ragged trail of destruction in its wake.

Silo was silent, looking out to the Hump, or rather where the Hump used to be, for now there was nothing visible there but a solid sheet of stormy foam-flecked water.

At noon that day, when the waters had started to recede, a group of Mudfords took the big raft out. All day long they poled slowly back and forth across the flooded marsh, but of the Zycos there was no trace, all but one having been seemingly swept from the face of the Earth. Silo found his own raft in the remains of someone's bedroom and spent all day on the water, retrieving bits and pieces of people's houses and towing them back to the Island, trip after trip from noon to sunset. He wanted to be too busy to think. He knew that his warning had saved lives, but he had been unable to help his own family, and the knowledge haunted him. Though they had been an unlovely crew they were all he had, and he felt he had failed them miserably. And he realized that he was also homeless. After tying off his raft, he stood undecided for a moment, then headed slowly uphill to find the only person who, like himself, had no family to call his own: Ryker. He found him crouched over a smoking fire outside the Chronicle Keeper's hut and poking at a pot of eels.

"Silo, you're just in time for supper," he said. "Go on up"—this with a grand sweeping gesture to the rickety steps up to the door of the hut. When Silo went in he saw that the table was set for two and that an extra hammock had been slung from the beams, and felt an immense sense of gratitude.

"I would have invited you before," said Ryker, coming in behind him with the pot of eels, "but your family were dead set against it. They seemed to think I wanted to get my hands on your Eel Rights."

"Do I have Eel Rights?" This was unexpected.

"Your mother owned the Eel Rights to Mud Island. She left them to you when she died."

Mud Island was a hump with a ruined hut on it, the loneliest spot on the whole marsh. It seemed a deeply depressing thing to inherit.

"Didn't they mention it to you? I'm surprised."

Silo wasn't. It seemed typical of his family. And now, he supposed, he would inherit all the Zycos' Eel Rights, together with their dark reputation.

That night Ryker made a new entry in the Chronicles: *Missing, presumed drowned* ... and here followed a list of forty names, all of them Zycos. *Sole survivor, Silo Zyco.*

Silo Zyco, the last of the Zycos, son of Zenda, son of mystery, Sole Survivor. It seemed he had been born under a dark star, and that misfortune dogged him like a shadow.

Thus did he come to live with Ryker. Ryker was not a talkative man, but then Silo was not a talkative boy. Where Ryker came from remained a mystery. He never talked about his past, and Silo, a natural respecter of privacy, never asked him about it—though he did begin to have his suspicions, for in time he discovered something about Ryker that no one else knew.

Ryker had never adopted the Islanders' casual attitude about dress. He retained his Uplander clothes, his shirt and breeches and jacket growing tattier and more patched as time passed, and one day while Ryker was washing his shirt Silo had seen an ugly mark branded across his shoulder. The burned flesh was raised in lumpy red scars and spelled out four letters, crimson against his pale skin: SOUP. It had been stamped there deliberately, presumably by people who had a powerful dislike of Ryker, for the process must have been horribly painful. So Ryker had enemies and was perhaps even a criminal of some kind. Given Ryker's good nature, Silo couldn't believe it was a very serious kind, but it did explain his long residence on the marsh, and Silo came to believe that Ryker stayed on the Island because he was a wanted man, hunted through the Uplands by unknown enemies.

Silo felt comforted by this evidence of Ryker's outcast status because, ever since the tidal wave, he had felt a bit of an outcast himself. He had never been popular—he was, after all, a Zyco—but since that day he had noticed a subtle change in the Islanders' behavior toward him. The other children mostly avoided him now, and even a few of the adults. He had somehow turned into a creature of ill omen. But worse was to come:

> *4 January 366: Died today Ryker, teacher and Chronicle*
> *Keeper, age unknown.*
> *Mistaken for a muskrat and shot in the eye by Vernon*
> *Bean.*

It was Silo's first entry as Chronicle Keeper and written in his most beautiful handwriting, but blurred a little here and there by tears. Silo very rarely cried, for his short life had taught him there was little profit in it, but on that occasion he had been unable to help himself.

Ryker had been out duck hunting and was lying flat on one of the little reed-fringed islands, wrapped in a length of muddy sacking for camouflage. Vernon Bean was out hunting too and, seeing Ryker's dark hair and whiskers protruding from behind a tussock, had let fly an arrow and killed him instantly. Despite Vernon's noisy remorse, Silo cursed him from the bottom of his heart and was sorely tempted to add "an idiot" after his name in the Chronicle entry, but Ryker was dead, and nothing he wrote or did could change that awful truth.

That had been almost four months ago, and the beginning of the worst times that Silo could remember. Life had become lonely and cheerless. Now not only his entire family but even the man who had taken him in had died sudden and violent deaths, and an aura of bad luck hung over him like a cloud. Silo Zyco, Death-Bringer, Family-Killer, Hoarder of Eel Rights.

But today the inspector had come. Standing in the shadows outside the meeting hall, Silo prayed that he would whisk him off to the Uplands, the Capital, or beyond: somewhere far away from the Island to a place where no one knew him and he could shrug off his miserable past like a snake shedding its skin. Emma Pattle had just finished telling the story of the great wave and its aftermath, and the inspector was making the exact same comment that certain members of the Bean family had: "I'm surprised he didn't think to warn his family." Silo scowled.

"There wasn't time," said Emma, then added, "Besides, they weren't the sort to listen."

"You are claiming, then," said the inspector, "that this boy can accurately predict the arrival of birds, beasts, fish, and floods. Let's put it to the vote. All those of you who think Silo Zyco is a seer will raise your right hand."

All the Mudfords and Pattles raised their hands, and most of the Beans too, until they noticed that their headman was sitting with his arms moodily crossed, then hurriedly put them down again.

"I take that to be a majority vote," said the inspector. "Where is Silo Zyco?"

Silo pushed open the door and stepped into the hall.

"Silo Zyco," he said, "your community believes you to be a seer. As you no doubt know, the Government has an interest in seers. Therefore, you will accompany us to the Capital, where your abilities will be examined by the relevant authorities."

There was a sudden buzz of excitement in the hut, but he silenced it with an upraised hand.

"It is your duty to name the next Chronicle Keeper, and I suggest you would be wise to choose an older person."

"Lula Pattle," said Silo without hesitation. Lula was eleven and had been one of Ryker's best students. She had an identical twin sister, equally clever, called Lily. Lula and Lily did everything together, and Silo was sure that between them they would do a good job.

"Meeting dismissed."

The Islanders stood up and headed for the door, everyone talking at once. It was the first time in recorded history that an Islander had been summoned to the Capital, and a crowd of Mudfords and Pattles gathered around to congratulate him, among them Lula, who shot him a look of radiant gratitude. Silo felt dazed by the success of his plan. He escaped from his well-wishers as soon as he politely could.

Silo went back to his hut and made his last entry.

> *I, Silo Zyco, was accepted as a seer and will accompany the inspector to the Capital.*

As he finished, there was a knock at the door and Lula and Lily Pattle edged their way into the room. Lily, Silo was happy to see, was carrying a plate containing a seaweed dumpling. They and their family were his next-door neighbors, and their mother, Emma, had often sent him plates of food since Ryker's death.

"Oh, Silo," said Lula, "thank you so much for making us—I mean, *me*—Chronicle Keeper. Mum and Dad are so pleased! We've come so you can show us—I mean, *me*—what to do . . ."

". . . and we've brought you a dumpling," said Lily.

"Thanks." Silo speared it with the tip of his knife and pushed the tools of the Chronicle Keeper's trade across the table: a bundle of goose-quill pens, a bottle of squid ink, and the precious book itself.

"Everything you write in the Chronicles must be true, and the hut goes with the job. Good luck with it."

"We get the hut?" Lula and Lily beamed at him.

Silo recalled that the twins had six younger brothers and sisters and that the Pattles' house was rather a small one.

"Thanks, Silo! This is brilliant." Lula and Lily lunged in at the same time, and both gave him great hugs and kissed him on the top of the head. Silo blushed scarlet, and at just that moment the door swung open to reveal Ruddle, guide to the government inspector.

"Saying good-bye to your little girlfriends, then?" He smiled what was probably meant as a friendly smile but, given the state of his teeth, was actually rather terrifying. Lula and Lily uttered small screams and scurried past him into the night. With as much dignity as he could muster, Silo waited for Ruddle to tell him why he was there. But Ruddle was in no hurry. He was a sturdy little man with unkempt brown and gray hair, which grew thickly from his scalp, chin, and ears. Set within its hairy frame, his face had a battered, weather-beaten appearance. His eyes were brown, as were his teeth, and he wore layer upon layer of patched, dung-colored clothing.

"Don't you worry, son—there's plenty of pretty girls in the Capital," he said at last; then, "So you're a seer, are you? A rare ability, that, but then you specialize in rare abilities, don't you? You mentioned earlier that you knew how to make coffee out of seaweed."

Now Silo knew. He reached for a jug of evil-smelling liquid under the table, filled a cleanish cup, and handed it to Ruddle. Ruddle peered into its oily depths, and for a fleeting moment a look of doubt crossed his hairy features, but then he tossed it back in a single gulp. It had the usual effect. He beat the table with his fists. He choked, tears ran from his eyes, and his whole body shook with powerful spasms. And then the power of speech returned to him.

"So you're a seer. There's lots that say they are, but the genuine item—now, that's very rare. Word's got around that the Government wants 'em, you see, and there's lots of people who want to go to the Capital and get a government job. That lad at the meeting, for instance—what a pack of lies! But then it stands to reason a swamp boy like him wouldn't know anything about the big city. Best to stick to things you know, isn't it, son?"

Here he winked at Silo and raised his empty cup, which Silo dutifully refilled.

"Geese, now, and eels and seals and floods. I dare say a smart boy like you, living in a place like this, knows all sorts about them. And the people here, they're . . . quite simple people, shall we say—maybe the kind of people that a smart boy could fool. So nice work, son. I'd like to know how you found out about us coming, though."

Ruddle smiled his unsettling smile and rose, a little unsteadily, to his feet. "I thank you for the coffee, and be sure you're ready early tomorrow. The inspector's in a hurry to leave. He's no great man for swamps, and eels don't agree with him."

He lurched out, leaving Silo puzzling over his words. Ruddle obviously thought he was a liar but seemed to have been congratulating him on being a good one. And then there was another knock at the door.

This time it was Ben Mudford, keeper of the lookout tower. Silo liked Ben for the simple reason that Ben had always been kind to him, and he had happy memories of the hours they had spent together at the top of the tower, staring out to sea. Ben was good at silence, but tonight it seemed he had something important to say.

"Well, Silo, you'll be leaving us tomorrow, but there's something I have to tell you before you go. She said I'd know when the time came and I think it has."

His tanned face flushed slightly. "I liked your mother a lot, Silo—asked her to marry me, in fact. But she wouldn't have me. She was a lovely woman, though, your mother. She wasn't like the rest of the Zycos."

Silo took this to mean that she was neither a thief, nor a liar, nor a homicidal maniac. He waited for more.

"No one knows who your dad is, but I think he was an Uplander and I think she was waiting for him to come back. She used to spend hours with me up the lookout tower, just standing there with you in her arms and staring northward. Like she was expecting somebody."

A long-forgotten memory rose from fathoms deep in Silo's mind. He remembered his younger, happier self sitting on the rail at the top of the tower and gazing out to sea. His mother stood behind him with her warm arms wrapped around him and her long hair swirling in the wind, whipping across his face and tickling his nose. For a moment it made him feel so sad he wished he had never remembered.

Ben delved into some hidden pocket in his sack. "The thing is, when she realized she was dying she gave me something to give you when the time came: something about your dad. Here!"

He handed Silo a large, much-folded piece of paper. Silo opened it and read, in huge black letters:

WANTED

SHILOH AQUINUS,

also known as **AQUINUS THE ACCURSED**,
for Dog Theft, Horse Theft, Tax Theft, Fire Raising,
Impersonating a Member of the Armed Forces,
Obtaining Weapons by Unlawful Means,
Consorting with Enemies of the State,
and the Destruction of Government Property.
A Reward of Fifty Gold Crowns to Any Person Providing
Information Leading to his Arrest or Capture.

"She left you a message too," said Ben. "She said it was your destiny to complete the great work your father started."

"What, stealing dogs?" Silo was stunned.

"Is that what it says?" said Ben. "That doesn't sound so good, but maybe someone was treating the dog unkindly."

Silo realized for the first time that Ben couldn't read—he

had been, after all, one of Miss Mudford's old students. He read the notice aloud and Ben's kindly face clouded.

"Well, he does sound like a bit of a wild one. But your mum liked him and she was a good sort of woman. She gave you his name, didn't she? Could be it's all lies."

Shiloh—Silo. Yes, she had given him his father's name, or tried to. Silo realized that not only was his father a dangerous criminal but he himself was a spelling mistake. Thoroughly depressed, he examined the paper again.

"It doesn't even say what he looks like. Shouldn't they have put a description?"

"Your father's a bit of a mystery," said Ben, then added, "You have your mother's feet, Silo—webbed, that is—but otherwise you don't look a bit like her. So I imagine your father's a blue-eyed man, and probably a bit on the short side."

He stood up, patted Silo heavily on the shoulder, and left him alone with his thoughts. Silo Zyco, last of the Zycos, son of Aquinus the Accursed, Spelling Error.

He rose very early the next morning, dressed as he had the previous day, then wrapped the poster detailing his father's many crimes into his spare sack and stuffed it under his belt. He was ready.

Ruddle was saddling the horses outside the meeting hall, smiling his ruinous smile. "Bright and early, I see! You'll be riding Blossom here."

Blossom was the huge white packhorse and smelled strongly, although not of blossoms.

"Don't you worry," said Ruddle, seeing his look of alarm. "She's a gentle beast. She'll see you to the Capital safe and sound—won't you, my lovely?"

Blossom towered above him and had hooves the size of dinner plates, but her dark eyes were kindly and Silo felt somewhat comforted. The inspector had stayed at Headman Bean's house for the night, and now he came striding up from the direction of the communal toilets, a look of barely concealed horror on his face.

"Everything ready, Ruddle? Then let's get out of this godforsaken hellhole."

And half an hour later Silo was looking back at said hellhole, his home for ten years, and wondering what the future held. His gift of the seeing had given him no clues, but considering what lay in store, that was probably just as well.

3

MAXIMILLIAN CROW

The first week was wet and painful. It rained nonstop and Silo, unused to horse riding, ached in every bone in his body. The Uplanders thought themselves greatly superior to the Islanders, but for the life of him Silo couldn't see why; the Uplands turned out to be a bleak, flat country dotted with huts that seemed to contain as many pigs as people. Silo had never seen a pig before and thought them endearing creatures, but even so he didn't think he'd care to share a room with one. On their second day they skirted a deserted town that dated back to the time of the Ancients, and even in ruins the buildings that remained looked more impressive than those of the Uplanders.

"Why don't people still live there?" Silo asked Ruddle.

"They're afraid to," he replied. "Fact is, the Ancients did a lot of things that don't seem quite right. There's legends that they could fly through the air and talk to people hundreds of miles away. There's plenty who think they were sorcerers who used dark powers to do all these things. But something went wrong, didn't it? Their world died in the Great Catastrophe, and maybe that was because those powers turned against them. The Government, now—they's very keen to make a new world like theirs, but most normal folk think they were a crew of black magicians and good riddance to them."

Silo was surprised. On the Island, people hadn't spared much thought for the Ancients. The only evidence of their existence had been the Causeway and the Island itself, and both were on such a massive scale that they had been seen almost as geological features, placed there long ago by a helpful race of giants. It seemed that he still had much to learn about the world.

They followed a meandering route through the Uplands so the inspector could extract taxes from every village, however small and remote. Silo and Ruddle were always left to fend for themselves. Their first job was to see to the horses, and Silo was glad to help with this, for he had grown fond of Blossom. She turned out to be a sympathetic, kind-hearted animal and on the occasions when he fell off she neither galloped away nor trod on him, but simply waited patiently for him to remount before resuming her stately progress. And once the horses were settled, Ruddle's thoughts turned to food. Silo thought the Uplanders a miserable bunch on the whole, but

Ruddle had a cheerful way about him, which, together with his huge stock of stories and keen appetite for gossip, made him a welcome guest in most of the villages they stopped at. Ruddle would introduce him briefly to the company:

"This here's Silo. Silo's coming to the Capital with us. Seems like he might be a seer. Excuse the way he's dressed, but he's from the Eastern Swamps and they do things a little differently there."

"It's not a swamp, it's a marsh," Silo would say, then spend the rest of the evening in silence.

Ruddle urged him to be more sociable. "You're a useful lad, Silo, but you're the quiet type—not much of a one for a laugh or a joke, are you? You should cheer up a bit. You'd find the world a nicer place for it. Smile and the world smiles with you, that's what they say."

Privately Silo thought that faced with Ruddle's smile, the world might reel back in horror, but he didn't say so because he had grown to like the man. He may have thought Silo was a liar, but he treated him kindly, which was more than could be said of the inspector. Silo didn't like him and was rather pleased to learn, listening to Ruddle's new friends talk in the evenings, that no one else did either. Everyone was very polite to his face, but behind his back it was a different matter. The Uplanders were poor, and the inspectors and their taxes were universally hated. But so were people who said they were seers, because so many had lied to get the job. This didn't bother him much, but at that particular moment he almost wished he didn't have the gift. He had just had another seeing and it was a bad one: Ruddle was going to be eaten by a zoo animal.

Silo didn't know much about zoo animals because there weren't any in the marshes, but he knew they were dangerous and could kill a man. People said that long ago the Ancients had kept them as pets, but times had changed, or maybe the animals had. Silo had heard stories about areas where people would only travel in armed bands, fearful of attack by hungry beasts. His seeing had been vivid. He had seen a track running through a meadow bright with buttercups. Ruddle had been sprawled on it, his horse galloping off into the distance, and a huge brown animal, fearsome of tooth and claw, had been lunging toward him with an evil expression in its eye. Ruddle had been struggling to rise, but it was obvious he wouldn't be quick enough, and Silo was relieved that the seeing had ended when it had, as what followed promised to be extremely gruesome. He wanted to warn Ruddle, but he knew he thought him a liar—at least when it came to his gift of the seeing—and he could hardly tell him to stay away from meadows full of buttercups without him thinking he was mad as well.

After the first week of their journey the rain stopped and the countryside changed for the better. Silo saw his first living tree, and within a few short days the whole landscape grew greener and hillier, and their road led them through dappled woodlands. Silo, used to the bleak expanses of the marsh, thought it a beautiful country and found that this new traveling life suited him. He liked to wake in the morning with no idea of what the day would bring but knowing there would be new sights to see on their journey and new stories to hear in the evening. This was adventure indeed for someone who had lived all his life on a marsh, and he felt at home on Blossom now and rode in comfort, lulled by the steady, plodding rhythm of her hooves.

One afternoon found them riding down a track overarched by trees, and Silo lay slumped against the baggage, enjoying the dappled pattern of sunshine and shadow that fell through the leaves. He felt extremely content. It seemed that his troubles were behind him and his new life would be full of days like this, full of adventure and possibilities. But then the sun was full in his face, and he saw to his horror that the trees had come to an abrupt end and the track continued on through a meadow bright with buttercups. It was unmistakably the site of his seeing. Ruddle was riding on ahead, but Silo shouted a warning.

"Stop! There's a zoo animal!"

Ruddle reined in his horse, nervously scanning the bushes that bordered the meadow.

"A zoo animal?" said the inspector. "Are you sure? Where did you see it?"

"Here." Silo tapped his forehead. "It was a seeing."

The inspector shot him a withering look. "Let us get one thing clear. I had to bring you with us because your village voted you a seer. However, it is one thing to convince a marsh full of morons, and quite another to convince me. It is just possible that you are a seer, but far more likely that you are a liar, particularly as there have been no zoo animals reported in these parts for years. We'll ride on."

With that he kicked his horse into a canter, on into the meadow where the buttercups grew.

What happened next was gratifying for Silo's reputation but must have been terrifying for the inspector and his horse. Silo's eyes darted to a clump of bushes just in time to see them stir, and then shake, and then explode in a flurry of crackling twigs as a huge brown animal burst snarling from their depths.

"Bear!" cried Ruddle.

It was a clumsy-looking creature, but still it managed to move at an astonishing speed as it bore down on the inspector in a series of great loping bounds. The horse gave a scream that sounded almost human and reared, twisting sideways and up, sending the inspector sprawling to the ground. The bear aimed a vicious swipe at its rump, but its claws caught empty air when the horse bounded forward to gallop wild-eyed across the meadow with its ears flattened to its skull and its tail streaming. The bear chased it for a little distance but, finding it too fast for him, spun around and headed back to the fallen man. But the inspector had leaped to his feet as though on springs and was up and running, his mouth open in a silent scream and his eyes popping with terror as he sprinted back toward the trees, leaving a trail of trampled buttercups and a whirlwind of petals swirling in his wake.

Ruddle spurred his little horse and rode bravely forward. "Shoo!" he cried as he fumbled for his bow. "Shoo!"

Distracted, the bear slowed its headlong charge, giving

the inspector just time enough to reach the edge of the wood where, with an astonishing burst of athleticism, he scaled the nearest tree with the agility of a squirrel. And finally the bear lumbered to a halt. It glowered at them, growling low in its throat, and then reared up on its hind legs, massive and terrifying, taller than a man, and roared—and roared and roared and roared, revealing foam-flecked jaws and a vicious set of teeth. Then it dropped back to the ground and, with a final malevolent glance, loped off into the woods. So that was a zoo animal. Silo was awestruck. Surely no one, not even an Ancient, would keep one of those as a pet. He glanced up at the inspector, clinging white-knuckled and trembling to a branch. Wisdom decreed that he remain silent, but the alternative was irresistible.

"I told you so," he said.

Silo's seeing raised him mightily in Ruddle's estimation. At the earliest opportunity he bought him a thank-you present—a black shirt and jacket and breeches. They were secondhand and patched in places, but Silo was grateful for the gift as he'd noticed that Uplanders sneered at his sack. Now he dressed himself as they did and, more reluctantly, took to wearing his boots. He found them a painful encumbrance at first, but Ruddle was insistent.

"It's not right, Silo, to go barefoot—not with you being a seer. It's a high calling, that, and a little dignity's required."

And now he introduced him to company as "Silo Zyco,

a genuine seer from the Eastern Marshes." Then he would launch into a long version of the bear story. It always went down well, especially Ruddle's impersonation of the inspector running screaming through the meadow, but Silo noticed that not everybody believed it.

One night someone commented, "Well, it's a fine story, but Maximillian Crow's the only genuine seer I've ever heard of."

Silo asked a rare question: "Who's Maximillian Crow?"

He regretted it immediately, for Maximillian Crow was, it seemed, the greatest seer on all Mainland, perhaps even the greatest seer of all time. He was only eight years old, but already he had predicted remarkable things. He said that the Unicorn Tower would burn down last autumn, and it did. He had predicted that Ingall the Unclean would attack the Southern Shires, and he had. He had known that Upland United would beat Capital City 5–0 at a goatball match. And so on and on and on. Apparently he could have as many as three seeings in a single day, all of them unerringly accurate, and his powers grew greater by the year. Recently he had predicted that the lookout tower at Herringhaven would fall down, and it duly did. Unfortunately his parents had been standing underneath it at the time, but the Government had requested that he come to the Capital this year, despite his young age. Silo listened with growing depression. He had hoped to become the greatest seer on all Mainland himself, and so this was very bad news. He began to suspect that he would dislike Maximillian Crow if he met him, and was about to ask why he hadn't warned his parents that a tower was about to fall on them, but then he thought of his own family and remained silent. He probably didn't have time, and besides, they may not have been the sort to listen.

But it did seem as if the mention of Maximillian Crow had put some sort of curse on their journey, because not only was Silo miserable now but so was the weather. It grew cold and wet, and they left the lush countryside behind them and traveled on over bleak hills. Here the work of the Ancients was everywhere in evidence and often they passed the ruins of their towns, but the tracks they followed gave these a wide berth, presumably lest their ghosts still lingered about their old haunts. The succession of miserable days and nights led to depressing thoughts, and during their long damp rides Silo found his mind turning more and more to Aquinus the Accursed.

His father had always been a mystery, but now that Silo knew his name he seemed an even greater one. His mother had left him only three things in this life: Eel Rights, webbed feet, and a wanted poster for a dangerous criminal. The first two he could live with, but the third was a problem. The question Silo asked himself was an unanswerable one: could his mother read? It could be that Aquinus the Accursed had given her the poster telling her it was his medical diploma, or a certificate thanking him for his noble work among the poor. She'd have to have been pretty dim to believe him, but it would mean that she was just a trusting girl deceived by an unscrupulous man. But what if she could read? Did she really want Silo to steal dogs and set fire to things? He hoped she had just been a bit thick, but he wasn't counting on it. She had, after all, been a Zyco. He burned the poster secretly one night, gloomily watching as it curled into ash. He knew it by heart now and it seemed a risky thing to carry around. As far as the world was concerned his father was a mystery, and it seemed better that he remained so.

The next morning they were toiling up a hillside, Silo and Blossom bringing up the rear as usual. Blossom had her own pace and wasn't to be hurried, but the view was well worth the wait. They were looking out over a forest that stretched as far as the eye could see, a carpet of rippling green that spread from horizon to horizon. Far in the hazy distance, just as Ryker had described long ago, Silo saw the great towers of the Ancients rising out of the trees. They were crumbling now, and their sharp outlines were blurred by the creeping vegetation that veiled their walls and hung from their many windows, but what windows they must have been once! Gigantic windows in neat, regular rows—Silo counted the ones in the highest tower—over twenty floors. The towers had stood neglected and silent in the woods for hundreds of years now, but even in ruin they were awe-inspiring. How could the Ancients build so high, wondered Silo, and why?

"There you are, son—civilization at last," said Ruddle. He pointed to the Fort-Before-the-Forest, which lay sprawled at the foot of the hill beneath them. It was by far the largest outpost they had yet seen, with high walls and a lookout tower on each of its corners. Within, Silo could make out a packed mass of buildings, and threads of smoke rose from dozens of chimneys.

"Looks like there's a goatball game this afternoon." Ruddle nodded to an enclosed rectangular space to the south of the fort with flags fluttering from its corners. He let out a great whoop and sent his little hairy brown horse downhill at a gallop.

Silo and the inspector caught up with Ruddle at the gate of the fort.

"There's a colleague of yours here, sir," he said brightly to the inspector. "Chief Inspector Hardacre's just arriving from the Southern Shires. That's his party coming up now."

Silo scanned the group of riders critically for potential seers. Chief Inspector Hardacre was followed by an armed escort, but there were two blond children riding behind, both a year or so older than Silo. The first was a tall, good-looking boy with flowing blond curls, dressed in a blue shirt and breeches and a purple cloak. A *rich boy*, thought Silo, eyeing his dapple-gray pony, for it was a magnificent beast and currently prancing on two legs. Blossom, perhaps sensing Silo's appraising eye, chose this moment to let off a great ripping fart, and the two of them turned in his direction. Studying their shocked faces, Silo got the impression that they thought it was he who was responsible. It didn't seem the right moment for introductions, so he stared at them coolly.

Chief Inspector Hardacre was obviously an important man, for Ruddle's inspector greeted him with extreme politeness and even managed to smile, something Silo hadn't thought him capable of. Ruddle, finding himself next to the blond boy, said, "You don't happen to be a seer, do you, son? Because Silo here has the gift."

Ruddle was determined to find Silo some little friends.

"Yes, I am. And so is Daisy here." He indicated the fair girl. Two of them. Silo's heart sank. The blond boy turned around and looked at him with clear gray eyes, a look that Silo thought lingered a little too long on his scruffy clothes and oversized boots. But perhaps that was just his imagination.

"I'm Elgarth Early. Pleased to meet you."

He didn't sound as though he was at all, but Blossom was towering over him by now and slobbering into his curls, which may have had something to do with it.

"I'm Silo Zyco." They were riding through the gate of the fort.

"Why don't you drop in on us this evening?" said Elgarth. "At six. We're staying at the Red Hand."

"All right, I will. Thanks."

They had arrived at a big inn and the inspector was dismounting. Ruddle, finding himself dismissed, rode off with Silo down a narrow street with tall buildings on either side, bright with painted inn signs: the Owl, the Bear and Bowman, the Forest Oak. Ruddle whistled cheerfully as they turned into the stable yard of the Running Dog.

"We'll get the horses settled, and then you're in for a treat," he said. He produced two crumpled bits of paper from his pocket. "I got us a couple of tickets for the goatball."

Three o'clock found them seated at the goatball stadium in the middle of an excited crowd, many of them waving flags and placing last-minute bets. Long ago on the marsh Ryker had told Silo about goatball, and he was greatly looking forward to the match. Goatball had been the most popular sport in the time of the Ancients; twenty years ago the Government had decided to revive it so that the modern generation could learn the skills of their forefathers. It had been difficult because the exact rules had been lost, but they knew that there was a net at each end of the field, two eleven-man teams, and that the winners were the ones who got the most goats. With this to go on they had been able to reconstruct the game very much as it must have been played in the time of the Ancients, and Silo could see before him a rectangle of smooth green grass with a goat pen at each end. The teams were coming onto the field now, Wildwood Rangers in brown shirts and Wildwood Wanderers in green. The goatkeepers, traditionally the tallest men on the pitch, picked up their nets and made their way down to their positions in front of the goat pens. Then the referee blew his whistle and the linesman let loose the first goat.

The game that followed was extremely exciting. The goat was an experienced one and very fast on its feet. The players had to catch it and then pass it down to their own pen, where the goatkeeper threw his net over it so it couldn't escape, but the game was much harder than it seemed as the goats were specially bred for their speed and agility and put up a spirited fight. Often it seemed that the goat was cornered and it would go down beneath a mass of brown and green shirts, only to squirm out of the scrum and race around the stadium with twenty men in pursuit. Even when a player succeeded in catching it, it kicked and butted him as he raced down the pitch to his pen, tackled as he went by members of the opposing team. The stadium echoed to the cheers of the crowd, the grunts and cries of the players, and the thunder of cloven hooves. After fifteen minutes of play the referee blew his whistle and the first goat was sent off and a fresh one substituted. It had got the game off to a scorching start and went out to a big round of applause. The game was played in two forty-five-minute halves and with a minimum of six goats, and the Wildwood Wanderers managed to put a goat away just seconds before halftime. Their supporters cheered as the Wanderers players ran around the field, punching the air in triumph, and the goat began to graze.

With one goat up, the Wanderers made a confident start to the second half, but their defenders had their work cut out for them, for now the game was being played on two fronts. They wanted another goat, but they also had to protect the one they already had, for the Rangers wingers came streaking down the field and tried to release it from its pen. The Rangers supporters roared their approval and chanted defiantly:

We are the Rangers!
We don't like strangers!

We'll get your goat,
And then we'll gloat!

But the Wanderers goatkeeper knew his job. He stood firm, a mighty oak of a man. His teammates rushed to his support, and soon the area before the pen was a mass of struggling bodies, whirling fists, and uncouth cries. And it was then that the Rangers caught the Wanderers on the break. The goat in play, feeling that its services were not needed for the moment, had let its guard down and began to graze. And a Rangers forward saw his chance. He burst from the struggling throng and streaked up the pitch, scooped up the unsuspecting creature, and headed for the goal, pursued by the Wanderers defense, a chorus of boos and a hail of dung thrown by the home support. But it was all in vain. The goatkeeper threw his net, the Rangers had tied, and the game settled into its final phase—a hard-fought battle between two stalwart teams and a speedy ruminant. Some games ended badly, with a pile of unconscious forwards or multiple goats loose on the pitch, but not this one, for, in the closing minutes of play, Wanderers star player Ron Alonzo made a sensational run. He was a powerfully built man and, with the goat clasped firmly in his arms, he simply ran at the Rangers defense, trampling them down like weeds. The last man stood firm and might have prevailed had not a turnip, hurled by a Wanderers supporter, struck him full in the face at the crucial moment. Alonzo seized his chance, the net was thrown, and the game was won. And the Wanderers supporters went wild, for it was three long years since they had beaten the Rangers at home.

"So, Silo," said Ruddle as they shuffled out of the stadium in the heart of a buzzing crowd, "what do you think of goatball?"

"Really good. Thanks for taking me."

They pushed out of the gate and the crush began to thin a little. Silo hated crowds. He was too small and tended to get trodden on, so now he and Ruddle leaned against the trunk of a tree and waited for the press to go by. But there were shouts from the direction of the highway and the crowd wavered, some heading on and others turning back to the source of the commotion. There was an excited stir and Silo heard someone speak the name of Maximillian Crow; in a moment it was on everyone's lips: "Maximillian Crow . . . Yes, he's coming. . . . Maximillian Crow . . . He's here. . . . That's him there, on the black pony. . . . It's Maximillian Crow. . . . Maximillian Crow's arrived."

There was cheering from the highway and a group of excited girls started climbing the tree to get a glimpse of the greatest seer on all Mainland. Silo could see nothing from his low vantage point, and found he didn't much care.

"Want to go and get a look at him?" asked Ruddle. "He's bound to want to meet you, you both being seers and all."

"No," said Silo shortly. "It can wait."

4

THE RED HAND

When Silo set out that evening to keep his appointment with Elgarth Early, there was a raging thunderstorm in progress and the streets of the Fort-Before-the-Forest were flooded. He waded through the torrent with his cloak pulled over his head, but he was very wet about the legs and feet by the time he arrived at the Red Hand. There was a fat lady counting coins at a desk, and he asked her where he could find Elgarth Early.

She gave him a happy smile. "So you're another of Master Elgarth's little friends! You've a treat in store tonight—he's got Maximillian Crow with him. Yes, the famous Maximillian Crow, so you'll get to meet him. Lucky old you! Up the stairs, first landing and second door on the left."

Silo sighed and supposed he might as well get it over with.

Elgarth opened the door to his knock and Silo found himself looking into a handsomely furnished room. The fair girl and an unknown boy were seated in front of the fire.

"Silo, I'm so glad you could come."

Studying Elgarth's face, Silo was not convinced.

"I'm sorry, but do you mind . . . ?" Elgarth pointed at his dripping boots and Silo reluctantly took them off and set them beside the door. He had no socks and was self-conscious about his webbed feet, but they weren't very obvious and he hoped no one would notice. "Thank you so much. Normally I wouldn't bother, but as you can see this is a rather expensive carpet."

Elgarth waved Silo to a chair and said, "Silo, meet Daisy. I'm sure Maximillian here needs no introduction."

Silo examined the great Maximillian closely. He wasn't what he had expected. He was a sturdy brown boy with a healthy, outdoors look about him, eyes so dark they were almost black, and a tangle of jet-black curls. And he was big, Silo noticed with dismay. He was acutely aware that he was small for his age, and it was depressing to discover that not only was Maximillian a great seer but also the tallest eight-year-old he'd ever laid eyes on. He nodded gravely to Silo.

"Silo is a fellow seer and comes from the Eastern Swamps," said Elgarth.

"It's not a swamp, it's a marsh," said Silo.

A brief silence followed, and then Elgarth said, "I see you have webbed feet, Silo. How very unusual."

Silo was beginning to dislike him. "All my family have—" He corrected himself. "All my family had webbed feet."

"Ah yes, your family. The inspector was telling me. You were the only survivor, I believe, saved by your gift of the seeing. I'm so sorry for your loss." He paused. "Of course I know nothing of the exact circumstances, but was there no way you could have warned them?"

"There wasn't time," said Silo shortly. Now he was beginning to really dislike this boy.

The girl called Daisy fixed him with huge, shining eyes. "Such a terrible tragedy, to lose all your family."

"Well, maybe not all." Elgarth gave Silo a smile, but it wasn't a very nice one. "From something the inspector said I gather there's a chance your father may still be alive. Have you heard anything from him at all?"

Now Silo hated him with a powerful passion. How did he know? Then he realized the inspector had read the Chronicle containing the "father a mystery" entry. This was no time to mention Aquinus the Accursed, dog thief, so he simply stared at Elgarth. Silo had a powerful, unsettling stare, and although Elgarth opened his mouth to say something else he thought better of it and dropped his eyes to the rather expensive carpet, now marked with a trail of wet webbed footprints.

Daisy broke the silence. "The gift of the seeing seems a dark one with you, Silo: tidal waves, the attack of zoo animals, things that bring sorrow and death. I see only lovely things—where the rainbow will shine, when the swallows will arrive in spring, the spot where the first snowdrop will flower. Mine is a joyous gift."

And a useless one, thought Silo. If he was walking in a

lonely wood he would rather know the whereabouts of a hungry bear than the first snowdrop, but he said nothing.

Daisy turned to Elgarth. "And you, Elgarth—what is it that you see?"

"Oh, a little bit of everything. I'm an all-rounder."

He looked modest as he said it, but Silo didn't think he really was. Silo thought he was rude and sly and obnoxious. "But obviously compared to Maximillian here, it's all pretty low-key stuff. He's a much greater seer than I am."

They all turned to the great Maximillian Crow. He had said nothing so far, but now he blinked and stared about him, as though the sound of his name had brought him back, reluctantly, from some remote realm of thought. Then he gave them a slow, dreamy smile and said, "No one seer is greater than another. All of us here are equals. We have all been blessed with a great gift, and it is our duty to use it for the benefit of humankind."

"How?" breathed Daisy.

Maximillian looked grave. "The gift of the seeing often shows us future sorrows. We should warn those who may be laid low by misfortune."

"Or tidal waves, perhaps," said Elgarth.

Silo stood up. He didn't have to be a seer to know that if he stayed any longer, he would punch Elgarth in the face. "I've got to go."

His boots stood in a puddle by the doorway and he picked them up and left, not even bothering to say good-bye, and took the stairs two at a time, his head buzzing with rage. He found Ruddle in the Bear and Bowman talking goatball with a couple of soldiers. He shifted up to make room for Silo.

"Had a nice evening, Silo? How were your little friends?"

"They're no friends of mine," said Silo shortly. "I hate them all."

After weeks of sleeping on floors it was a real luxury to have a bed, and when Silo woke up in his tiny attic at the Running Dog next morning it was already late. He decided to pay Blossom a quick visit before going out to look around the fort, but he got no farther than the lobby. The inspector, who seemed to be in an extremely bad temper, poked his head out of a door.

"I want a word with you," he said, beckoning Silo into the room. He settled himself behind a desk, and Silo got the distinct impression that he was in trouble.

"I believe you accepted an invitation last night from Governor Early's son Elgarth."

So his father was a governor, thought Silo. He would be.

"Elgarth tells me your behavior was odd. He said you barely spoke a word, and that your manner was hostile. And that you left in a great hurry."

Silo thought back over his visit. That seemed to sum it up quite well.

"I didn't bring you here to discuss your manners, or rather your lack of them, but a theft took place at that time and it seems likely that you are responsible. Have you anything to say for yourself?"

Silo hadn't. Seething inside, he waited to hear more.

The inspector continued. "The facts are these. Elgarth put a red purse containing forty silver quarters on a table just inside the door of his room. Then he heard that Maximillian Crow had arrived and went to meet him—leaving the door locked, I might add. He invited Maximillian back to his room and left him there while he went to fetch Daisy. You arrived a little later, and Elgarth noticed the money was missing shortly after you left."

He looked at Silo as though expecting him to say something. He didn't, and the inspector went on, "Daisy is the daughter of a village headman. Her family provided her with ample funds for her journey. She has no reason to steal. Maximillian Crow is spoken of very highly by all who have met him, and Elgarth would hardly steal his own money."

Silo wasn't quite so sure about that.

"And so that leaves you. I am aware of your unfortunate family background. Your village headman told me all about their dishonest habits. And Elgarth mentioned that you left without putting your boots back on. Rather an unusual thing to do on a wet night—unless, of course, you had a purse of coins hidden in them."

"I didn't do it. You can search my room if you like."

"We did so last night."

Silo blessed his foresight in burning the Aquinus the Accursed poster. He stood glaring at the inspector. It seemed pointless to offer explanations, as it was obvious they wouldn't be believed. So much, he thought bitterly, for getting away from his past and the reputation of the Zycos.

There was a knock on the door, and it swung open to reveal none other than Maximillian Crow. He was wrapped in an emerald-green cloak and wandered into the room with the same dreamy look that Silo had seen the night before.

"I just heard about . . . Elgarth said . . ." He seemed painfully shy.

"Have you something to tell me, Maximillian?" asked the inspector.

Maximillian nodded. "About yesterday evening. When Elgarth went to fetch Daisy I had . . . well, some visitors came."

"How many visitors?" said the inspector.

"Oh, about twenty, I suppose."

"Twenty?" The inspector was startled. "Who were they?"

Maximillian looked embarrassed. "I don't know their names. They were just people who wanted my autograph."

"Why didn't you mention this earlier?"

"I only just heard. And besides . . ." He shuffled his feet. "It would seem as if I were boasting." Then he added, "I'm sure Silo wouldn't steal from a fellow seer." He smiled his dreamy smile at them both and wandered out. He had just gone up in Silo's estimation. Thanks to Maximillian he had gone from being the only suspect to one of twenty-odd and it was a great relief.

The inspector seemed almost annoyed. "What Maximillian has told us changes the situation somewhat. You may leave, but remember that I personally am not convinced of your innocence in this matter. I will be keeping a very careful eye on you in future."

Silo left, raging with the injustice of it all. He went into Blossom's stable and leaned against her leg, absently scratching her great belly. Elgarth had been very quick to accuse him, he thought, and he had been deliberately unpleasant the night before. Silo half suspected him of setting the whole thing up to get him into trouble. But why? He and Elgarth hadn't liked one another from the first, but that hardly seemed reason enough. He decided to find Ruddle. A man of his sociable habits might have picked up some useful gossip about Elgarth Early and his family. He set out to check the inns, starting with the Bear and Bowman. Ruddle wasn't there, or at the Forest Oak or the Owl, and after checking all the possible places on the main street, Silo started investigating the roads that ran between.

Within five minutes he was lost in a tangle of alleys. His way was blocked by herds of foraging pigs, and the area was home to a host of unfriendly dogs that growled at his approach. He was about to retrace his steps when a flash of emerald green caught his eye. Maximillian Crow had stepped out of a turning and was hastening down the alley ahead of him. Silo was about to call him but he paused, for there was something odd about Maximillian. His dreamy, wandering manner had gone and he walked briskly, scanning the houses on either side. And as Silo stood hesitating he saw him stop beside an open window, then turn to check the alley behind him. Hardly knowing why, Silo ducked behind a dunghill. And when he cautiously raised his head from behind its reeking mass he saw, as clear as day, Maximillian reach through the window and lift out a plate bearing a steaming jam roly-poly.

Silo was flabbergasted. Maximillian Crow, the greatest seer on all Mainland and pudding pilferer! And suddenly a dark suspicion took possession of him, for experience told him that those inclined to steal desserts were often capable of more desperate crimes. But he held his indignation in check. He watched Maximillian pad off down the street and then set to follow at a safe distance, flitting softly from shadow to shadow. The pursuit ended in a quiet square. Maximillian rounded a corner, and when Silo reached it in his turn he found himself hemmed in by a huddle of tumbledown houses. Maximillian had vanished, but Silo's eye was drawn to a ruinous pub called the Dead Lion. Although its windows were shuttered its door was ajar, and a plate stood upon its windowsill, a plate still warm to the touch and containing traces of jam. Silo had tracked down his quarry. He peered through a chink in the shutters and saw Maximillian sitting down with a ragged man. He saw him take a red purse from beneath his cloak and push it across the table to him, and then he had seen enough. His suspicions were confirmed. Maximillian had taken the money that Silo had been accused of stealing. Silo fought down a powerful urge to burst into the Dead Lion and kick him viciously on the bottom, but instead he sidled into a shadowy doorway and settled down to watch and wait, and in about ten minutes he saw the pair come out and walk away quickly in opposite directions.

When they were out of sight Silo entered the dark interior of the Dead Lion. The bartender was a sinister man with milky eyes and a forehead studded with boils.

"Those two who just left. What were they talking about?"

The man glared at him. "Is it any of your business?"

"No," said Silo.

This was obviously the right answer. "I heard them mention goatball."

"Thanks."

Silo picked his way out of the alleys and headed back to the Running Dog, his head full of dark thoughts. So Maximillian Crow was a thief. And it seemed as if he was using the money to place goatball bets. It wasn't even as if he really needed it. Silo fumed with a savage resentment as he stalked through the streets. They seemed more crowded than usual, and he stood back to let a woman carrying two pails of water go by, then two men carting a barrel of water, and then a tiny girl with a jug of water. He looked around and realized that the whole street was carrying water in bottles, buckets, barrels, anything that would hold water and some things that wouldn't. Mystified, he turned into the stable yard of the Running Dog and found Ruddle standing there with a bucket of water.

"What's the water for?"

"This is for Blossom. As for the others, they've heard about Maximillian Crow's new seeing. He says there's going to be a big fire tonight. Caused a bit of a panic, that."

There was one thing you could say for Maximillian, thought Silo; he did have a certain style. Thieving from governors' sons, lying to inspectors, betting in seedy pubs, and throwing a whole community into a state of panic—these things were all in a day's work to him.

"And good news! A couple more inspectors came in from the south this morning, and they brought some new seers with them."

This didn't seem particularly good news to Silo. "How many?"

"Two. Sisters, by the look of them, and round about your age."

Silo suddenly remembered what the inspector had said about Daisy. "Is their dad a village headman?"

"Now you come to mention it, I think he is."

This was getting to be too much of a coincidence. Three headmen's children and a governor's son. Silo found himself wondering what Maximillian's parents had been before the unfortunate incident with the tower.

Ruddle was eyeing him sadly. "It won't do, Silo, you always being so suspicious and unfriendly. You need some little friends. No harm in dropping by the Red Hand and saying hello, surely? You should go and see them, be pleasant and all."

"All right, I will."

Maybe Maximillian Crow would be with them, and there were many things he wanted to say to Maximillian, none of them particularly pleasant. He strode to the Red Hand, dodging the crowds of water carriers as he went. But as he walked he turned Ruddle's words over in his mind and realized that he was right. It would be nice to have some friends. Ruddle was always kind to him, but he wanted someone of his own age to talk to. He was lonely, he finally admitted to himself, and had been for a very long time. He slowed his pace and soon found himself hoping that Maximillian wouldn't be there, and by the time he arrived at the Red Hand he was even trying to think, unsuccessfully, of some pleasant things he could drop into the conversation. Looking through a window, he saw Elgarth and Daisy sitting at a table with two mousy-looking girls. Maximillian wasn't with them, and Silo's spirits lifted.

The same fat lady was sitting at the desk, this time with a row of brimming buckets lined up in front of her, and she smiled at Silo and directed him to the room down the hall. But just as he was about to enter he heard his own name mentioned and stopped outside the door. It was sometimes useful to know what people said about you when they thought you weren't listening, but on this occasion it was painful. Elgarth was speaking, interrupted now and then by little cries of horror from the girls, and although Silo couldn't hear all of it he heard quite enough.

". . . father a mystery . . . headman of his village said . . . notorious family . . . thieves . . . reign of terror . . . webbed feet . . . gift of the seeing . . . didn't warn them . . . some sort of inheritance apparently . . . valuable Eel Rights . . . yes, very shocking . . ."

Silo turned and ran from the Red Hand. Silo Zyco, Silo the Accursed, Silo the Friendless and Falsely Accused, Web-Footed Wanderer in a Hostile World.

He went back to the Running Dog. A bucket of water had appeared in his room and he was grudgingly impressed by the power of Maximillian's reputation, for his seeing had thrown the whole fortress into turmoil. No smoke rose from the chimneys and, as dusk fell, no candlelight appeared in the windows and men marched the streets, buckets in hand, on the lookout for fires. The houses were all built of wood and packed tightly together, so he supposed that almost any fire here would be a serious one, but in his black mood he found he really didn't care, and he went to sleep hoping that the whole place would burn to a cinder and take him with it.

Woken several hours later by the cry of "Fire!" he found his feelings had changed dramatically. He sprang out of bed and fumbled his way into his clothes in the dark, suddenly remembering Blossom and the other horses shut in the stables. He ran down the stairs into chaos. People were milling around carrying bundles of belongings, shouting and shoving, and two men were trying to manhandle a huge chest out the door. Silo ducked underneath it and ran to Blossom's stable. A pall of smoke drifted overhead. There was a red glow in the southern sky and a vicious crackling, popping sound in his ears. And then someone was bellowing something in the street outside: a confused string of words with "goatball" somewhere in among them.

Ruddle suddenly appeared at his side. "It's all right, Silo. It's outside the walls. The goatball stadium is burning."

As the news spread, the panic slowly subsided. Men climbed up onto the roofs on the southern side of the fort to beat out wind-borne sparks, and people started returning to their homes. But others wanted to get a view of the fire and crowded up the steep steps that led onto the walls of the fort, and Silo was among them. The fire had taken a firm hold by now, and the goatball stadium was a mass of flame. Above it was a great twisting pillar of fire, dusky red at its heart and roaring, sending a mass of whirling sparks high into the night sky and lighting up the whole countryside for miles around with a harsh, unearthly glow. But Silo had no eyes for the spectacle. He wormed his way through the crowd until he spotted a familiar figure in an emerald-green cloak. Maximillian Crow, admiring his handiwork.

Silo prodded him in the back. "You and I need to talk."

Maximillian's face flickered orange and red in the firelight and he gave Silo a huge, beaming smile. "I knew you'd be on to me soon. You must admit, though"—he nodded to the inferno—"it's a good show for forty silver quarters."

5

ORLANDO

Silo and Maximillian walked through the thronging streets in silence, but back at the Running Dog, with the door closed firmly behind them, Silo got straight to the point.

"You stole Elgarth's money."

"Yeah, I'm sorry about that. But believe me, the boy has plenty. I had a quick look through his room while he was getting Daisy and there was cash everywhere—gold crowns under his bed, silver crowns under his pillow, you name it. I didn't think he'd miss a few quarters. And I did try to help you out with the inspector."

"You paid a man to burn down the goatball stadium."

"There weren't any goats in it. I checked."

"Why did you do it?"

"I had my reputation to think of. I hadn't had a seeing for weeks. People might have started to ask questions."

"But you don't need to fake seeings. You're Maximillian Crow."

"No, I'm not."

Silo was shocked. Maximillian Crow was even more villainous than he had imagined. He wasn't even Maximillian Crow.

"Who are you, then?"

"My real name's Orlando Bramble."

"So what happened to Maximillian Crow? The real one, that is."

For the first time Orlando looked slightly ashamed of himself. "Well, I feel bad about that, but he should be all right." He thought for a moment, then said, "I know they say he was a great seer and all, but he was a bit dim as well, if you know what I mean."

"No, I don't," said Silo. "You're going to have to explain it. From the beginning."

"Well," said Orlando, settling himself comfortably on Silo's bed, "I guess I'm a bit like you, really. No parents to speak of— they got killed in a riot a few years back. So I lived with my older sister for a bit, till she took up with a Raider. She went off with him and I haven't seen her since. I hear she's done well for herself, though, captains her own ship now and everything. So she left me with my uncle and he—well, he did quite a few things, but the one they got him for was fixing a goatball game. So then he got shipped out. And that left me on my own and I did a few things too. Nothing serious, you understand, but a boy has to eat. Then I got myself into a spot of trouble."

Here was a family that put even the Zycos in the shade.

"What sort of trouble?" asked Silo.

"I was in Herringhaven. It's a harbor town out west. Got caught stealing. Anyway, the authorities said they'd found me an honest job as a cabin boy. That was fine by me, but then I realized where the ship was headed. Turned out they were shipping me out."

"Stop!" said Silo. "Explain this shipping-out thing."

Orlando looked at him in surprise. "You don't know much, do you? Is it true what Elgarth said, that you come from a swamp?"

"It's not a swamp, it's a marsh," said Silo.

"Whatever. Anyway, 'shipping out' is what happens to people who upset the Government. They get shipped out to work someplace, the sort of work that no one else wants—so chances are my uncle's in the Northern Isles by now, working down the silver mines."

"So where were you being shipped out to?"

"That's the problem. It was to the Us of Ay."

"I've never heard of it," said Silo.

"I'm not surprised. Chances are it doesn't exist. Most people think it's just a legend from the time of the Ancients."

"But why would the Government send people to a place that isn't there?"

"That's really complicated. It's all to do with the Ancients. You know how the Government's always going on about how wonderful the Ancients were? About how we must find out how they did all those weird things and do them again?"

Silo didn't. But then he thought of goatball and nodded wisely.

"They want to find out what the Ancients' power was so they can use it again."

"But they already have power, don't they?" said Silo. "What about all their soldiers and inspectors and governors?"

"Not that kind of power," said Orlando. "The Ancients had things called power stations and power supplies and power lines. They want all that back. It's a different kind of power—some sort of force, I think, not like a solid thing."

Silo thought he understood. "Something like the wind or the tide."

"I suppose so. No one really knows. Anyway, they say that in the time of the Ancients there was a place called the Us of Ay, and the Government is sending a ship to check it out, just in case it really exists. To see if there's anyone there who understands the power stations and stuff."

"So they were going to ship you out to the Us of Ay."

"Yeah, but obviously I didn't want to go. I mean, they say it's thousands of miles away—if it's there at all, that is. It just sounded really dangerous. And that's when I met Maximillian Crow."

Silo was beginning to feel sorry for Maximillian Crow. "What did you do to him?"

Orlando yawned and slumped back on Silo's bed. "It's been a long day. Can't it wait until tomorrow?"

"No."

"Oh, all right, then. Well, after they caught me for

thieving, the headman of Herringhaven said he felt sorry for me, what with my bad family and all. He said he was going to give me a second chance, and that he'd found me a job as cabin boy on a ship called the *Leviathan*. Said it was sailing to Parris Port. Well, I was really pleased. Parris Port's only thirty miles from the Capital and I've always wanted to go there. So he gave me a letter to hand to the captain and I went down to the harbor. And that's when I realized he was lying."

"How?"

"I watched them loading the ship. Sailing to Parris Port's just coast-hopping—loads of places to pick up stuff on the way. But they were putting serious supplies on board the *Leviathan*. It looked to me like they were stocking up for a long ocean voyage. So I opened the letter, and it said that I was a dangerous criminal from a long line of criminals. Told the captain to lock me up below until they were out of sight of land, and then it wished him luck in finding the Us of Ay. So I had a problem. Seemed like the best thing to do was just run away, and fast. And I would have done, but then I met Maximillian."

"What's he like?" Silo was beginning to suspect the fate of his old rival, but he was curious about him all the same.

"He was kind of sweet, really. Very small, seemed much younger than eight. He was a bit muddled, though. He was meant to be meeting an inspector to get an escort to the Capital, but somehow he'd got himself lost. He asked me to help him. A trusting sort, I'd say. Anyway, he showed me a letter they'd given him."

Orlando reached into his breast pocket and produced a thick sheet of parchment. "A very useful letter."

He handed it to Silo, who read:

To Whom It May Concern:

The bearer of this letter, one Maximillian Crow, is traveling to enter into the service of the Government. Said Government commands that he be given all possible assistance on his journey, financial or otherwise, from whatever person or persons he requests it of. Any person or persons failing to comply with the above order will incur the wrath of said Government, and a fine of ten silver crowns.

Beneath was an impressive array of stamps and seals and signatures.

"You swapped the letters," said Silo.

"Yes. And then I told him the inspector was waiting for him on board the *Leviathan* and took him down to the harbor. Just in case he got lost again."

"But didn't he tell the captain he was Maximillian Crow?"

"I expect he did, but I'd already thought of that. Before I resealed the letter I added a PS. I'm quite good at forgery—it was a sideline of my uncle's, so he taught me a few things. I put: *This boy is a shameless liar. Don't believe a word he says.*"

"He was only eight," said Silo. "That was a horrible thing to do."

"I don't know," said Orlando. "He was a weedy little boy.

It might do him good, lots of fresh sea air and healthy exercise."

Silo stared at him, and Orlando dropped his eyes.

"All right, then, it was a horrible thing to do. I still feel awful about it. I remember his little trusting eyes looking at me—*Thank you for being my friend.* I should have just run away like I'd planned. But I was in a spot."

"You still are, aren't you? You're not a real seer. You can't just go on paying people to burn down goatball stadiums."

"I've thought of all that. After tonight I can just cruise on my reputation for a while. And when we get to the Capital I'm going to get brain damage, fake a head injury. Then I'll say I've lost my gift and then I'll be free to do whatever I like."

Orlando had a sudden inspiration. "I've just had a thought—perhaps you could slip me the odd seeing every now and then. Sounds like you're really good at it."

"It's not that easy," said Silo. "Seeings are rare. I don't have very many."

"Never mind," said Orlando. "At least they're good ones. Not all that rubbish about rainbows and snowdrops."

He stood up and stretched. He was almost a head taller than Silo.

"How old are you really?" Silo asked.

"Getting on for eleven. Anyway, must go now, been a busy day. It's been nice talking to you. It gets really tedious being Maximillian Crow all the time, hanging around with that creep Elgarth and listening to Daisy banging on about sunbeams. And thanks for not telling the inspectors about me burning down the goatball stadium and stuff."

"How do you know I won't?"

"Elgarth told me all about the Zyco family. Doesn't seem like their style somehow. See you tomorrow." He grinned at Silo and left.

Silo had a little friend. A little criminal friend.

⌯

They left the Fort-Before-the-Forest at noon the next day. When Ruddle and Silo arrived at the north gate it was obvious that the next stage of their journey was going to be done in much greater style than the first. There was an escort of sixty mounted soldiers waiting, for their road skirted the Wildwoods, and the Wildwoods were home to zoo animals and savage woodland tribes. The soldiers rode at the head of the party, followed by Ruddle and his fellow guides, then the inspectors, then the seers, then a group of servants, and finally three wagonloads of baggage. Silo supposed he should be riding with the other seers, but Blossom was set in her ways and liked to be last. She settled herself comfortably behind the baggage wagons and he was happy enough with her choice, for he had no wish to mix with anyone who thought him a web-footed psychopath obsessed with Eel Rights. But he was pleased when Orlando rode out of the column on his fat black pony and waited for him.

He grinned up at Silo, who towered over him on

Blossom. "Good idea to ride at the back. Now we can talk. I told them I'd try to talk you out of your evil ways. They think I'm a saint—all except Elgarth. He said I was wasting my time."

"Why has Elgarth got it in for me?" said Silo.

"I was wondering that myself. I think it must be the competition. I mean, how many seers does the Government need? There's five already and maybe we'll meet up with more. Mind you, Daisy seems pretty useless and so do those two new girls, Bella and Stella."

"What are they like?"

"A bit deranged. They had a seeing this morning—according to them there's going to be a big fire at an outpost. Not very original, are they?" Orlando laughed. "I'm pretty good at predicting fires myself—pair of arsonists if you ask me. But you're a proper seer and I don't think Elgarth's too happy about it, so he's spreading stories about your nasty criminal ways. The Government's not too keen on employing criminals. I found that out in Herringhaven. Although I can't see why you want to work for them anyway."

Silo was surprised. "But seers always work for the Government, don't they? They use their seeings to help them—warn them about attacks from Raiders, stuff like that."

"Why not be different? Why not work for the Raiders and warn them about attacks from the Government?" Orlando sounded annoyed.

"Sorry," said Silo, "I forgot your sister was a Raider."

"Yeah, Val always had a taste for travel. Or Valeria the

Violent, as I suppose I should call her now. That's what it said on her wanted poster, anyway."

Silo was struck by a sudden blinding thought. "Was Ingall the Unclean a Raider too?"

"Yeah. He burned all the coastal forts in the Southern Shires last summer."

"Are they always called Something the Something? Like Valeria the Violent or Ingall the Unclean?" He hesitated for a moment. "Or Aquinus the Accursed?"

"Not all of them, only the really respected ones. It's considered a great honor among Raiders to have 'the Repulsive' or 'the Undesirable' or whatever added after your name. It means you've performed great deeds."

"Things like fire raising and tax evasion and destroying government property? Or stealing dogs maybe?"

"I've never heard of them stealing dogs before," said Orlando, "but the other stuff, yeah, that's all standard for a halfway decent Raider."

So Silo's father was a Raider. He rode in silence for a while, turning it over in his mind. After a while he asked, "Why aren't they ever called nice things? Like 'the Great' and 'the Good' and 'the Kind'?"

"They take the names their enemies give them," said Orlando. "To show that they think they're a real pain in the bum. A bit unfair sometimes, though. Val had a temper on her, but she wasn't that bad."

Maybe Aquinus the Accursed hadn't been either. Silo hoped not, anyway.

Later that day, when the shadows were lengthening and Silo was beginning to think hopefully of supper, Ruddle pulled out of the column ahead. When Silo and Orlando drew level with him he was on foot, and his little horse was lame at his side.

"Rusty here's got a loose shoe," he said. "There's a village up ahead—place by the name of Baldock, if I remember rightly. Best I stop off there, see if I can find a blacksmith."

"I'll come with you," said Silo. He didn't like to think of Ruddle alone and prey to zoo animals, although he wasn't sure what use he and Blossom would be if they were attacked by another bear. Maybe Blossom could sit on it.

"I'll go ahead and tell the others," said Orlando, and muttered to Silo as he rode past, "I suppose I'd better go and be Maximillian for a while. I've been neglecting him a bit today."

Ruddle and Silo made their way to Baldock. It was a compact cluster of huts, ringed with a high fence to keep zoo animals at bay, and as they approached they could hear pigs and chickens, and then the unmistakable *clink-clink-clink* of a blacksmith's hammer.

"Sounds like we're in luck," said Ruddle. He led Rusty through the gate in the fence, but Silo stayed outside for a moment. Blossom wanted to graze, and Silo trusted her not to run away. Running anywhere was not something she much enjoyed, so he took off her bridle and turned her loose. He walked through the gate, but then suddenly, in the blink of an eye, day turned to night and a mass of confused images rushed through his mind. It was a seeing. It was the village, but the village at night. The wooden huts were burning and people were running, their dark figures flashing before a backdrop of flames. There were horsemen in among them, and the air rang to the sound of commands and curses and screams. For a brief instant Silo saw a hulking figure on a rearing horse. A club was raised high over his head, and behind him a banner streamed out for a moment, glowing crimson in the light of the flames: the sign of the red hand. And within seconds it was gone. Silo found himself standing on the threshold of the sunlit village with a group of friendly pigs snuffling around his feet. Head pounding, he hurried toward the sound of the hammer.

While the blacksmith saw to Rusty, Ruddle held forth to a group of ragged villagers, and he introduced Silo as he approached.

"This here is Silo Zyco, a genuine seer from the Eastern Marshes."

Silo didn't even pause to say hello. "Your village will burn. Horsemen will come here. They ride under the sign of the red hand. I don't know when exactly, but soon."

He never had been much good at small talk. He stared at their astonished faces for a moment, then turned on his heel and walked back out of the village, throwing himself down in Blossom's shadow. Twenty minutes passed and then Ruddle, his face expressionless, came out leading a newly shod Rusty. A group of villagers gathered at the gate to see them off.

"Thanks for the warning," said the blacksmith. "We'll be ready for them when they come."

"That seeing of yours . . . ," said Ruddle as they rode away. "Might be best not to mention that to anyone. Especially not the inspectors."

"I wasn't going to," said Silo.

6

THE CAPITAL

So far their journey from the fort had led them along muddy woodland tracks, but on the morning of the third day they came to a wooden sign bearing a single word: MOTORWAY.

"We're entering godforsaken parts from here on in," said Ruddle. "This here's the old highway and we'll be following it a step of the way."

He looked glum at the thought, and Silo followed him out of the trees to find himself on a vast road, stretching off dead straight in either direction. The size of it took Silo's breath away, for it was wide enough to march an army down, and their column seemed suddenly dwarfed as it rode out onto its great expanse, the sound of the horses' hooves loud amid the silence of the woods that grew thick on either hand.

"Why's it so big?" he asked in wonder.

"Who knows?" grumbled Ruddle. "All I know is that it's

hard on the horses' feet. But government folk don't seem to give a thought to that. The Ancients rode this way once, and they reckon that if the Ancients did so, it must be the smart thing to do. But mark my words, we won't find any normal folk riding this road along with us."

And he was right. Once a herd of deer flitted across their path in the far distance, but as the day wore on they met no other travelers. The road swept through the landscape regardless of the natural lay of the land, gouging its way through hills and soaring up on embankments over valleys, bisected by crumbling bridges that bore the ghostly traces of other, lesser roads that had long been engulfed by the surrounding forest. And one day this one, mighty as it was, would vanish too, for slowly but surely nature was taking its course. Leaf mold was piled deep upon the verges and its surface was starred with dandelions; here and there great oaks had fallen, and their little procession had to weave its way around their mossy trunks. They rode in silence save for the beat of the horses' hooves and the creak of harnesses, for their strange surroundings seemed to throw an oppression over their whole party, and Silo was greatly relieved when, as dusk began to fall and the skies grew clamorous with home-going rooks, they finally saw signs of human life. A trickle of smoke rose up out of the forest ahead, and beside it a tall lookout tower. It was an outpost, more heavily fortified than any they had yet seen, and with a sign affixed to its gate:

"What's a motel?" said Silo as they pulled up outside.

"An inn without any booze," said Ruddle. "Blooming useless places."

But to Silo it seemed no worse than his usual lodgings. He had a room to himself, for in the evenings Orlando abandoned him and reverted to being the saintly Maximillian Crow. He confessed to finding the role rather tedious, but luckily none of their fellow seers seemed to have noticed. Daisy and Elgarth had become inseparable and Daisy had a way of looking at Elgarth, wide-eyed and adoring, that turned Silo's stomach. And as for Bella and Stella, they seemed to spend all their time huddled together in corners, alternatively whispering and giggling. Silo, who found gigglers intensely irritating, didn't think he would ever wish to count them among his little friends, and that evening he became certain of it.

Blossom was a horse of gargantuan appetites, and it was Silo's habit to look in on her before he went to bed to give her a fresh bucket of water and something extra to eat, but he had discovered that innkeepers, and doubtlessly motel keepers too, took a dim view of horses that ate twice as much as all the others—which was why he left his boots in his room that night and went tiptoeing to the feed shed, silent on webbed feet. But Bella and Stella had arrived before him. When he eased open the door he found Stella piling hay in a corner.

She was giggling as she did so, and Bella was poised over it with a lighted candle in her hand and an unhealthy gleam in her eyes.

"Don't," said Silo.

They spun around and stared at him, their eyes wide with shock.

He stepped forward and snatched the candle, amazed at their stupidity. "No fires tonight."

They shook their heads numbly, then Stella said, "Promise you won't tell."

"If you don't, we'll tell you a secret," said Bella. "It's about Elgarth's seeing. Maximillian had a seeing, and now Elgarth's had one. That's why we . . ." She looked wistfully at the candle.

Silo sat down on a bale of hay. "Tell me about Elgarth's seeing."

"He had it three days ago, but we didn't hear all of it. He only told Daisy. We had to listen behind the door. But he said that something bad is going to happen to Maximillian."

It already had, thought Silo, then remembered she was talking about Orlando. "What?"

"It's going to happen when he gets to the Capital. He's going to hurt his head, get a brain injury. There was a letter involved—at least I think he said a letter. It was difficult to hear. They were whispering."

Silo was horrified. How had Elgarth found out about Orlando's plan? And did he know about the letter that Orlando had stolen from Maximillian Crow? It didn't sound like a seeing to him; more as if Elgarth had been listening in to their conversations, for these were both subjects they had discussed on their rides.

He stood up and blew out the candle. "I won't tell anyone I saw you tonight."

He scooped up a double armful of hay and headed off to Blossom's stable.

Silo had lied, for he told Orlando the whole story as soon as they were alone together at the back of the column next morning.

"Heck!" said Orlando. "So Elgarth's on to me—but that can't be a seeing, can it? I stole that letter weeks ago—seeings are always about the future, aren't they?"

Silo's were. It certainly didn't sound like any of his own seeings.

"He must have paid someone to spy on us," said Orlando. "Hid them in the last baggage wagon or something. But he hasn't said anything to the inspectors yet, and he told Daisy it was a seeing. I think he's going to try to pass it off as one somehow—try to make people think he's a real seer. And the Arson Sisters said it was going to happen in the Capital, so he's biding his time."

"But why?"

Orlando shrugged. "He probably wants to make a big deal of it, wait until we get to the city before he reports me to the authorities. But never mind—at least we know now. As soon as we get within the city walls I'll be off and running."

"Where will you go?"

"I'll spend a few days in the Capital first—always wanted to see it. Then I'll hitch a ride down the river Rampage to the coast, see if I can find Val and the Raiders. Shouldn't be too difficult. They say she leaves a trail of destruction wherever she goes. She always did, actually. You should have seen the state of her bedroom."

Silo's heart sank. He'd never had a proper friend of his own age before, and suddenly the prospect of a world without Orlando seemed a very lonely one.

That afternoon they finally met some fellow travelers on the great highway. Silo heard a slow drumbeat from up ahead— *bam-BAM*, *bam-BAM*, *bam-BAM*, *bam-BAM*, *bam-BAM*, *bam-BAM*—growing louder by the minute, at once menacing, insistent, and strangely irritating. A party of horsemen was approaching in the distance, and Orlando scowled.

"It's the Bucket Heads," he said. "I guess we must be getting back to civilization."

As they watched the horsemen approach, Silo felt the hairs prickle on the back of his neck, for their leader carried a black banner on a tall pole, a banner that unfurled lazily in the breeze to reveal the sign of the red hand.

"What does that sign mean?" he asked. "The hand with the hole in it?"

"That's not a hole," said Orlando. "It's a coin. They're the collectors—the Government's tax collection squad, and they are one evil, evil bunch of Bucket Heads. They're the ones my mum and dad tangled with."

The horsemen were moving at a fast trot and in a moment they were sweeping by. Watching them pass, Silo was not surprised at the fate of Orlando's parents, for they were a formidable-looking bunch. There were thirty in all, big men in black uniforms with studded leather breastplates and huge, crushing boots. As well as swords and bows, each carried a hefty club strapped to his saddle, and a shield slung on his back: a black shield decorated with a bloodred hand, a black coin in its palm. The bucket-shaped helmets they wore made them look even more sinister, for they covered their entire heads and necks, leaving just a slit to see out of. They moved to the jingle of harness, the clink and clank of weapons, and the deafening drums—*bam-BAM, bam-BAM, bam-BAM, bam-BAM*; in his mind's eye Silo relived his seeing—the burning village and the fleeing villagers, the horseman with his upraised club—and felt a quick chill in his heart. The Government employed some very strange people, and he suddenly wondered if he really wanted to be among their number.

That evening brought them almost to the end of their journey. The forest petered out and the old highway suddenly ran riot. Instead of one road it branched into many, roads that swept high above the Earth supported on giant pillars, then around and above and beneath each other in long, looping curves like a vast nest of snakes, coiling off into the great plain that stretched before them. Smoke rose from the fires of a dozen villages and, dark and ominous against a flaming sunset, the mound of the Capital rose up in the distance. They had arrived at the last outpost and Silo and Orlando were making plans.

"There are four gates in, but one of them is for river traffic," said Orlando. "My guess is we'll be entering through the south one. Bound to be a big crowd there. I'll just mix in with it and slip away."

Silo had half a mind to go with him. Working as a government seer had been a simple decision to make back on the marsh, but things had grown more complicated since then. He would miss Orlando badly, and he didn't like the inspector or the collectors, but he wasn't as worldly-wise as his friend—or a thief or a forger, come to that. His gift of the seeing was the only talent he had. He would see how things worked out first, and if they didn't, well, maybe then he would consider joining Orlando.

"Is there anywhere we could meet up?" he said. "If I decide to come with you?"

"My uncle spent a bit of time in the Capital. There's a street called Great Sewer Alley, and he said there's an inn there called the Invisible Worm. It's next to a dung works."

Silo sighed. Presumably Orlando's uncle had not frequented the smart side of town. "Why there?"

"Well, if you knew my uncle, you'd understand that he's got a gift for finding places—the kind of places where you might meet useful people."

"Would that be criminals?"

"Some of them, yeah, but the sort of people who might

know what the Raiders have planned for the summer. We can meet up there in a week's time."

So that was their plan. Silo wasn't sure if it was a good one, and the next day he felt sick with apprehension as they set out on the last stage of their journey, watching the Capital looming slowly larger on the horizon. The smoke from a thousand fires hung over the city, and through its fog they could dimly discern a mass of rooftops rising above the city walls, dwarfed by the huge old buildings that stood among them. In the center, dominating the skyline, stood the famous Lion Tower. Silo saw that its balconies were strung with washing lines and he noticed a pig standing on one of them, giving the whole place a rather scruffy, domestic appearance. The great stone lion that stood at the tower's apex was impressive enough, though, and it stared angrily down the road to the Capital with its jaws open in a savage, silent roar.

Their way was slowed by wagons, herds of animals, and the seemingly endless squads of tax collectors traveling in and out of the city. The ceaseless *bam-BAM, bam-BAM, bam-BAM* of their drums seemed like an evil omen as they finally found themselves within the shadow of the great walls, soaring thirty feet into the air and studded with guard posts. They gave the place a grim, fortresslike air; somehow Silo had expected the approach to the Capital to be much grander. The inhabitants seemed to be in the habit of throwing their rubbish over the walls and so their way led past piles of festering garbage, picked over by buzzards and pigs and stray dogs. And children, Silo saw with sudden shock. He watched a tiny girl beat off a buzzard with a stick and snatch up a loaf of moldy bread.

The image of the Capital that had formed in his mind long ago, his shining city on the hill, died a sudden and painful death. The crush on the road had grown so great by now that they were almost at a standstill, and all at once a group of soldiers shouldered their way through the crowd and surrounded their party. For one dreadful moment Silo thought that Elgarth had told all he knew, but then the soldiers started shoving people roughly to one side.

"Make way for the government inspectors!"

They were beating a path through the crowd.

"Make way for the inspectors! Make way for the seers! Stand back, make way!"

A soldier seized the bridle of Orlando's pony and bawled, "Make way for Maximillian Crow!"

A girl rummaging through a nearby garbage pile heard the name and sprang to her feet: a tall girl dressed in a ragged gray vest and breeches, with long bony arms and legs and a mass of wild tawny hair. Her bottom lip was thrust out, giving her face an expression of savage discontent, and her green eyes blazed with hatred. She glared at Orlando, then stooped, picked up a rotten lettuce, and threw it, with astonishing force and accuracy, at his head. He was taken completely by surprise. He reeled back in his saddle, lost his balance, and fell off his pony. His head hit the ground with a dull thud and he lay motionless among the garbage, blood oozing from a gash in his temple. Silo slid off Blossom and knelt by his side, stunned into a sudden, shocking realization. The words of the Arson Sisters rang in his head—something bad happening when he got to the Capital, a brain injury, something about a letter. A lettuce. Not a letter, a *lettuce*. This was Elgarth's seeing. He had known this would happen all along and kept it secret. He was a genuine seer. Silo sought out his face in the crowd and knew that this time at least he was right, for Elgarth was smiling and his eyes were shining with triumph.

Two days later Silo found himself standing in front of a grimy door. Screams came from behind it. A sign depicting a severed arm hung over his head, and the door had a big cross on it, executed in two broad slashes of dripping red paint that looked like blood. He hated visiting the hospital. Steeling himself, he pushed open the door and walked quickly down the corridor ahead, trying to ignore the cries that came from the rooms on either side. He found Orlando at the end of the hall with his head swathed in bandages.

"Hi. How's your head feeling today?"

"Awful. Like Blossom trod on it. And I can hear this weird screaming noise."

It didn't seem the right time to tell Orlando that it was the sound of his fellow patients. But Silo was relieved to hear him making sense again, for on his previous visit Orlando had been semiconscious and rambling on about goats, and Silo had begun to worry that his brain was well and truly damaged.

"What happened to me?"

"Some loony lobbed a lettuce at you. You fell off your pony. And no need to worry about Elgarth. He won't be talking to anyone." He explained why.

Orlando was mightily relieved that his secret identity was safe but enraged that Elgarth hadn't warned him of the impending lettuce attack. "So he's a real seer, then, curse him, and the evil beast didn't say a word! Just my luck, I suppose. I'm stuck here feeling rubbish and you're having fun exploring the Capital. What's it like?"

Silo shrugged. It was a question he found almost impossible to answer. One thing was for certain: the place wasn't anything like he'd expected.

The Capital was chaos. As he shoved his way through its crowded streets, Silo could dimly see that it had once been designed to some kind of plan, but that had been a long, long time ago, and although many of the buildings and broad avenues of the Ancients still remained, the passing years had changed them out of all recognition: imprisoned within its encircling walls, the Capital was bursting at the seams. The great stone buildings and concrete towers were home to thousands now, surely far more than had originally been intended, and they bulged under the strain. Whole families camped on balconies, huts perched on rooftops, and the gaps between the old buildings had been filled in with tenements. Rows of huts had mushroomed down the center of the once-wide streets, and squashed into these narrow confines the daytime traffic was almost unbearable: thousands of pedestrians and riders and wagons shunting back and forth, along with goats, chickens, dogs, and pigs. Buzzards and vultures wheeled overhead, making even the skies seem crowded.

Looking at Orlando's eager face, Silo hadn't the heart to tell him that he lay in bed at night and dreamed he was out on Goose Creek again, alone on his raft under a great sweep of sky, with the fresh salt breeze blowing in from the sea and only the cry of the marsh birds for company.

"Wait and see," he said. "You'll be up in a few days."

"Where are you staying?"

"At the Academy in Cowcross Street. It's where they train seers."

"Is it any good?"

Silo shrugged. "I don't know yet. We don't start classes until tomorrow. We're waiting for some woman from the State Archaeological Division to arrive—she's the headmistress, apparently."

"Heck!" said Orlando. "You may have a problem, then. I've heard a few things about the State Archaeological Division, and they sound like seriously bad news."

"Why?" asked Silo.

"Well, it's all to do with that stuff about power supplies and power stations again. And how my sister got to be Valeria the Violent instead of just Val Bramble. The story they told me was that there's a peninsula somewhere on the west coast. It had a big ruin on it, something left over from the time of the Ancients. So a bunch of people from the State Archaeological Division turned up there one day and said they'd found out it used to be a power station. They got all the people from the nearest village to start digging it up, to see if they could find the power. But it was like the Ancients had left a curse on the place or something, because after a few weeks people started getting sick. First they got blisters on their skin and then they got really ill, but when they tried to leave, the people from the Division got Bucket Heads to guard them, made them keep on digging. Well, a few of them managed to get away in a boat, and that's when they met Val. She was sailing down the Horse Island Straits—her along with a few other Raiders' ships. When they heard what was happening, they sailed to the peninsula and had a big battle with the Bucket Heads. Val took in the first ship, led the first assault. That's how she got to be called 'the Violent'—for her heroic deeds. Anyway, they won the battle and took the villagers away with them to the Horse Islands."

"Did they get better?" said Silo.

"Some did, but lots of them died. So that's the sort of people the State Archaeological Division are. Not very nice ones."

Silo scowled. Already he had formed a dim view of the Academy, and the news that his future headmistress might be party to mass murder was deeply depressing.

"I just realized something," said Orlando. "That screaming's not in my head, is it?"

"No. They've got a few cases of crab pox down the hall, but it looks like they caught it in time. No one's gone terminal yet, anyway."

A grim-faced nurse came in holding a spoon and a bottle

of something that looked nasty. She gave Silo an unfriendly look and jerked her thumb in the direction of the corridor. "End of visits."

"See you tomorrow," Silo said to Orlando. "Good luck with it."

Silo was in low spirits as he weaved his way through the crowded streets, for he was on his way to say good-bye to Ruddle. He found him saddling Blossom outside the Burning Buzzard, and his parting words awakened a suspicion that had long lain lurking in some dusty corner of his mind.

"Shame I have to leave so soon," said Ruddle. "I'd've liked to see you settled in that school of yours first."

"I'll be fine," said Silo.

"Maybe so. Been wondering what happens to all these seers, though. Every year half a dozen or so arrive, but you never hear much about them afterward. A bit of a worry, that."

Silo thought so too. "Don't worry about it. Me and Orlan—Maximillian have made plans. If we don't like the Academy, we'll leave."

"That's what I was coming to. If things go wrong, you're to let me know. You can send word by any of the guides as are headed west."

"Are you guiding the inspectors again?" said Silo.

Ruddle shook his head. "I'm through with the Government and its inspectors. When we were back in the Wildwoods and you warned those villagers about the tax squad—well, I found I was glad you had, and when a man gets to thinking like that it's high time he works for someone new." His face brightened. "And it's coffee merchants I'm guiding this trip, so it's all worked out for the best."

Silo had known he would miss Ruddle, but he didn't realize quite how much until he watched him ride out into the teeming streets, turning in his saddle to give him a final wave. As he watched the crowd close over Blossom's vast rump, Silo wished with all his heart that he were going with them, but then he remembered his days on the marsh, when being a government seer had been the height of his ambition. He had traveled many weary miles to get here and he might as well give it a try—or at least until Orlando was well enough to travel.

He took a roundabout route, for he was in no hurry to get back to the Academy. Ever since the incident with the lettuce he found it difficult to be in Elgarth's company without being overcome by the desire for violent revenge, and so it seemed safest to avoid him as much as possible. Now his way led him down a street lined with stalls where market traders bawled for custom. For the first time in his life Silo had money in his pocket, for Ruddle had given him a fistful of coins as a parting gift, and he paused before a stall selling buzzard products.

"They flies in the skies and they goes in our pies! Buzzard pies! Buzzard pasties, fresh baked this morning! Get your lovely buzzard burger here!"

Silo bought one and regretted it instantly, for it took inedibility to new and hitherto unsuspected heights. He took a mouthful, froze where he stood, and then apprehensively lifted the lid of the bun. Concealed within was a lump of grayish matter clotted with feathers and claws, and he promptly spat violently into the gutter.

"I'll have it if you don't want it."

A ragged boy had appeared at his side.

"It's vile," said Silo as he handed it over.

"Buzzard's fine. You should try the vulture burgers."

Silo made a mental note never to do so. The boy took a ravenous bite and Silo hurried away. It was not just the buzzard burger that sickened him. He had been in the Capital only two days, but he was already aware of a mysterious twilight world that existed behind its bustling façade. The Capital was home to an army of watchful, ragged children who kept to the shadows and alleyways, emerging at dusk to scavenge for the spilled fruit and rotten vegetables that lay in the mud. In his darker moments Silo feared that he might come to share a similar fate, for it seemed that the Capital was a cruel place for children who, like himself, had no parents to watch over them.

7

THE SCHOOL FOR SEERS

Silo's new home was an uninviting one. The Academy's dark edifice soared above Cowcross Street like a cliff face, and its entrance was flanked by two towering statues of warriors. They wore stern expressions but little else and held swords in their hands. An inscription ran above the massive bronze door they guarded—THIS INSTITUTION IS DEDICATED TO SERVICE, OBEDIENCE, UNITY, AND PROGRESS—and Silo's tiny figure was dwarfed by the structure. Two sentries stared suspiciously, then opened the door a crack for him, and as he slipped into the cavernous hall it swung shut behind him with a sound like a thunderclap. The school for seers took up a wing on the second floor, but the rest of the Academy was devoted to military training, and Silo climbed a flight of stairs lined with paintings of bloody battle scenes and severe-looking soldiers. He passed other students as he went, hulking teenagers in black uniforms. Silo didn't like the Academy, and he sensed that the feeling was mutual, for students and portraits alike seemed to stare down at him with mistrustful eyes as he passed.

He shoved open the door and steeled himself to meet the vile Elgarth. Presumably Elgarth disliked him quite as much in return, but Elgarth was much better at concealing his feelings, and as Silo walked into the room he turned to him with a look of grave concern.

"I hear you've been to the hospital. How's Maximillian? We've all been so worried about him."

"He's so caring," Daisy whispered admiringly to the Arson Sisters as Silo stared at Elgarth and willed his head to explode. But he was spared the effort of replying, for at that moment Orlando himself came staggering through the door. He looked terrible, and Daisy ran up to him uttering sympathetic cries.

"Poor Maximillian! How are you feeling today?"

"Rubbish."

"Shouldn't you be at the hospital?" said Silo.

"Too dangerous. A crab pox case has just gone terminal. Now, if you'll excuse me I really, really need to lie down for a bit."

Silo led him to his room, and he threw himself down on the bed. Drifting up from the quadrangle below came the tramp of marching feet and the bellowed commands of cadet training officers.

Orlando groaned. "I was hoping this place might be a bit quieter than the hospital. Still, at least no one's screaming."

But that was before they met Mrs. Morgan.

She arrived the next morning as they were sitting over breakfast. Silo was just polishing off his scrambled eggs when he was startled by a sound like a thunderclap. Turning, they saw a tall, thin woman between forty and fifty years of age standing in the doorway. She was smiling at them, but she held a stick in her hand and the door was still reverberating with the blow she had given it.

"Good morning, children! I am Mrs. Morgan, your new headmistress. I understand that you must all be very excited to be here, but we have work to do."

The general impression she gave was one of blackness, for she wore a long black dress that clung to her bony body, a necklace of black jet beads, and long earrings of black jet, and her black hair was parted in the middle and skewered back in a bun with long black jet pins. Her eyes were black too, startlingly so in the pallor of her face. Even her lips were colorless, and they were parted now in what Silo supposed was meant to be a welcoming smile, but her teeth were long and yellow, like the keys of an ancient piano, and they gave her face a hungry, wolfish quality.

"Now! Classroom One, if you please, and quickly!"

Silo trooped into the classroom with the others, and Mrs. Morgan began the proceedings by giving them a little talk.

"Well, children! It will surprise you to learn that not all who have applied to this Academy in the past have been genuine seers. It is well known that government-approved seers are generously provided for, and there have been unfortunate cases where dishonest, lying children have attempted to pass themselves off as seers to reap rewards they in no way deserve. I'm sure that is not the case with any of you"—Mrs. Morgan gave them all a thin smile—"but even so, it would be foolish of us not to make absolutely sure! So we like you all to have at least one officially witnessed seeing to your name, one verified by a government representative, before you can be considered a true student of this Academy."

Silo felt the Arson Sisters stirring uneasily at his side.

"Now!" said Mrs. Morgan. "Maximillian Crow! Your reputation has preceded you. No one can doubt that you have remarkable talents. And as for you, Elgarth, Governor Early has vouched for your gift and given us numerous examples of your seeings. Silo Zyco—one of our inspectors tells us you accurately predicted the attack of a zoo animal. That will do nicely. And so that just leaves you, my dears." She turned her glittering eyes on Daisy and the Arson Sisters. "I know the gift of the seeing is not always a reliable one, but I will need proof of your abilities, and quickly. That way we can be *absolutely sure* that you are fit to be part of our little class. And now"—she produced a great bundle of papers from her desk—"I always ask my new students to fill out a Character Appraisal Form."

Silo took his form. It started simply enough: name, age, date of birth—that much was easy, but after that the questions became increasingly strange:

Do you believe in elephants?
Why is goatball our national sport?

Have you ever committed a crime rated three or higher
   on the Scales of Justice?
Do you hear voices in your head?

There were pages and pages of them. Silo gave up after page four and just wrote no to everything. The others were obviously more conscientious as they took hours over it, and by the time Mrs. Morgan had collected all the forms it was nearly lunchtime.

"Girls, you shall stay. I have a little test for you," she said. "The boys may go."

"I think we made a mistake coming here," said Silo as he and Orlando made their way back to their room. "How long before you're fit to travel?"

"Give it a day or two. That appraisal form did my head in, and it's done in already. *Do you hear voices in your head?* I do now. They're saying, *Run, Orlando, run.* That Mrs. Morgan is one evil-looking woman."

Silo left Orlando to nurse his headache and wandered through the empty hallways of the Academy. For a school with only six pupils it seemed unnecessarily large, and Silo was curious to know what else it contained. He set off down a corridor, opening each door in turn, and examined a series of shuttered classrooms full of cobwebs, then a lumber room and a long-neglected toilet. But when he opened the very last door two pairs of eyes stared back at him: huge, unblinking emerald-green eyes. Two sleek black cats lay lounging in the gloom. But they were gigantic, gargantuan cats, ten times bigger than a cat had any right or reason to be. Silo stared at them in astonishment, and as he did so one made a deep rumbling noise in its throat and rose to its feet with a liquid grace, eyes fixed on his. And then it licked its lips. Silo leaped back and slammed the door behind him. And as he stood before it, aghast and trembling, he heard footsteps approaching. Instinctively he backed into a shadowy doorway, his heart racing. There were zoo animals in the Academy! But why?

Mrs. Morgan was pacing down the corridor with Daisy and Stella and Bella in tow, and to Silo's horror she stopped directly in front of him. She stood with her back to him, the girls ranged in a row before her.

"Well, girls," she said. "Time for your test! You claim you can see into the future, so tell me—what would you find if you were to enter this room?"

They stared at her miserably.

"Come now! This should present no problem to a seer. I'll give you one minute to come up with the answer, and if it is not forthcoming, I shall be very disappointed." She gave them a thin smile. "It would be a great shame, would it not, if I had to let you enter the room to discover the secret?"

And Silo suddenly believed her quite capable of such a cruelty. He realized it was down to him to spare them a hideous, and perhaps deadly, surprise. He stepped out of the shadows, laying a cautionary finger to his lips as he did so, and stood behind Mrs. Morgan.

"Well?" she said.

Silo raked the air with imaginary claws.

"It's an animal of some kind," said Daisy.

Silo licked his paws.

"A cat," said Bella.

He stretched his hands wide apart.

"A big cat," said Stella.

He stretched them wider.

"A very big cat," said Daisy.

He bared his teeth in a ferocious, silent snarl and stuck two fingers up—and found himself staring up into Mrs. Morgan's glittering black eyes. She had turned around at an unfortunate moment, and her fury was frightening to behold.

"How *dare* you insult me? You insolent, skulking child!"

She struck Silo a vicious blow with her stick, knocking him sprawling to the floor. He uttered an involuntary cry of pain and it was answered, immediately and terrifyingly, by a low growl from behind the door. The girls froze in horror and then turned, wide-eyed, to Mrs. Morgan.

Daisy spoke in a faltering voice. "There are . . . there are zoo animals behind the door. Two of them. Big cats."

"Indeed there are, but what kind? I had hoped you would be able to give me a more exact answer."

"We were just about to," said Bella, "but then Silo came creeping up and being rude."

"He did it on purpose," said Stella. "He was trying to put us off."

Astounded, Silo rose to his feet, just in time for Mrs. Morgan to box him around the ears.

She addressed the girls. "I am satisfied for the time being. You may go to lunch now. But you"—she seized Silo by the scruff of the neck and shook him—"shall have none, nor supper either! You shall spend both periods writing lines, for I'll not take insolence from a dirty little swamp child."

Daisy shot him a compassionate look as she scurried away, but the Arson Sisters did not so much as glance at him. Silo fought down a red tide of fury, and as Mrs. Morgan hauled him off down the corridor his mind seethed with bloody, vengeful visions of her, Stella, and Bella being consumed, down to the very last morsel of bone and gristle, by ravening zoo cats.

That afternoon Mrs. Morgan addressed the class in front of a blackboard inscribed one hundred times with the legend: *I will not be rude to my teachers.* The general effect was rather fine, for Silo had worked off his rage by using a variety of scripts and swooping calligraphic flourishes. Now he sat and surveyed his work with pride for, rude though he might be, no one could deny the excellence of his handwriting.

Mrs. Morgan began her class with a bombshell: "All of you here claim to be able to see into the future, and those skills will have to be developed," she said, "but we expect more of you than that—much more. You must expand your gifts so that you can see things that are happening in the present too, and more importantly, you must learn to look back into the distant past. That is the most vital thing of all."

A stunned silence followed. Then Daisy put up her hand.

"But, Mrs. Morgan—seeings are always about the future, aren't they? No one has them about the past. It's impossible."

Mrs. Morgan smiled at her. "My dear child, you are quite mistaken. A great many ignorant people no longer believe in seers. They say it is impossible that anyone can see into the future, but all of you gathered in this room, you have that gift. You have been blessed with minds that are not fettered by the usual human limitations. A seer has a mind that is capable of overstepping the boundaries of time itself. If you can see forward in time, it follows that you must be able to see backward also. You may find it difficult at first, but you will learn. It is just a matter of hard work and discipline, no more."

Orlando put up his hand. "Why would anyone want to see backward? What's the point?"

This was obviously the wrong question to ask, for Mrs. Morgan frowned and struck the desk with her walking stick. "Ignorant boy! Because of the marvelous things you might learn about the ways of the Ancients, that's why! How do you think we rediscovered the rules of goatball? That was the work of seers—seers who worked in this very classroom twenty years ago. But that is a trivial thing, a mere entertainment. There are far greater things yet to discover: the secrets of the power stations; the purpose of zoo animals; how the Ancients flew through the skies."

"Did they really fly?" said Orlando. "I thought maybe that was a myth."

"Of course they flew!" Miss Morgan beat the desk again. "The Lion Tower is twenty-two stories high. Do you think the

Ancients had nothing better to do with their time than climb stairs all day?"

She scanned their faces with her weird black eyes. They were so dark they seemed to be all pupil and no iris, and the effect was unsettling, as though she had black holes in her head.

"So this is the work we have planned for you, and I hope you are proud to be a part of it, but we expect you to work very, very hard to achieve our fourfold aims of service, obedience, unity, and progress. Much is expected of you, but there are exciting prospects ahead for those of you who shine at their lessons. Well, children! Are you prepared to shine?"

There was a short silence, then Elgarth said, "I'm sure we'll all do our very best."

But Mrs. Morgan was asking the impossible, and Silo had a creeping conviction that their very best would never be good enough for her.

However, Elgarth had meant what he said, and that evening he lounged on his sofa, giving serious thought as to how best to shine. The answer seemed a simple one—eliminate the competition. But how exactly? It was the kind of problem he enjoyed, and he smiled as he stretched himself out upon the velvet cushions. The other seers had been housed in comfort, but Elgarth had been housed in luxury. He had been allocated his own apartment, a splendidly furnished one that reflected his status as the son of Governor Early. And it was to his father that his thoughts turned this evening, for Elgarth's father was a difficult man. He came from a long line of dung collectors but had risen from his humble origins to become a regional governor through hard work, ambition, and an ability to terrify all who met him. Elgarth was among them, for his father wished his sons to be as successful as he himself had been, and he was not a man who took kindly to having his wishes thwarted. Already Elgarth's older brother was making a name for himself as a commander of the tax squads, a role to which he seemed ideally suited due to his violent and uncomplicated nature, and Governor Early had hoped that Elgarth would follow in his footsteps. But Elgarth believed that his gift of the seeing would enable him to carve a glittering career that would equal, if not surpass, that of his brother: one that would spare him the mud, blood, and general discomfort of a soldier's life. However, it was essential to succeed if he was not to incur his father's displeasure. He was confident in his own abilities but it seemed wise to leave nothing to chance, which was why he was currently contemplating ways of ridding himself of Silo Zyco and, more particularly, Maximillian Crow.

As he lay musing, his servant, Rankly, entered with a plate of cakes and a pot of tea. His father had given him Rankly for his eighth birthday. He'd been disappointed at the time because he'd asked for a hamster, but four years had passed since then and he was resigned to his loss, for Rankly took care of his needs with admirable diligence.

"I want you to keep an eye on Silo Zyco for me," Elgarth said. "See if you can catch him up to something dodgy."

"Gladly, master." Rankly busied himself with the teapot. "Has he annoyed you in some way?"

"Yes," said Elgarth with admirable candor. "He's a genuine seer, for one thing."

"And one seer is quite enough for the Government, especially if that one is as talented as yourself."

"Exactly. But I think I can deal with him. I can't prove it, but I'm almost sure he stole my money at the Red Hand. So he's a thief. And he comes from a long line of homicidal maniacs—rather an unusual background for a government-approved seer, so I'm sure they'll be keeping an eye on him. But he'll slip up sooner or later. I may even give him a helping hand."

"Any plans for the others?" said Rankly hopefully, for he entered wholeheartedly into the dastardly schemes of his master.

"No need to bother with the girls," said Elgarth. "I'm almost certain Bella and Stella are fakes, and I don't think Daisy has a genuine gift either."

"And if she has, it's not a useful one—snowdrops and so on."

"Exactly. So that just leaves Maximillian Crow." Elgarth considered. "I've been thinking about him. Given his reputation, he's going to be my main problem. There is one thing I'm curious about, though. They say he had a seeing about the lookout tower in Herringhaven falling down. It did, and it killed his parents—strange, that. Why didn't he warn them? There must be a story behind it, and ten to one it doesn't do him much credit. Maybe he didn't like them, or he stood to inherit a fortune or something. I want you to make some inquiries for me."

"Gladly," said Rankly, "but I'll need some expenses."

"Here!" Elgarth tossed him a silver crown and Rankly snatched it eagerly. His wages left much to be desired, and it was only when engaged in research for Elgarth that he was able to afford a pleasant day out.

"Thank you kindly, master! I'll be on the case first thing tomorrow."

Meanwhile Silo was standing gloomily at the window of his room, while Orlando lay slumped on his bed complaining about the noise, for the quad below was a scene of seething activity. That evening it was brilliantly lit with flaming torches, for hundreds of military cadets had gathered to listen to a speech. Silo was dismayed to see dozens of collectors mingled in with the crowd. They were wearing their black uniforms but had left their helmets at home, and surprisingly, they had closely shaven skulls, which were glowing a hectic orange in the firelight. A tall man was striding up and down a platform at the far end of the quad, in the middle of a stirring and impassioned speech. He waved his arms and shouted, but from his vantage point Silo could only hear odd snatches of his words:

". . . wonders of the Ancients . . . learn from their . . . glories of goatball . . . overhead power lines . . . example to our youth . . . our great nation . . . crush . . . destroy . . . tax evaders . . . Raiders . . . painful lingering death . . . mighty work we have undertaken . . . end to the dark ages . . . new dawn . . . noble cause . . . fourfold aims . . . ."

He raised his voice in a final mighty bellow: ". . . of service! And obedience! And unity! And progress!"

The cadets and the collectors took up his words, punching the air with their fists and chanting, "Service! Obedience! Unity! Progress!"

Orlando groaned and buried his head beneath his pillow.

Louder they chanted, and louder: "Service! Obedience! Unity! Progress! SERVICE! OBEDIENCE! UNITY! PROGRESS!"

And Silo saw a scene pass rapidly before his eyes—not a seeing but a memory. He was back on the Island. It was a wet evening and he was entering the Chronicle Keeper's hut carrying an armful of fishing nets. Ryker was crouched before a bucket washing his shirt, and Silo saw the ugly red brand seared onto his shoulder: SOUP. Service. Obedience. Unity. Progress. Silo felt a sudden icy chill that reached to the very marrow of his bones. These were the people who had hurt and hunted Ryker. They were the reason he had sought refuge on a lonely marsh at the far fringes of the civilized world. Ryker had been an enemy to Service, Obedience, Unity, and Progress.

He sprang back from the window as if struck, and spun around to face Orlando. "We have to get out of here!"

"Yeah, I was thinking along the same lines myself," said

Orlando. "The whole place is crawling with Bucket Heads, and the headmistress is in with a bunch of murderers. We're keeping seriously bad company here."

"We should leave tomorrow."

"Be nice, wouldn't it? Have to work out how, though. They've got sentries on the door. I think our best bet is to bide our time, act normal, and then slip away the first chance we get. And when we do I plan on throwing in my lot with the Raiders."

Swiftly Silo considered his options. Ryker had been the cleverest man he had ever known, and it was stunning to learn that Silo had traveled countless miles to work for the very people that Ryker had fled from. He might be dead, but Silo knew he could still trust Ryker's judgment and good sense.

He made a momentous decision. "I'll come with you."

It seemed that he was fated to fulfill his destiny, and to follow in his father's footsteps.

"My father's a Raider. His name is Aquinus the Accursed."

"Really?" Orlando sat up and grinned at him. "You kept that pretty quiet! But I'm really glad we'll be sticking together. I was hoping you'd change your mind about being a government-approved seer. I don't like to go on about you coming from a swamp and stuff . . ."

"It's not a swamp, it's a marsh," said Silo.

". . . but I've been around a bit, seen the way things work on Mainland, and it strikes me the Government isn't ever going to approve of you. You're just not their type."

8

THE SEEING

Sleep would not come to Silo that night. His mind was made up, but his future seemed perilous and uncertain. He thought of the vast range of the Kingdom Isles and then beyond, to the wild and boundless oceans—oceans on which he would sail if he was to become a Raider. It may have been his mother's dying wish, but even so his heart quailed at the prospect. His life had been lived on the margin of the sea and he had observed it in all its moods, summer and winter, year in, year out. He thought of its sucking tides, its shifting sands, and the wild fury of its storms and didn't think he cared to get more closely acquainted. But then he thought of his father. He must be out there somewhere on that vast expanse of ocean, standing at the helm of his ship under a star-spangled sky, bound for strange and uncharted lands beyond a dark horizon. Perhaps he would find him—if he was still alive, that was. But the thought gave Silo hope, and he fell asleep with a lighter heart. However, it was not to be sleep that came to him that night, but a seeing.

The darkness melted about him and suddenly he was standing on the Causeway under a wet gray sky, between the open sea and the flat expanse of the marsh. Even though he knew it was a seeing, and in reality he was far, far from home, his heart stirred at the sight of it. A sudden and unexpected homesickness swept through him like a flame, and eagerly he sought out the familiar mound of the Island, that tumble-down heap of huts and hovels that rose proud above the mud-brown waters of Goose Creek. But it was gone. He gazed in disbelief at the spot where it had stood and saw only open sky and the swirling tidal waters, and in the whole great expanse of the marsh there were no people, no rafts, no huts, not one single solitary sign of human life; the only sounds were those of the wind and the waves and the crying of the marsh birds. The Island and all who had lived on it had vanished. And the Causeway itself had changed. He saw that it was lined with driftwood markers, jutting from the damp earth like a row of rotten teeth, and on each one was a name. They were graves, he realized, his blood prickling with dread: Mudfords, Beans, and Pattles lay beside the sea and under the sweeping skies for all eternity in a long, low line. He saw Ben's name, and Lily's and Lula's, and all the old familiar names of his child-hood. Some great horror had visited this place, and death had closed the long Chronicles of the Island. And then his seeing ended and he was back in the heart of the Capital, sitting bolt upright in bed with his fists clenched and his heart racing.

"What's wrong?" Orlando murmured sleepily in the darkness.

"I've just had a seeing."

"Anything nice?"

"No. Something dreadful."

Orlando sighed. "That's always the way with you, isn't it?"

The next morning Silo and Orlando huddled together at the far corner of the dining table conversing in low, anxious voices. Silo was in a fever of anxiety, and his sausages lay forgotten and untasted before him. He must warn the Islanders, but of what? For the umpteenth time he unwound the familiar sequence of the Chronicles in his head. Many disasters had befallen the Island in its long history—floods, famines, epidemics, the great tidal wave—but he could think of no catastrophe so terrible as to wipe out the entire population. And how could the Island itself disappear?

"These seeings of yours—how far into the future are they?" said Orlando.

"Not very long."

"Hell! Then we need to be on our way tonight."

"Are you fit to travel?" asked Silo.

"I'll do," said Orlando. "And the Academy's not a healthy place to be at the moment. You're not the only one who had a seeing last night. The Arson Sisters say there's going to be a fire in Cowcross Street—a bit of a worry, that. I can cope with a sore head, but not being burned to death."

Tonight it would be, then. The bell rang and they went, with mutinous hearts, to their classroom.

Here Mrs. Morgan lectured them on the wonders of the Ancient world. Ryker had taught Silo about the Ancient world too, but he had stressed that what little people knew about it was mostly guesswork, for the Ancient world had ended abruptly and violently. First came the Great Catastrophe, when legend held that the Earth itself had moved. A chain of volcanic islands had risen off the northern coast and a time of chaos had followed. Tidal waves had swept the coastlines, plague had spread throughout the land, and the great cities burned. Countless numbers of people had died, and those who survived fled into the countryside and struggled to scratch a living from the land. Ryker thought they must have been very poor farmers, or maybe the weather had been exceptionally bad, for it was over a hundred years before things began to improve and they entered into their own era, the age of the Newcount. But by then the thread that had bound the old world to the new was broken. Records had been burned or destroyed, wise men and women were long dead, and the knowledge of the Ancient world was lost forever. Silo thought that maybe the Ancients hadn't been so wonderful after all, as they seemed to have made a fearful mess of things, but Mrs. Morgan obviously disagreed. Silo had not expected great things of her, at least not after Orlando had told him about the doings of the State Archaeological

Division, but she had exceeded all his worst fears. The incident with the zoo animals had been warning enough, but now, as he listened to her talk obsessively about a world that was lost beyond hope of redemption, she struck him as deranged and dangerous. He longed to be free of the Academy, and to be headed home again to warn the Islanders of the unfathomable disaster that was about to sweep them from the face of the Earth.

Elgarth was peevish too. Rankly was not around to serve his lunch and he resented it.

So when he did arrive, and looking remarkably cheerful, Elgarth was sharp with him.

"Where have you been?"

"At the Burning Buzzard, master, by the west gate. Those as travels in from the west often stop off there to refresh themselves when they arrive, and I spent the morning there. Mingling and chatting, I was."

"And drinking," said Elgarth, for Rankly's face was flushed, and he rocked slightly on his feet.

"I did take a drop, but only to make my presence there seem natural," said Rankly with dignity. "But good news, master! I met a man from Herringhaven who was a neighbor of the Crow family and we talked some. It seems that Maximillian had nothing to gain from his parents' deaths—an affectionate family, he said, and poor. But he does know what Maximillian looks like."

"So what?" said Elgarth. "So do we."

"Maybe not, master. He described him as a pale little chap with fair hair."

Elgarth sat very upright in his chair, an incredulous smile spreading across his face. "Are you absolutely sure?"

"Yes, master. The man was adamant."

"So our Maximillian's an impostor! Brilliant, absolutely brilliant! I should have guessed! The greatest seer in all Mainland, and he's only had one seeing in a month! He must have paid someone to burn down the goatball stadium, and chances are he stole my money to do it. And to think I thought it was Silo! But can we prove he's the wrong boy? Have you got the address of this neighbor?"

"I have better than that, master. I have the neighbor himself."

Rankly opened the door with a flourish to reveal a cheerful drunken man.

∾

Silo and Orlando were the first back in the classroom that afternoon; they leaned casually out the window, surreptitiously inspecting the alleyway below. Compared to most streets in the Capital it was a tranquil backwater, for the only sign of life was a pile of pigs that lay slumbering against the wall of the Academy in a happy communal heap. Silo eyed them with resentment, for they exuded an enviable air of peace and serenity, and their grunts of contentment, together with a powerful piggy aroma, drifted up to where he and Orlando stood, gloomily weighing up their options.

"It's a fair old drop," said Orlando, "but this looks like our best bet. All the other windows face onto Cowcross Street, so no way can we slip out without the sentries spotting us. I reckon it's this or nothing—we'll need a rope, though."

"We can make one out of knotted sheets," said Silo. "We'll leave tonight and find that inn your uncle told you about. You said it's a meeting place for Raiders—do you think they'd help us?"

But Silo would never discover Orlando's thoughts on the matter, for at that very moment Mrs. Morgan swept into the room and a series of startling events, each more unpleasant than the last, crowded in upon her heels.

"Maximillian!" cried Mrs. Morgan. "You have a visitor. One of your old neighbors from Herringhaven is here, and is anxious to pay his respects."

Horror-stricken, Silo and Orlando turned to see a small red-faced man. Elgarth stood beside him with a bright smile on his face, which brightened even further when the man stared indignantly at Orlando and cried, "But that's not Maximillian Crow—don't look a bit like him!"

For a boy of such indolent habits Orlando reacted with blinding speed. He sprang onto the windowsill and balanced there for a few frozen seconds, his face blanched with terror as he gazed down at the drop beneath his feet. And then he jumped. For a brief moment he seemed to hang suspended against the bright square of sky; then he plummeted down two stories to land squarely on the pile of sleeping pigs. They exploded beneath him like a pig-bomb. In the blink of an eye the quiet alley was transformed into a seething mass of outraged swine, torn rudely from their slumbers and shattering the peace of the afternoon with earsplitting squeals. They scattered in all directions—and astonishingly Orlando was among them. He had suffered no ill effects from his audacious leap for he had landed soft, bouncing on the back of a mighty sow. No doubt he would have preferred to make his own way from there, but she shot to her trotters as though electrified, and with the hapless Orlando still astride her. Thus it was that Silo's last glimpse of his friend was of him being borne away on the back of a stampeding pig, clinging on for dear life as he hurtled down the alley amid a cloud of dust and the thunder of indignant trotters. Within an instant he was whisked around a corner and out of sight, leaving Silo gazing after him openmouthed in astonishment.

Not so Mrs. Morgan.

"Alert the guards!" she barked to the helpful neighbor.

He stared at her in drunken befuddlement until she raised her stick.

"Immediately!"

He lurched for the door, and in a moment his roars of alarm reverberated through the Academy. Deprived of a living target, Mrs. Morgan struck the wall a vicious blow and stood in a drifting cloud of plaster dust, quivering with fury.

"An impostor! He shall pay dearly for this!"

Desperately Silo glanced out the window, scanning the

alley for another handy pile of pigs, but only a puzzled piglet remained, gazing reproachfully up at the sky. When Silo's gaze fell upon it, it squealed in terror and scampered away, almost upending a guard who had appeared at the end of the alley. Confused cries from below told him the hunt was underway. For him there could be no escape and, sick at heart, he turned to face the wrath of Mrs. Morgan.

Hectic red spots glowed on her cheeks and her eyes sparked with fury. "This is an outrage! How could such a thing happen? In *my* school!"

The ever-helpful Elgarth had a suggestion. "Perhaps Silo can help us," he said. "I don't suggest for a moment that he had any knowledge of this shameful impersonation, but he and Maximillian—I mean, the boy who claimed to be Maximillian—were such *very* good friends. It is just possible that he let something slip, something that would help us to understand his motives."

"Indeed it is!" Mrs. Morgan turned on Silo with a face like thunder. "As Elgarth says, the two of you were friends—or should I say co-conspirators? Surely you must have suspected something?"

"Why should I?" said Silo desperately.

"Why?" said Mrs. Morgan, her voice heavy with menace. "Because the two of you are inseparable, that's why! I believe you to be an accomplice in this, a traitor and a spy: a lying, conniving, ungrateful swamp child."

She raised her stick and advanced upon him, her face twitching with rage. Silo backed away, praying for intervention. And his wish was granted, but in a manner that seemed likely to compound rather than alleviate his woes.

"One moment, please! I have some questions to ask of the Zyco boy."

The grating voice was depressingly familiar. The inspector was standing in the doorway.

"Inspector!" Mrs. Morgan paused. "Forgive the violence of my language. A regrettable incident has just occurred, and I have reason to believe that we are nurturing a viper in our bosom."

"You mean Silo Zyco?" said the inspector. "I am of your opinion. That is, in fact, the reason for my visit. I came to warn you of his treasonous nature, but it seems I am too late."

"Explain yourself, Inspector."

"I have just received disturbing news from the provinces," said the inspector. "It seems a squad of our collectors have been subjected to an armed assault."

He stared at Silo, but Silo remained silent, mystified as to what this had to do with him.

The inspector continued. "They were sent to collect taxes, rightfully owed to the Government, from a village whose inhabitants had refused to pay. But they were ambushed on the road and viciously attacked. They were taken completely by surprise and regrettably came off very much the worse in the encounter. To date only one of the miscreants has been captured, but he told us they were warned of the collectors' arrival by a seer—a seer named Silo Zyco."

Silo froze in horror. It seemed that the villagers of Baldock had excelled themselves.

"And there is worse to follow. They stole weapons from the collectors and went on a lawless rampage. They have burned two of our outposts to the ground. They have stolen tax money and, they claim, 'returned it to the people'—by which they mean squandering it on public feasts and goatball tournaments. Even as we speak they are marauding about the Wildwoods, urging people to join them in revolt." He glared at Silo. "Can you deny that you are at the root of this anarchy?"

Suddenly Silo was wild with indignation. "Yes, I did warn them," he cried, "but why wouldn't I? I didn't know those collectors worked for you lot! They were burning things and beating people up. I thought they were just a bunch of psychos."

"You are not qualified to judge such matters," said the inspector, and he gave Silo a shrewd, calculating look. "I confess you surprise me. At first I did not believe you to be a genuine seer. It is a rare gift, and one that our Government values—if it be used in their service, for the maintenance of law and order. But rogue seers—that is another matter altogether."

"Indeed it is!" cried Mrs. Morgan. "They are the lowest of the low! Despicable child! You are in *very* serious trouble."

"Yeah," said Silo heavily, "I figured that one out for myself."

THE UNICORN TOWER

To the north of the Capital, hard by the river Rampage, stood the Unicorn Tower. It had loomed over the tangled streets for centuries past but it was a smoke-blackened ruin now, and its windows were rimmed with fangs of shattered glass. All around it ran a high wall topped with spikes. Guards stood watch at the gate, and above was a notice that read PROPERTY OF THE STATE ARCHAEOLOGICAL DIVISION: DEDICATED TO SERVICE, OBEDIENCE, UNITY AND PROGRESS. In the forecourt before the tower stood an untidy clutter of huts, one of which had SUPERINTENDENT FRISK written on the door in letters of gold. It was an office, and at this moment in time it contained a guard, Silo Zyco, and the superintendent himself.

The superintendent was dressed in a black uniform. The dignity it conferred was somewhat diminished by gravy stains and straining buttons, for he was a big man in both directions. His head was as round as a billiard ball and covered in coarse

gray bristles, his eyes unfriendly. The object of thei[r]
a disheveled and sulky-looking Silo.

"So! You're the Zyco boy. Mrs. Morgan's told me
you. Scum from the Eastern Swamps, she tells me, [r]
raised by criminals. A nasty Zyco; a lying Zyco, frien[d of trai]
tors and rebels. So they've sent you here to learn t[he error]
of your evil ways." He gave Silo a malicious smile. [You've]
been sentenced to ten years of voluntary labor for t[he]
Archaeological Division."

With that he opened the ledger that lay before h[im and]
added Silo's name to the bottom of a long list. Silo w[as]
seething with indignation, as his life was signed aw[ay. But]
the words of protest that rose to his lips were silenced [as]
two words sprang out at him from the page: *Orlando* [Gum-]
ble. Even upside down they were unmistakable. So the[y'd]
caught Orlando too! This was news of the worst kin[d, but]
at least it meant that he was not alone in this grim [place.]
He had one friend here at least, and a faint glimmer of [hope]
stirred within him, for perhaps between the two of them [they]
could work out some means of escape. A great bell tolled [out-]
side, and Superintendent Frisk laid down his quill and s[poke]
to the guard who stood behind Silo.

"Now get him out of here."

The guard led Silo to a dining hall, a filthy shed lined w[ith]
trestle tables, and no sooner had he entered than his nost[rils]
were assailed by an appalling stench. Apparently mudfish w[as]
on the menu. About thirty children were seated before bow[ls]

of something greenish that bubbled, and Silo scanned their faces eagerly, searching for Orlando. And his resolve wavered a little, for they were a sad-looking crew: thin, spectacularly dirty, and unnaturally pale, like a race of creatures that had never seen the sunlight. All wore sacks over their tatty clothes, with holes cut for their heads and arms, and on each was stenciled a bold black number. They were young too, he noticed, mostly younger than himself. And very hungry, for they dared to eat their mudfish broth. He took in this unwelcome information, then walked boldly up to the nearest table and addressed the largest of the children seated there, a hefty girl with a number 2 stenciled on her sack.

"Where can I find Orlando Bramble?"

The girl stared at Silo with an expression of bovine suspicion. She appeared to be thinking but evidently found it something of a struggle, for after a few painful moments she abandoned the effort and pointed to a forlorn figure seated alone in a corner. Silo headed over, but as soon as he got a good look at the boy he knew it wasn't Orlando; not his Orlando, anyway. His Orlando was still at liberty, for this was a puny, fair child even smaller than Silo himself, with a head that looked slightly too large for his body and a pale, freckled face. Silo sat down opposite him, and the boy looked up at him apprehensively with huge brown eyes.

"You're not Orlando Bramble," said Silo.

"That's what I told them," said the boy eagerly, "but they wouldn't listen to me."

"Who are you then?"

"My real name is Maximillian Crow."

Silo stared at him in wonderment. So here, finally, was the famous Maximillian Crow! He felt suddenly ashamed of himself for ever having nursed so powerful a hatred for such a sad and pathetic-looking little boy. "I thought you'd be in the Us of Ay by now," he said.

"How do you know?" said Maximillian, his eyes wide with wonder. "I told them again and again. The real Orlando Bramble is an unkind boy. I thought he was my friend, but he tricked me. He stole my letter and gave me another one full of lies."

His eyes filled with tears at the memory, and Silo found himself judging Orlando severely for playing so mean a trick on the hapless Maximillian, however desperate his circumstances had been at the time.

"How did you manage to get off the *Leviathan*?" he asked.

"They said I had to be a cabin boy. I had to do the cooking, but I didn't like it. The ship rocked up and down so much it made me feel very sick. I was sick often, and sometimes I was sick in the cooking. The captain got very angry. He said bad words, and once he threatened to throw me overboard. But when we'd been sailing for a week we met a ship that was going back to Mainland, and our captain told them to take me back with them. I was sick on that ship too. Once I was sick in the captain's boots. He was a rude man. When we got back to land the captain gave me a letter and told me to deliver it to the State Archaeological Division. I told the people there that I was Maximillian Crow but they laughed at me.

They said I was a liar called Orlando Bramble and they sent me here to dig things up. I think they're rude, mean people."

It struck Silo that Maximillian was not cut out for seafaring—or probably any other profession, come to that. He had the gift of the seeing, and for vomiting in inconvenient places, but it was an unusual combination of talents and not one that guaranteed a smooth passage through life.

"They say you used to have three seeings in a single day," Silo said. "Is that true?"

"It used to be," said Maximillian sadly. "But not anymore."

"Why not? Have you lost your gift?"

"No. Now I have dozens and dozens. They get in the way. Sometimes I don't know where I am or which time I'm in, or if what's happening is true or not. It's awful. I had a seeing where the lookout tower in Herringhaven fell, but I didn't know when it would happen—tomorrow, or next week, or next year. I was going to tell my parents about it when they came home. But they never did."

His eyes brimmed with tears again and Silo, who was use-less at coping with weeping people, racked his brains for a more cheerful subject. But it was unnecessary. A tall girl came striding across the dining room and stood before him. She was wearing a number 28 sack and gray breeches, and had long bony arms and legs and a mass of wild tawny hair. Her bottom lip was thrust out, giving her face an expression of savage discontent, and her bright green eyes blazed with anger. Silo recognized her immediately as the lettuce thrower from the south gate; to his horror, for he had already seen the havoc she could cause with a simple salad vegetable, he saw that she held a fork in her hand.

He sprang to his feet and fixed her with his most powerful stare. "What are you doing here?" he said.

"They arrested me for braining your friend." She scowled. "I'm charged under Section 303 of the State Criminal Code—Deployment of a Vegetable with Malicious Intent."

"Serves you right."

"Yeah, well, I thought he was Maximillian Crow."

Behind him, Silo heard the real Maximillian emit a squeak of terror.

"What's your problem with Maximillian Crow?" asked Silo.

"Everyone hates government-approved seers," said the girl. "Most of them are useless, but they use the good ones to spy on people, tell them what they're going to get up to in the future. And Maximillian Crow was supposed to be a very good one."

"The Government don't approve of him anymore," said Silo. "He was an impostor."

"Yeah, so I heard. The guards were talking about it. And they said you started a tax rebellion out in the Wildwoods."

Silo sensed faint approval in her voice. He shrugged. "So?"

"So it sounds like you and I are fighting on the same side."

She dropped the fork and offered him a grimy hand. "I'm sorry about beaning your friend. My name's Ruby."

Silo took it with some reluctance, for he was not a boy who easily forgave an injury. "I'm Silo Zyco."

"Yeah, I know," said Ruby. "And word has it you're a genuine seer. Could be useful, that. I'm working on an escape plan—maybe you could help." She nodded toward Maximillian. "Is he a friend of yours?"

"Yes," said Silo.

Ruby gave him a pitying look, and at that moment a bell rang, deafening in the narrow confines of the dining room. When it finally fell silent she said: "We'll talk this evening. I'll be waiting for you in the washroom."

"Back to work, the lot of you!" Superintendent Frisk had appeared in the doorway. A gigantic bunch of keys hung from his belt, and they jangled with his every movement. "Move it!"

The children rose as one and scurried for the door. Silo followed at a more leisurely pace, with Maximillian trotting at his side. He looked up at Silo with anxious eyes.

"Is it true what you said to that rough girl?" he said. "That you're my friend?"

Silo sighed. Maximillian seemed badly in need of one. "Yes, I suppose so," he said grudgingly.

"Thank you! I've never had a friend before."

Silo was not altogether surprised. Maximillian slipped a small and grubby hand into his, and together they walked out of the dining hall and toward the Unicorn Tower.

It stood, partially collapsed, amid a great mound of rubble. Maximillian led him to a well-worn path twisting upward between chunks of concrete and twisted girders. When they entered through one of its many windows, Silo stood astounded on the threshold.

The scale of it was awesome. For the first time in his life he was standing in one of the great buildings of the Ancients, and the sheer size of it took his breath away. High above his head, rusting girders protruded from the smoke-blackened walls, but the floors they had supported had collapsed long ago, and now the shafts of sunlight that fell through the shattered windows illuminated a vast open space. And jutting out into the void was a great platform, crudely constructed from heavy planks. Silo walked to the end of it, peered cautiously down (for he hated heights), and saw an area the size of a field way below, the sunlight barely reaching its depths. At its center a tall stone plinth rose like an island, and on it were carved in letters a foot high: INVEST IN UNICOM FOR A BETTER TOMORROW. Two gigantic bronze statues stood upon it, a man and a woman dressed in the strange garb of the Ancients. They held briefcases in their hands and strode forward arm in arm, with radiant smiles on their faces, into what Silo presumed was a Better Tomorrow. But if this was the Better Tomorrow, he shuddered to think what kind of day yesterday had been, for the scene below him seemed like a vision of hell. He was staring down into one of the State Archaeological Division's excavation sites, and the area around the statues was a chaos of pits and piles of earth bisected by serpentine paths. The dizzying drop made his head spin, and he raised his eyes only to see a vulture glide down to perch on the shoulder of the Unicom woman.

It seemed to eye him with interest, and Silo hastily backed away and examined the platform on which he stood. To his right was a big wooden bucket beside a pulley, and crates labeled FRAGILE — ANCIENT ARTIFACTS were stacked all around them. And to his left stood a treadmill, a great wheel supported by upright beams, positioned on the very edge of the platform. It was evidently used as a winch to haul loads up from below, for its circumference was wrapped with heavy chains from which hung a huge basket. And it was powered by children, for as Silo watched, the bigger boys and girls were filing into it and taking their places inside its giant wheel.

"You! New boy!" Frisk handed Silo a sack with holes cut in it. "You'll wear this at all times. You have no name here, only a number. You're Twenty-Nine. And you're a small boy, and a bony boy, and not strong enough to work the treadmill, by the looks of you. So you'll dig. Why is it that all our volunteers are so very weedy?"

"Because you feed them on mudfish?" said Silo. He instantly wished he hadn't, for Frisk struck him a savage blow around the ear.

"You'll not answer back to me! Ever! And you will address me as Superintendent Frisk. Always! Now get yourself down to the diggings!"

Twelve children were now in position inside the treadmill, preparing to winch down the great basket. The rest of the children were scrambling into it, ready to be lowered into the darkness below and commence work on the Division's mysterious digging. An anxious Maximillian tugged Silo toward it, and Silo, averting his eyes from the nauseating drop beneath them, climbed cautiously aboard.

"Lower away!" roared Frisk. The children in the tread-mill strained forward, and then the great wheel creaked to life and, with a rattle of chains, the basket began its descent into the void.

Down and down they went, a hundred feet or more, down to below ground level. When they reached the bottom there was a damp, dank earthy smell, and Silo examined his new workplace with growing depression. There was a deep layer of mud and rubble underfoot and great pits had been dug in it. In their shadowy depths he discerned jumbled objects protruding at strange angles from the earthy walls; a ferret-faced man in a black uniform was waiting to greet them.

"Get to work, all of you. You! Number Twenty-Nine! My name is Officer Feeton, but you may call me sir. Come over here!"

Silo came, with Maximillian hard on his heels.

"Is Number Thirteen a friend of yours?"

"Yes," said Silo resignedly.

"That's 'Yes, sir' in future. If he's a friend of yours, you're to stop him from daydreaming. And if he's sick one more time, he's in for a beating. Got it? You can begin here. Get a shovel and start digging in this spot. Any interesting objects, you're to ease them out carefully."

Silo eyed the surrounding junk. "Define *interesting*. Sir."

"All of it, Number Twenty-Nine, all of it. Everything in

here is a genuine Ancient artifact, and the Division is interested in every single little piece of it."

Silo was exhausted when he emerged from the Unicorn Tower that evening. He and the others were herded into a cavernous dormitory lit by skylights in the roof twenty feet above. They were barred, and the evening light fell through them in broad stripes of light and shadow, illuminating rows of bunk beds. On each was a little nest of straw and a few pitiful possessions—spoons, combs, and battered tin mugs. The aisles between them were strung with lines of washing.

"You can sleep in the bunk under mine," said Maximillian. "It's empty."

"Why?" said Silo suspiciously.

"I have bad dreams," said Maximillian. "Sometimes I scream in the night. And sometimes I'm sick."

"In that case I want the top bunk," said Silo firmly.

Being Maximillian's friend was evidently going to be something of a trial. He saw a battered sign in the corner—WASHROOM—and beneath it a door guarded by the hefty girl he had spoken to in the dining hall. He walked over and discovered, to his intense irritation, that when standing up she positively towered over him.

"I've come to see Ruby," he said, and she shoved the door open a crack.

Ruby was awaiting him in the dim, candlelit interior. "This is Drusilla, my lieutenant," she said, then added, in a lower voice, as she shut the door behind them: "She's a bit thick, but she's big."

Silo scowled. As a small person he thoroughly disapproved of this method of recruitment. The room he found himself in was the merest box, about eight feet by eight. It contained a few buckets full of dirty water and its walls were chalked over with a sketch of what appeared to be a giant maze, but a maze with teeth, a striped tail, and claws.

"It's a map of the building, to plan escape routes on," Ruby explained. "I disguised it as a drawing of a tiger. It's not complete yet, though. I only arrived here two days ago. Just as well really—they're a bit wet, that lot." She jerked her head in the direction of the dormitory. "Some of them have been here for ages, and they hadn't even organized an escape committee. But things have moved on a lot since then."

"Good," said Silo. "What's the plan?"

"The courtyard's out," said Ruby. "High walls and guards on the gate. Same with the dormitory—the skylights are barred, and we're always locked in. I think we're going to have to escape during working hours, and the drains are our best bet. I was living on the streets for almost a year before they arrested me, and I used the drains sometimes to hide from the SAD patrols—"

"The what?" said Silo.

"SAD. The State Archaeological Division. The idiots we're working for. They go grubbing around in old rubbish dumps looking for Ancient artifacts. They have problems finding staff, though, so they send patrols out at night to

round up homeless children. They say they take them to or-
phanages and look after them, but they don't really. They put
them to work in places like this."

Silo thought of the buzzard burger boy—he and all the
other ragged children who haunted the Capital. "Why are
there so many homeless children here?"

"Because their parents have been shipped out," said Ruby.
"That's what happened to mine, anyway."

She looked so angry that Silo swiftly changed the subject.
"About the drains . . ."

"Yeah. There's a whole labyrinth of them under the city.
We're working underground, so hopefully we can dig our way
in and find a way back to the streets. I noticed you and that
little weird boy were digging by the north wall today. That's
good. The river Rampage runs to the north, and the drains
must empty into it."

"I'm on the case," said Silo.

Thus began the most miserable period of Silo's already rather
miserable life. Their days at the Unicorn Tower began early.
The bell rang when the light that filtered through the skylights was still pearly with the dawn, summoning them rudely
from their bunks and dreams. Within ten minutes of waking
they were expected to be seated in the dining room, where
a mug of water and a slice of stale bread awaited them by
way of breakfast, and then they were herded into the Unicorn
Tower and their day's work began. The twelve largest children

worked the treadmill and the rest were lowered down to work in the chaos below, and Silo was always among this party. He found it filthy, backbreaking work, toiling in the gloomy half-light digging pit after pit after pit. Sometimes the sides caved in, half burying him in earth, and sometimes it rained and the pits flooded, leaving him toiling waist-deep in water. The excavated mud was loaded first into barrows and then into the great basket to be hauled up to ground level, and the route there was a perilous one, pushing heavy loads along paths that snaked around the crumbling edges of pits, where a single misstep meant a long fall. And Maximillian was an additional worry to Silo, for wherever he went Maximillian tracked him like a shadow. From the day of their first meeting he had attached himself, limpetlike, to his side, for Silo had told him he was his friend and Maximillian had taken his words to heart. Unfortunately he was a hopelessly impractical boy, much given to tripping over shovels and stumbling down holes, for he seemed to live in a strange twilight world of seeings where the present and the future mingled inextricably in his mind, and it made him dangerously absentminded. Often he froze where he stood and simply stared vacantly into space, prey to who knew what strange visions—at which point Superintendent Frisk would roar with rage and throw missiles at him.

For Frisk was an inescapable evil. The titanic statues of the Unicorn couple soared high above the chaos of the diggings, and it was the superintendent's habit to climb up to the plinth that supported them and pace around and around their gigantic feet, surveying his little empire of mud and misery. His beady eyes were everywhere and his bullying voice carried into even the most distant corners of the tower:

"Number Sixteen—move it with that barrow! Numbers Twenty-Nine and Thirteen—why so slow? Number Eight—stop picking your nose and start digging!"

Officer Feeton patrolled the paths that wound amid the heaps and holes, and nothing escaped his eyes as he urged the children to work harder, dig deeper, move faster. Frisk bellowed and bullied from his plinth, his keys clanking with his every movement, but it was Feeton whom Silo came to hate more, for he moved swiftly on silent feet, creeping up on weary children and hurling clods of earth at them if he found them snatching even a moment's rest.

And so their days passed to the dull thud of picks and shovels, the shouts of the overseers, and the trundle of barrow wheels, but loud over all came the rumble of the treadmill that towered above them, its great wheel creaking and its chains rattling as the basket was lowered, loaded with earth, and raised up again; up and down, up and down, from dawn until dusk. It paused only once, at noon, when the children were hauled back into the daylight for lunch. The menu was unvarying—mudfish broth. Lunchtime lasted for forty minutes precisely, and then they descended back into the gloom. And their work seemed meaningless to Silo, for the Ancient artifacts they found seemed singularly useless: bits of rotted wood and rusty metal, fragments of pottery, lengths of cabling, and the mangled remains of mysterious objects shattered beyond all hope of repair or identification. But on this, as on so many things, he and the State Archaeological Division disagreed. These precious finds were loaded into a big wooden bucket and hauled up to the platform by means of a pulley. When they arrived at the surface they were packed carefully into straw-lined crates, for the Division wished to inspect each and every one of them.

At six in the evening work finished for the day. A meager ration of boiled turnips was served, and then finally they were allowed what was called "recreation"—though by that time most of the children were so weary they headed, zombie-like, to their bunks. Silo yearned to do likewise, but instead he forced himself to join Ruby in the washroom to sit, dazed with exhaustion, as she pored over her ever-expanding map in the vain hope of finding an escape route. But as the long summer days crept past, even Ruby began to sound despondent. Silo was dismayed to learn that some of the children had been there for six months or more. The grinding labor and meager diet were taking their toll on him, and he found himself thinking less and less of escape and more and more about food; and the things that had preoccupied him when he was at liberty began to seem distant and strangely unimportant. But one question at least was answered for him, and in an unexpected way.

One morning the children were gathered beside the treadmill, about to begin their daily grind. Silo was glowering at the Unicom couple. Their gigantic heads were on a level with the platform and so were the first thing that met his eye when he entered the tower each morning. Their toothy smiles seemed to mock the miserable children ranged before them, and Silo had grown to hate them with a passion. Frisk was strutting about in his usual self-important manner.

"New girl!" he cried. "We have no names here, only numbers. You are Number Thirty, and will answer to that number at all times. And you will join the party on the treadmill."

Silo turned to see what new unfortunate had fallen victim to the Division, and was surprised to see it was someone he knew. "Hello, Daisy," he said.

"That's Number Thirty to you," roared Frisk, poking him painfully in the back of the neck. "And you're here to work, not chat. Into the basket immediately!"

Daisy was taking her place on the treadmill, her eyes redrimmed with weeping. So now Silo knew where seers ended up—at least, those who pretended to be seers to get a government job. Poor Daisy was working for the Government now, but Silo doubted she would derive much joy from it.

10

NEWS FROM THE ISLAND

One morning, in the third week of Silo's captivity, something finally occurred to break the monotony of their days. The great treadmill juddered to a halt and Frisk's cries of rage, loud in the sudden silence, told Silo that it was not a scheduled stop. A single ladder led from the diggings to the platform high above. He and Feeton went storming up it to see what was amiss, and the children gratefully dropped their tools and slumped down to rest. Lunchtime came and went, and finally Feeton's face appeared, scowling down at them over the edge of the platform.

"On your feet, little vermin! Form a line by the bucket."

They did so, and were hauled up one by one in the bucket used to transport artifacts. Silo was the last to arrive and his eyes were immediately drawn to a mangled metal object, an Ancient artifact no less, protruding from the workings of the treadmill. He realized, with a thrill of pleasure, that it was an act of deliberate sabotage, and he suspected Ruby was responsible.

"You the last one, Number Twenty-Nine? Right! The superintendent wants a word, so get along to his office, the whole pack of you."

The children trooped out of the tower and into Frisk's office, and instantly all eyes were fixed longingly on his desk, for sitting before him was a plump chicken roasted to golden perfection, garnished with crispy bacon, nestling amid a mound of vegetables and smelling mouthwateringly delicious.

"Well, you little maggots," he said, dousing his plate in gravy, "don't any of you be getting any bright ideas from Number Twenty-Eight."

So it had been Ruby, thought Silo.

"Thought she'd disrupt work, she did, so she could have a rest and a sit-down maybe, but she got a beating instead. And she'll be having no food for three days either"—he speared a roast potato and stuffed it into his mouth—"so let this be a warning to the rest of you." He glowered at them, gravy dripping from his chin. "You two! Numbers Six and Seven!"

"Yes, sir!" Two brothers called Basil and Rodney Bolton sprang to attention.

"You're to take her place on the treadmill tomorrow. Number Twenty-Eight won't be given a chance to play her nasty tricks again. She'll be working in the diggings from now on."

Ruby had planned this, Silo realized. From now on she would be able to hunt for drains to her heart's content; he was impressed by her fortitude.

"So no more monkey business," Frisk continued. "We're way behind schedule as it is. You need to work harder, the whole pack of you."

He tore off a chicken leg and leveled it at them in a menacing manner. "What do you need to do?"

"Work harder, sir," chorused the children, their ravenous eyes fixed on his plate.

"That's right!" he cried. He took a bite of chicken, his words issuing forth amid a rotating mass of mangled meat. "Now get out of my sight, you shirking little scumbags." He gave them an evil smile. "And enjoy your lunch."

It was boiled buzzard. Silo stared at his plate for a moment, torn between hunger and revulsion, then drank the gravy and wrapped what remained in a rag and stuffed it into his pocket. He nodded to Daisy as he left the dining room. He had barely spoken to her since her arrival, for she had been a friend of Elgarth and that he found hard to forgive, but time had worked an unexpected change of heart.

Daisy had spent her first evening weeping quietly in a corner, but that was nothing out of the ordinary. The sound of sobbing was commonplace in the dormitory. But on her second day she seemed to pull herself together. She, Ruby, and Drusilla were the three oldest children in the group. Ruby was preoccupied with her escape plans and Drusilla was frankly scary, but there was a gentleness about Daisy that seemed to draw the youngest children to her. Some of them were very young indeed, no older than four or five, and perhaps she reminded them of big sisters from happier times. She dried her tears and took them in hand. She patched up their cuts and bruises, combed their matted hair, and encouraged them to brush their teeth. She taught them an annoying song about a puppy called Cuddles. Sometimes a little group, about a dozen in all, would cluster around her and she would tell stories. Silo found the stories repellent, for they invariably featured fairies and elves, but the little ones seemed to enjoy them and Silo discovered, somewhat to his surprise, that Daisy had risen in his estimation.

Now he made his way to the washroom with Maximillian padding at his heels. Ruby was perched on an upturned bucket. She had a split lip and the beginnings of a spectacular black eye, but even so there was an air of quiet satisfaction about her as she sat surveying her map.

"Here." Silo took the unsavory package from his pocket and handed it to her.

"Thanks!" Months of living on the streets had inured her to the taste of buzzard.

"Maybe now that I'm in the diggings we can move things on a little." She spat out a stray talon. "But I was wondering— you two are seers. You haven't seen anything useful, have you, about the future? Something that might help us?"

Silo shook his head. His own gift had lain dormant within him since his last terrible vision of the Island. When he first arrived he had hoped that Maximillian, as the greatest seer on all Mainland, might see a path through the troubles that beset them—though in this, as in so many things, he was doomed to disappointment. But Ruby could find out for herself.

"Tell her what you've seen today," he said to Maximillian.

Maximillian thought for a moment, then stared into space with unseeing eyes. "Two bulls will fight on a hillside. The spotted one will win. A man will buy a horse called Clover, but Clover will tread on his foot and break his toe. The man will say a bad word. Pigtown will lead Killvale ten–nil at goatball, but then they'll run out of goats and the Killvale fans will riot. A woman wants to surprise her husband for his birthday. She'll make a pudding and pour booze on it, then set it on fire. But the pudding will set fire to the curtains. Her husband will be very surprised—"

"That'll do," said Ruby. She looked wearily at Silo. "Is he always like this?"

"Yeah," said Silo.

Being the greatest seer on all Mainland was obviously not all it was cracked up to be.

The next afternoon he and Maximillian were set to work in the corner where the north and west walls met, toiling in the gloom with the usual layer of mud and junk underfoot. Silo had just dug up an old panel, cracked, chipped, and caked in dirt. It was one among dozens they had excavated to date— little boards made of a strange material, not wood or metal or stone but something smooth and light. On one side were written numbers, symbols, and mysterious words—CTRL, ALT, ESC, PGDN—and the whole alphabet in a strange, random order, not A to Z but Q to M. Silo was mystified as to their original use, but they had obviously been considered precious once, for they had lids that folded down to protect them.

"I wonder what these were for," he said idly.

"They're all dead now," said Maximillian sadly, "but once they used to glow. The Ancients pressed the letters and the lids showed them pictures and writing. And sometimes they sang."

"Why do you think that?"

"I've seen them doing it."

Silo dropped his pick in amazement. "You mean seen as in *seeing*?"

"Yes."

"Do you mean that you have seeings of the past, from way back before the Newcount? From the time of the Ancients?"

"Sometimes," said Maximillian.

Silo's mind reeled. It was possible, then. Mrs. Morgan had been right. He suddenly realized, with a blinding flash of revelation, that the fragile form of Maximillian Crow embodied the wildest dreams of Mrs. Morgan and the entire State Archaeological Division: a seer who could unravel the mysteries of the Ancients and describe the workings of their strange artifacts, maybe even find the source of their mysterious power. He stared in wonder at him, a boy whose mind ranged freely through unimaginable realms of space and time but was incapable of finding a sensible place to be sick.

"What was it that Number Thirteen was just talking about?"

Silo turned, and to his horror he saw that Feeton had

crept up, in his usual silent manner, and was standing right behind them. How much of their conversation had he heard?

"Number Thirteen was saying something about seeing into the past. Is he a seer like yourself, Number Twenty-Nine? The Division is interested in seers—leastways, those of them that behave themselves."

"Number Thirteen gets confused, sir," said Silo, appalled. "He . . ."

He what? Silo desperately racked his brains for a way out of his predicament; anything that would prevent the Division from getting their hands on Maximillian and forcing him, by who knew what horrible means, to divulge the secrets of the Ancients. He needed a miracle and—astonishingly—he got one.

There was a wild cry from overhead, a sudden shower of rubble, and Silo looked up just in time to see a figure plummeting through a window high above him. Its fall was arrested violently just six feet short of the ground, and the three of them stared in amazement at the sturdy dark boy who revolved slowly before their eyes, suspended upside down in a tangle of rope. It was Orlando.

"What is the meaning of this?" cried Feeton. "Trying to escape, are we?"

"No, sir!" cried Orlando. "I was trying to get in."

"Why?!"

"Because I'm an orphan, sir! My parents died of crab pox, and I'm all alone in the world. I heard that the Division was a friend to poor orphans, took them in and fed them and gave them a roof over their heads. I know I should have asked, but I was afraid you'd turn me away. So I thought I'd just sneak in, and that perhaps you wouldn't notice one more among so many. Please don't send me away, sir—don't let me starve on the streets! I'm willing to work for my keep. My name is Titus MacGurk."

"A volunteer," said Feeton in wonder. "A genuine volunteer! Usually we has to catch them."

Then he pulled himself together, shaking Orlando free of the ropes that held him. "You'll report to Superintendent Frisk immediately! Come with me."

"Bless you for your kindness! You'll put in a good word for me, won't you, sir?"

Feeton took Orlando firmly by the scruff of the neck and hauled him away. A moment of stunned silence followed their departure; then Maximillian burst out indignantly, "He's not Titus MacGurk! He's a dirty great liar called Orlando Bramble!"

"I know he is," said Silo, "but keep it to yourself, will you? I'll explain later."

So his friend had come to rescue him. It was a pity he had made such a mess of it, but in his heart of hearts Silo was deeply touched. He had missed Orlando badly, and the sight of him stirred within him a renewed resolve to be free of this dreadful place. He had allowed himself to succumb to despair, he realized, and it was vital that he, Orlando, Maximillian, Ruby, Daisy, and all the other wretched children forced to labor in the gloom of the Unicorn Tower escape, and soon. The Island was in danger and every day counted, and now there was a new cause for urgency—what if Feeton repeated the conversation he had overheard? Silo realized there and then that it was his sacred duty to take Maximillian somewhere far, far away from the Capital—somewhere the Division could never find him or set him to work in pursuit of their dark designs, for he hated them with a passionate intensity. They abused the powers they already had, and the thought of them unleashing the mysterious powers of the Ancients was too horrible to contemplate. He had no time to waste. Silo took up his pick and, with all the strength at his command, dealt the wall a mighty blow.

"Rauuugh!" he cried.

That evening he sat in the dining room with Orlando, Maximillian, and Ruby. The atmosphere was rather strained as Maximillian, quite understandably, had a very low opinion of Orlando, and Orlando knew Ruby only as a girl who assaulted strangers with vegetables. He had just joined them, fresh from Frisk's office, and wore a sack with the number 31 stenciled on it.

"How did you find me?" said Silo.

"Simple. Everyone in the Capital knows the Division uses stray children to work on their sites, and the Unicorn Tower's their biggest digging right now. I had it all planned out, but then the windowsill gave way—bit of a pig, that."

"Wasn't Frisk suspicious about you?"

"At first, yeah," said Orlando, "but I just pretended to be really, really thick. He didn't need much convincing. After all, he needs more slaves to shovel dirt for him."

"Did you get the chance to have a look around before you got caught?" said Ruby. "Can you add to our map?"

"We're close to the river," said Orlando. "The north quay's only a stone's throw from the gate. There's shipping there, so that would be our best way out of the Capital."

"We have to get out of the building first," said Ruby.

"I think I know how," said Silo. "I found a drain this afternoon." He spoke with quiet satisfaction. He had been saving up this happy news until after supper, and was rewarded by a look of joy on Ruby's face.

"Maximillian and I are working in the northeast corner. I broke through the wall today and there's a pipe behind it, a huge one. And when I put my ear to it I could hear gurgling."

"Brilliant! Finally things are going our way! Tomorrow we can—"

But Silo silenced her with a quick motion of his hand, for Superintendent Frisk was advancing toward them.

"Number Twenty-Nine! You've been sent an official communication from the State Archaeological Division."

He placed a thick sheet of parchment before Silo and stamped back to his office. Mystified, Silo unfolded it and read:

To Silo Zyco, former resident of the Island in the Eastern Swamps.

This is to notify you that the State Archaeological Division has identified the above-mentioned Island as the site of a power station from the age of the Ancients, and therefore an area of Priority Archaeological Interest. The department will begin excavation of the site in July this year. All owners of property and/or Eel Rights are hereby notified that, on the arrival of the Division's team, their property and/or Eel Rights will be considered official government property under Decree No. 255 of the State Archaeological Division. This decree is absolute and no appeals will be considered.

By Official Order of the State Archaeological Division, dedicated to Service, Obedience, Unity, and Progress.

Silo read it, and then reread it, his brain reeling with disbelief. So this was the great catastrophe that would lay waste to the Island! He recalled, with a sudden rush of dread, the story that Orlando had told him of the power station in the west; of the villagers who were forced to dig, and of the terrible consequences that followed. This, then, was to be the fate of the Mudfords and the Pattles and the Beans! He thought of his seeing, and of the long row of graves that lined the Causeway, and the hairs prickled on the back of his neck.

"What's wrong? What does it say?" cried Ruby, watching the dawning look of horror on his face. Silently he handed her the letter.

—:—

Elgarth was lounging in an armchair. A pedicurist was crouched at his feet seeing to his toenails, and the remains of supper lay on the table beside him. He picked up a bell and rang for Rankly.

"Clear up this mess, would you? I'm expecting Mrs. Morgan."

"She's just arrived, master," said Rankly.

"Excellent! Show her in." Elgarth kicked his pedicurist aside with practiced ease and pulled on his boots, and a moment later Mrs. Morgan entered and bared her long yellow teeth at him in an exultant smile.

"Good news!" she cried. "Our expedition is finally ready to depart! In a few days' time I set off to begin work on a most important project. Members of our Research Department have been hard at work, and they have unearthed old documents that reveal, beyond the shadow of a doubt, the exact site of an Ancient power station. We mean to excavate it immediately."

"What a splendid opportunity to find out more about the source of the Ancients' power!" said Elgarth.

"Yes indeed," said Mrs. Morgan. "And it is all the more gratifying after the setback we suffered last year, when the Raiders, those seaborne vermin, had the audacity to mount an attack on our power station in the west. The Government was extremely displeased, and so it has taken a great deal of convincing on my part, but happily I have finally brought them around to my way of thinking. We shall take an army with us this time, and I am certain that our endeavors will be crowned with success!"

Her dark eyes glittered at the prospect. "Only imagine! It could be but a matter of weeks before we unlock the secrets of the power stations, and what a blessing that will be to those of us who aspire to revive the glories of the Ancient world, and to see the dawn of a new age of Service, and Obedience, and Unity, and Progress!"

"It is a privilege to live in such exciting times," said Elgarth.

Mrs. Morgan favored him with her wolfish smile. "And obviously, as a government-approved seer, I wish you to accompany us. It could be that the Raiders will seek to interfere again, and your gift could be of use."

Not only was Elgarth an official government-approved seer now, he was the lone survivor of his class. Silo Zyco had been neatly disposed of, and Maximillian had been exposed as an impostor. Getting rid of the Arson Sisters had proved a little more difficult. They and Daisy had been asked to produce accurate seeings within the space of three days, and all had failed miserably. Daisy had talked of rainbows and sunbeams with increasing desperation, but the Arson Sisters were made of sterner stuff. They had predicted another fire, and on hearing this, Elgarth felt he really must put his foot down, for he had no desire to be burned in his bed. So the Arson Sisters had to go. It had proved to be extremely simple. Even they realized that it was only a matter of time before they were exposed as frauds, and so he had paid them the sum of ten silver crowns on the understanding that they disappeared. And disappear they had. There had been a spate of small fires around the Capital, it was true, but that could have been mere coincidence. And Daisy had disappeared too, although in an altogether more mysterious way. She'd had a seeing that the Academy's resident mouser would give birth to a litter of beautiful fluffy kittens. Unfortunately it was a tomcat, and the next day Daisy's place at the breakfast table was empty.

So Elgarth was victorious. He had but one worry, and that was that the real Maximillian Crow might reappear, and with his formidable gift of the seeing put his own more modest one in the shade.

"I was wondering," he said to Mrs. Morgan, "if you have any news of the whereabouts of Maximillian. If he is as gifted as everyone says, his services would be a welcome addition to the expedition."

"Indeed they would," said Mrs. Morgan. "But you may rest assured that we are on his trail. Maximillian is an orphan, and with no home to return to it could well be that he has been wandering the streets, alone and friendless. But our government is compassionate. It is their policy to collect up stray children and send them to be cared for at one of the Division's many archaeological sites. A most humane plan, for there they are given food, shelter, and constructive work to occupy them. It could well be that Maximillian is among their number, and the inspector and I are visiting these sites in the hope of finding him. In fact, we had planned to visit one tomorrow—the project Superintendent Frisk is overseeing at the Unicorn Tower. It is a most promising location, and we expect to make exciting discoveries there. Perhaps it would interest you to join me?"

"Isn't that where they sent Silo Zyco?" said Elgarth.

"Indeed it is."

Elgarth didn't care much for Ancient ruins, but he knew they were a subject close to Mrs. Morgan's heart, and he felt it would be diplomatic to join her. And besides, Silo was there. Elgarth had disliked him from the first, not just as a rival seer but also for being so distressingly ill-mannered and ill-bred, and his presence at the Unicorn Tower would add interest to the expedition.

"I'd be delighted to accompany you," he said with his ready smile.

11

DRUSILLA CREATES A STINK

Next morning Elgarth arose bright and early to keep his appointment with Mrs. Morgan and the inspector. Superintendent Frisk, bowing and smiling, was waiting to greet them at the entrance of the Unicorn Tower.

"Good morning, Inspector. And Mrs. Morgan! A right pleasure to have you with us again. And you must be Master Early. But come on in! You'll be wanting to see how we've been getting on with the excavation."

"Indeed we do," said Mrs. Morgan. "But there is another purpose to our visit. We are looking for a small fair boy of about eight years old. Do you have such a child working here?"

"We've several," said the Superintendent, "and you can examine them at your leisure. They're at work down in the diggings. This way, if you please."

They walked out onto the platform and into the shadow of the great treadmill.

"Magnificent!" cried Mrs. Morgan, gazing rapturously around the ruin. "I never cease to be struck by the grandeur of Ancient architecture."

It was well that she was so happily occupied, for frenzied activity was taking place behind a stack of crates just to her right. A hefty girl was scrambling into the bucket used to transport artifacts, and a desperate figure in a number 31 sack was fumbling with the ropes of the pulley, preparing to lower her down to the diggings.

"Warn Silo and Ruby!" he hissed. "Tell them to hide Maximillian! Heck, what if they see me? Curse the beasts! What kind of lunatics are they to come and visit a rat pit like this, anyway?"

"Lower the bucket," said Drusilla, her dark brows knitted with concentration.

Orlando did. She was much heavier than he had supposed, and descended at record speed. Then he pulled his sack up over his head, so that just his eyes were showing, and scuttled back to the treadmill. He was just in time, for the unwelcome visitors had stepped into the basket and were preparing for their own descent.

"Lower away!" cried Frisk.

"Oh no!" muttered Orlando as the great wheel stirred to life. "How long before he notices Drusilla's missing? This is a disaster! I suppose we could just drop them," he added hopefully. But Daisy thought otherwise.

"Please, no violence! It sets a shocking example to the little ones."

Orlando's reply was a rude one, so it was probably just as well that it was drowned out by a mighty bellow from Frisk.

"Where's Number Two? Why is she not at work?"

"She's not well, sir," said Orlando desperately. "She just nipped outside for a breath of fresh air."

Frisk uttered an inarticulate howl of rage and strode toward the entrance of the tower.

"Damnation!" said Orlando. "Silo and Ruby need to come up with a plan, and fast."

Silo, Ruby, and Drusilla were scuttling between the piles of earth at lightning speed. They had hidden Maximillian beneath an upturned barrow and given him strict instructions to stay there until further notice.

"We've not got much time," said Ruby as they arrived panting at the northeast corner. "Drusilla! You're the strongest. Take a pick to the pipe. And Silo—keep an eye out for Feeton, would you? That's the last thing we need, him creeping up on us."

Silo scanned the diggings. Feeton was nowhere to be seen, but his eye was caught by another and even more unwelcome figure. The inspector and Mrs. Morgan had completed their descent and had scaled the plinth beneath the Unicorn statue, the better to examine the extent of the excavations, and a blond boy, resplendent in a fur-trimmed cloak, was just climbing up to join them. It was Elgarth. Silo fixed him with his most powerful stare. And it seemed as if Elgarth sensed it, for he paused and scanned the chaos of churned earth beneath him as though seeking something there, and finally his eyes met Silo's. Silo cut a small, spectacularly dirty figure and his eyes blazed with hatred, but Elgarth seemed delighted to see him, for he smiled and gave him a cheerful wave. Beating back the red tide that threatened to overwhelm him, Silo turned on his heel and watched, seething with rage, as Drusilla squared up to the gigantic pipe with a pick.

"Go easy," said Ruby. "Just a small hole to begin with, so we can see what's inside."

But Drusilla and subtlety were strangers to one another. She struck the pipe a mighty blow and a huge chunk of concrete flew out. There was a sudden dreadful stench, so potent that the three of them gagged and staggered back. As they watched, something dark, viscous, and vile trickled from the hole that Drusilla had made, and a network of jagged cracks formed about it, creeping slowly but inexorably across the surface of the pipe.

"Oh hell!" said Ruby. "I think it's the main sewer."

Silo backed away. "And it's going to burst."

"Of all the filthy luck!" cried Ruby.

Filthy was the word for it. Silo's eyes met Ruby's and he knew, from the horror that he saw there, that she too was contemplating the catastrophic consequences of a tidal wave of sewage. He spun around and surveyed the diggings, racking his brains for ways to avert a terrible and malodorous tragedy. The great basket lay at the foot of the platform, and Silo counted sixteen children at work in the diggings. That meant there were eleven on the treadmill—surely not enough to haul their companions to safety.

Ruby was obviously thinking along the same lines. "I'll go and warn them," she said, "but we'll need more on the treadmill. You two get up there and help them."

Easier said than done, thought Silo.

They ran over to the lone ladder that led up to the platform, but Feeton was, as always, in the last place you wanted to find him, and stood guard at its foot. He looked down at Silo with an unpleasant smile. "And why aren't you working, Number Twenty-Nine?"

Silo opened his mouth to reply, but at that very moment a brick, thrown with astonishing force and accuracy, came hurtling out of the gloom. It struck Feeton squarely on top of his head, and he keeled over and collapsed in a heap at Silo's feet.

Drusilla bent over his crumpled form. "Ruby threw a brick at him!" she said, in a voice in which astonishment and pleasure were equally mixed.

"Let's get up to the treadmill," said Silo, "and fast."

As Drusilla went storming up the ladder he cast a nervous glance over his shoulder. Mrs. Morgan, the inspector, and Elgarth were still standing on the plinth of the statue, but mercifully they were staring up into the tower, seemingly reveling in the glories of Ancient architecture. The brick-throwing incident had gone unnoticed. Swiftly Silo followed Drusilla, and as he did so a whiff of something ghastly wafted up from below. The sewage was stirring. Time was running out, and yet the ladder was an immensely tall one, and its rungs seemed to stretch on to all eternity. And worse still, it began to move beneath him, shuddering and jerking. He looked down to the ground, now far distant below him, and saw that Feeton was moving. He was evidently still stunned from the blow, but even so he had laid hands upon the ladder and was tugging at it, yanking it sideways. Drusilla reached the top and, without her weight, the movement intensified. The ladder was going to fall. Whimpering with terror, Silo redoubled his efforts, fairly flying up the rungs, but he was too late—it was sliding, moving with a strange, slow-motion drift. But by now the safety of the platform was only inches away, and Silo made a mighty upward lunge and clutched the edge of it with one desperate, white-knuckled hand as the ladder slid out from under his feet and began its descent to the ground way, way below.

He hung suspended over a long drop to certain death, and as he did so the scene below him presented itself with a sudden and startling clarity, and every tiny detail was indelibly imprinted on his brain. Discarded shovels and barrows lay strewn about the diggings, and the giant basket was packed with children, their pale faces staring up at him. It rocked slightly as the chain that held it drew taut, and above him he could hear fearsome grunts and cries.

"Nuur-ugh! Urr-urgh! Nnnn-ugh!"

Drusilla had arrived at the treadmill and was applying all her strength, but to no avail. The load was too heavy. Ruby was the biggest of the children, and nobly she stepped out of the basket. Thus lightened, it began, with painful slowness, to judder its way upward. She had sacrificed herself that others might be saved, but when Silo contemplated the dreadful fate that awaited her, he felt his terror drain from him and a powerful resolution took its place. The basket was gone, the ladder was gone, but there was still . . . Yes! There it was! The bucket used to haul up artifacts sat beneath its pulley at the foot of the platform. Silo's eyes met Ruby's and he pointed his boot at it. Ruby understood. She nodded back at him, and as she did so Elgarth uttered a cry of warning. He stood on the plinth beneath the statues and pointed an accusing finger.

"Silo Zyco's up to something!"

Finally the inspector and Mrs. Morgan realized that all was not well.

"Superintendent Frisk!" cried Mrs. Morgan. "The children are up to mischief. Stop them immediately!"

Silo turned his eyes to the platform above him. He had a hand on it. Two hands. He wriggled and swung. The tip of a boot. Grunting with exertion, he forced himself up, desperately scrabbling for handholds on the rough wooden floor but finding only splinters. But then his bleeding fingers found a gap between the planks. He jammed his hand in and heaved, slowly hauling himself out of the dizzying void. He squirmed a knee onto the platform, then an elbow; then he was up and over the edge and finally—finally—he was safe. He had no time to reflect on his brush with death, for Ruby needed him. He ran to the pulley and hauled in the slack on the rope, then peered over the platform's edge. Ruby was standing in the bucket, and she gave him a wan smile and a thumbs-up.

"Frisk! Frisk! Where are you? The brats are escaping!" cried Mrs. Morgan.

Silo had very little time. He set his shoulder to the rope and pulled with all his strength. But it was not enough. Ruby was too big and he was too small. He was not strong enough to save her. Desperately he glanced over at the treadmill, which was just now gaining a slow, ponderous momentum, and saw that he could call no help from there. Drusilla was performing heroic feats, but she and her companions were working at the very limits of their strength, groaning with exertion as they turned the great wheel, and it was obvious that not a single one of them could be spared. Far below him Silo could hear terrible, ominous noises coming from the northeast corner: strange rumblings and gurglings and then—horror of horrors—the dull thud of falling masonry. And then Frisk appeared in the entrance of the tower. Cursing, Silo ducked behind a crate of artifacts.

Frisk strode past him and stopped at the edge of the platform, glaring down at the overladen basket that was jerking its way up, inch by painful inch, to safety, and then at the children toiling on the treadmill.

"Lower that basket immediately! Back to work, the lot of you!"

A glorious and audacious plan sprang fully formed to Silo's mind. With lightning speed he tiptoed up behind Frisk, slipped the rope of the pulley through the heavy ring of keys on his belt, and knotted it tight in a trice. The keys jangled beneath his trembling fingers and Elgarth was shouting a warning, but Superintendent Frisk heard nothing, for he was roaring at Drusilla and Orlando and Daisy and all the other children desperately working the treadmill:

"Stop that immediately, d'you hear? Or there'll be beatings before bedtime, you villainous little vermin!"

Silo dashed back twenty feet and appraised the mighty bulk of the overseer as he stood raging on the brink of the platform. He prayed that he had strength enough for this at least, and then he began his run-up. He sprinted up behind Frisk and, with a great howl of rage and desperation, sprang high into the air, launching himself feetfirst into the small of Frisk's back. His boots struck home with a dull thud, and Frisk gave a grunt of astonishment and teetered on the platform edge, his arms windmilling. And as he did so there was a great rending, rumbling roar from below and then the most appalling smell: a noxious, rotten-eggy, eye-watering, vomit-inducing stench, as though every stinking thing that festered upon the face of the Earth had united for one brief moment to glory in their own loathsomeness. Frisk overbalanced and plunged into the void, and as the rope on his belt drew tight Silo heard the rumble of the pulley wheel: his weight was drawing Ruby and her bucket soaring up from the depths.

And in the nick of time. Frisk would land softly, for even as he fell a stinking tide burst forth. The sewage was unleashed. Ruby leaped out of the bucket and ran to help at the treadmill, yelling to Silo as she passed, "Sort the guards! Get them away from the gate!"

Silo dashed to the entrance. The guards were holding their noses and staring at the Unicorn Tower with bemused expressions on their faces.

"Help!" cried Silo. "Help! The sewer's exploded! Save them! Superintendent Frisk will drown!"

He could but dream. And his words did the trick, for the guards abandoned their post and ran to the rescue. Silo followed hard on their heels. The basket had just arrived at the platform and the children were leaping out. A green-faced Maximillian was the last of them, and Silo grabbed his hand and hauled him, retching violently, to safety.

"It smells so awful, Silo! It makes me sick."

He wasn't the only one. The stench was enough to fell an elephant.

"Get to the main gate, all of you!" Silo hissed.

Children were pouring off the treadmill now and, with Ruby in the lead, the whole crew made a desperate dash for freedom. Silo was the last of them, but he could not resist turning back for one last, lingering look.

The diggings in which he had worked for so many weary weeks was changed beyond recognition. The pits and piles among which he had toiled had vanished, buried deep beneath something brown and terrible that swirled about in a great steaming whirlpool, bubbling and burbling as it went. Stifled cries came from the depths, and the guards were hurling ropes from the platform.

"We're coming, Superintendent!" they cried. "Hold on there, Feeton! Help's at hand!"

Amid the brown tide two titanic figures rose up, submerged

to the waist but still smiling their improbably bright smiles. The Unicorn couple had survived the deluge, and they had company. Driven by desperation, Elgarth, Mrs. Morgan, and the inspector had managed to scale their heights. The inspector was crouching on the man's shoulder like a dark and dismal crow, reaching down for Mrs. Morgan as she clung for dear life to the knot of the giant's tie. Elgarth was not so lucky. He had gained a purchase on the ledge formed by the breast pocket of the giantess, but it was a temporary perch at best, for still the terrible tide was rising, slowly but inexorably. He had a hand clamped over his nose and his eyes were wide with horror. They met Silo's for a brief moment, and Silo responded with a smile and a cheerful wave. And then, reluctantly, he tore his eyes away and raced to join the others outside. His life was set on a strange, uncharted course and he knew that there would be dark days ahead, but at least he could now boast one brief moment of transcendental joy: the sight of Elgarth surrounded by a shuddering, stinking sea of . . . something nasty.

"Get rid of your numbers!" cried Ruby. "We'll head for the north gate."

"This way," said Orlando.

Within an instant the courtyard was empty. In the open gateway lay a heap of sacks numbered 1 to 31, but already their contents were racing through the teeming streets of the Capital, cheering and whooping as they went. They stopped briefly at the north gate, for two watchmen barred their way.

"Not so fast! Where do you think you're going?"

Orlando stepped forward. "There seems to be a misunderstanding," he said, smiling his sunniest smile. "This will explain everything."

He delved into his pocket and produced a letter. It was a familiar letter to Silo, a little crumpled now, but the very same one he had read long ago in the Fort-Before-the-Forest. He watched as the watchmen unfolded it and read:

To Whom It May Concern:

The bearer of this letter, one Maximillian Crow, is traveling to enter into the service of the Government. Said Government commands that he be given all possible assistance on his journey, financial or otherwise, from whatever person or persons he requests it of. Any person or persons failing to comply with the above order will incur the wrath of said Government, and a fine of ten silver crowns.

It had a dramatic effect.

"I'm sorry, Master Crow!" cried the first watchman. "Step right in. Excuse my rough manner just then—if only I'd known who I was talking to! I trust you'll take no offense."

"None whatsoever," said Orlando. "You were merely doing your job. But I and my colleagues here from the State Archaeological Division"—he waved an airy hand at the ragged children behind him—"are on a mission of some urgency."

The second watchman looked puzzled. "You do know, Master Crow, that the Division is searching all over for you?"

"Of course! That's my mission—to report to them

immediately. But evil forces are at work: even as we speak I'm being pursued by enemies who seek to prevent me. It may be that they'll come here and ask questions. They may even claim to work for the Division itself. But you know better than to help them." He smiled trustingly at the watchmen.

"We do now that you've warned us, Master Crow! Mum's the word!"

"Thank you!" said Orlando. "Now if you'll excuse us, we must be on our way."

The watchmen stepped back, and the children poured onto the docks.

Silo sprinted off at their head, scanning the mass of rafts tied along the quay for a suitable craft. His long residence on the Island had given him an eye for such things. And there it was, the perfect vessel—a great raft laden with cargo, and written along its side in bold letters: GOVERNMENT PROPERTY. TRESPASSERS WILL BE PROSECUTED. Silo beckoned to the advancing children, and in an instant they were streaming aboard.

"Ruby!" cried Silo. "Cast off the stern line. Orlando— you take the bow line. Drusilla—we need you on the steering paddle. You need to turn it hard left as soon as we're under way. And the rest of you—go to the middle of the raft and sit down."

He took up a boat hook and shoved the raft away from the quay. The watchmen at the gate were waving them farewell, but already they were growing distant, separated by a glittering sheet of water that grew wider by the second as the raft drifted out into the broad breast of the Rampage. Silo ran to help Drusilla on the steering paddle (for she seemed to have some trouble in distinguishing her left from her right), and in a moment he heard the chuckle of white water under their bows. The raft had caught the current and was moving out into the stream, picking up speed as it did so. Silo had his work cut out for him at first, weaving among the small craft that dotted the river's margin, but finally he brought the raft safe into the main channel. The current there was ferocious, and within moments they were fairly sweeping along. For the first time Silo dared to look back, and he saw the walls of the Capital receding rapidly into the distance. He saw the clustered rooftops rising up above them, and the Lion Tower looming over all, but already they seemed very far away, and with every second that passed they were borne farther from Mrs. Morgan, the inspector, and all their evil minions. They had done it, he realized. They had effected a daring and audacious escape under the very noses of their enemies. He imagined the looks of baffled rage on their faces when they realized that they were gone, and let out a great howl of joy. He was Silo Zyco, last of the Zycos, Unleasher of Sewage, Enemy of the State, Master of Escape, Raft-Rider of the Rampage, Genius.

Ruby, as ever, had more practical things on her mind.

"I hereby commandeer this cargo! All of you—open the crates and report on their contents."

The children untied the tarpaulin that covered the cargo and rummaged among the boxes and barrels and sacks beneath, and in a moment joyful voices were ringing out all over the raft.

"Cheese!"

"Jam!"

"Apples!"

"Spuds!"

"Bread!"

"Sausages!"

"Plum cake!"

"Booze!"

Ruby was disappointed, but she was the only one.

"I was hoping it might be weapons," she said, "but never mind. I suppose we may as well have a picnic."

12

ON THE RAMPAGE

They made good progress that afternoon. The first few hours were tense ones for Silo, for the Rampage ran fast and dangerous, and it took all his concentration to keep the raft on course, but as they traveled farther downstream the river gradually grew tamer. It was wider in these lower reaches, running swiftly between woods and pasture, and studded with shingle banks and wooded islands. For Silo and all the other escapees from the Unicorn Tower it was a joy to be out in the sunlight again, and a gleeful, carnival atmosphere reigned aboard the raft. Silo was in such a good mood that even Daisy, leading the little ones in a chorus of the "Cuddles the Puppy" song, could not puncture his mood. It was a perfect summer day: the riverbanks were bright with wild flowers, and willows trailed their delicate branches into the water. Swallows and dragonflies skimmed over its shimmering surface and cows stood knee-deep in its shallows and watched the raft sweep past with mild, curious eyes. The Rampage had become an altogether gentler river now, and finally Silo was able to relax. He stretched himself out luxuriously on a heap of sacks beside the helm, occasionally nudging the steering paddle. Ruby brought him a massive jam sandwich.

"Lucky there's all this food on board," he said.

"Yeah," said Ruby, "but I think you should know where it was headed for."

She lugged over a crate labeled TOP SECRET—ONLY TO BE OPENED BY AN OFFICIAL EMPLOYEE OF THE STATE ARCHAEO-LOGICAL DIVISION, and ripped off the lid. It was full of papers, and she handed Silo the topmost document. It was a list of the cargo on board, but it was the heading that caught Silo's eye: *Provisions for the Eastern Swamps Expedition, for Delivery to the Government Fleet at Parris Port.*

"They must be almost ready to sail," Ruby said.

"We've not much time, then," said Silo, "but at least we're headed in the right direction." He cast his mind back to his school days on the Island, and to the muddy maps Ryker had drawn on the classroom wall. "The Rampage runs out to the sea at the Great Gutfleet Flats. There's a town called Mudville to the south, but we have to pass Parris Port to get there— could be a problem on a stolen raft."

"Could we slip past at night?" asked Ruby. "Is it safe to navigate this thing in the dark?"

Silo shrugged. It would have to be. He began to ferret about in the crate. "Anything else in here that could help us?"

"I don't think so," said Ruby. "Looks like Ancient manuscripts to me."

And so it was. Silo was curious despite himself. He had heard a great deal about the Ancients but had never, until now, had a chance to read any of their writings. Such things were exceedingly rare, and he examined the crumbling papers gently. Most were odd pages and fragments, but there were a number of complete books, and he marveled at their strange titles: *IT for the Home PC, How to Raise and Train a Rottweiler, Making the Most of Your Microwave.* Who knew what rare and precious knowledge they contained? When Maximillian brought him a slice of plum cake ten minutes later, he was examining a worm-eaten page titled "Football Frenzy" and pondering over the extraordinary picture it bore.

Silo thought it must be a painting of some kind, but it was like no painting he had ever seen before, for it was incredibly, perfectly detailed, as though the artist had somehow captured a little rectangle of reality and frozen it forever in time. It showed a group of young men in red shirts and white shorts lined up neatly for their portrait, the back row standing and the front row squatting. The background showed smooth green turf and banks of seats—surely an Ancient goatball team. There was a picture on the other side too, and this one had a caption: *Golden goal for Arsenal.* The goatkeeper lay sprawled on the ground and a man in a red shirt was kicking a ball into an upright net with mighty force. He was surrounded by hapless defenders but they carried no clubs and, stranger still, there was not a goat to be seen.

Silo had a sudden and terrible thought. "Maximillian—when you see the past, do you ever see goatball games?"

"Only once, but it looked quite boring. They just ran around kicking a ball. Maybe the goats had escaped. But the Ancients seemed to enjoy it very much."

Aghast, Silo remembered what Mrs. Morgan had said about the rules of goatball being discovered by seers at the Academy twenty years ago. They had, he realized with a blinding flash of revelation, quite simply made it up. Not goats: *goals*. Goatball, like his own name, was down to a spelling error. But what a wonderful and ingenious invention it was! He tried to imagine it played with a ball, but it simply didn't work for him without the skill, speed, and exciting random element that goats brought to the game. He made a momentous decision. Part of him hated to destroy so rare and miraculous a thing, but much was at stake. Regretfully he dropped the tattered page into the Rampage and watched as it sank into the depths.

"Maximillian—don't ever, ever tell anyone that the Ancients played it with a ball."

"All right, I won't. It's more fun with goats anyway."

Meanwhile, back in the Capital, Mrs. Morgan was sitting in her office leafing through a sheaf of reports that had just been delivered. Two vast black cats lounged in the corner. They were the very same beasts that had so startled Silo, for Mrs. Morgan kept a pair of pumas as pets. They seemed restless and ill at ease with domesticity, and many of her visitors thought her unwise to so faithfully emulate the ways of the Ancients. Elgarth and the inspector were evidently of this opinion, for they were sitting as far away from the pumas as possible and looking distinctly uneasy. They and Mrs. Morgan all looked ultraclean and freshly scrubbed, but even so there was a faint odor about the room, a ghostly whiff of sewage.

"Aha!" said Mrs. Morgan, laying aside a sheet of paper. "I think this is what we have been looking for. It seems that a government vessel, a cargo raft, has been stolen from the north quay. The watchmen claim to have seen nothing, but the location is suggestive."

"It's certainly very close to the Unicorn Tower," said the inspector.

"Indeed it is! I'm convinced that if we find this raft, we will find the children responsible for the monstrous outrage that took place there. We must dispatch some reliable agents to track them down. The river Rampage will carry them down to Silo Zyco's old haunts in the Eastern Swamps, and he must be stopped at all costs."

"They're bound to catch him soon," said Elgarth soothingly. "After all, he's pretty dim."

Mrs. Morgan frowned. "There I disagree with you," she said. "I have discovered much in these last few hours, and I think there is more to Silo Zyco than meets the eye."

"And why is that?" said the inspector.

"Well, first there is his background. He comes from a legendary criminal family, and in my experience such people do not usually seek employment with the Government. And then there is his friendship with the boy who impersonated Maximillian Crow. We now know this is actually one Orlando Bramble, the brother of one of the Government's most dangerous enemies—Valeria the Violent, the notorious Raider."

The inspector looked thoughtful. "You suspect, then, that the Raiders are involved in this?"

"I'm sure of it," said Mrs. Morgan grimly. "So far they have been content to stir trouble on our sea coasts, but now it seems they grow more ambitious. Silo Zyco succeeded in inciting a rebellion in the Wildwoods, in the very heart of Mainland itself. I am convinced he is in league with them. And there is another thing. I have here a report from the guards at the Unicorn Tower. They say that the other children did not speak much to the real Maximillian Crow, but that no sooner had Silo arrived than he sought him out and befriended him. I am convinced he knew his true identity and was trying to recruit him to the cause of the Raiders. I believe there is a plot against us, a dangerous and deep-laid plot, and that Silo Zyco is far more cunning than we supposed. Where is your manservant, Elgarth? We must send him to Division Headquarters with instructions to have wanted posters circulated immediately."

"I sent him to the hospital to inquire after Superintendent Frisk and Officer Feeton," said Elgarth.

"I have done so, master, and returned." Rankly had materialized silently in the doorway.

"And how did you find our unfortunate officers?" asked the inspector.

Rankly looked grave. "Not well, sir. Their lives are not in danger, but the doctors say that the psychological scars will stay with them forever. The trauma was very great.

"But Officer Feeton does not forget his duty. He asked me to give a message to you. He remembers that he overheard Silo Zyco and the little Crow child talking about the gift of the seeing. He would have mentioned it earlier, he says, but the unexpected arrival of the Bramble boy put it out of his mind. Crow told Silo Zyco he could see into the distant past, right back to the time of the Ancients."

Mrs. Morgan sprang to her feet, her pale face tinged pink with fury. "You see? Maximillian's powers are even greater than we had supposed! He is the key to rediscovering the se-cret power of the Ancients, and yet Silo means to deliver him into the hands of the Raiders! Rankly—arrange transport for us immediately! Thank heavens the government fleet awaits us in Parris Port. It seems we must kill two birds with one stone: first put an end to Silo Zyco's schemes and then com-mence our eastern expedition. Elgarth—I'll meet you at the north jetty within the hour. Come, Inspector! We have no time to waste, and I find I must leave the cleanup operation at the Unicorn Tower in your capable hands."

The inspector looked depressed beyond measure.

Elgarth was left alone, and in an extremely bad mood. He suspected that Mrs. Morgan was wrong about Silo's alliance with the Raiders, and it infuriated him to hear Silo described as some kind of criminal mastermind. He had disliked him from the first, but since his terrible experience in the Unicorn Tower his dislike had deepened into a dark and unyielding hatred. Already the event had become the talk of the Capital, and for some reason the scum of the city found it extremely funny. It could only be a matter of time before the story reached his father, and Elgarth knew that he would not find it in the least amusing but rather a shameful blot on the family name. As he sat brooding a woman's voice drifted up from the street below: a voice both tuneful and unfeasibly loud, upraised in a rollicking ballad.

Silo Zyco was a seer, the future he could see!
He hated the Division just as much as you or me!
They said he was an anarchist—he was too mad for words,
And filled an Ancient ruin with a tidal wave of—

Her song broke off abruptly, for Elgarth had hurled a potted geranium at her. Seething, he slammed the window shut. Rankly was watching him, the expression on his face unfathomable.

"Well, don't just stand there!" snapped Elgarth. "Pack my things."

An enraged bellow came from the street:

His writing's neat, he has webbed feet, some say he is a
    psycho,
But if you care for freedom, drink a toast to Silo Zyco!

There followed the musical tinkle of breaking glass, and a turnip came hurtling into the room, thrown by an unseen hand.

❧

That evening the subject of the song steered the raft to a wooded island. A weeping willow grew on its banks, its branches sweeping down into the stream, and when the raft was secured to its trunk it was completely concealed behind a dense green curtain. Then Silo did what he had been longing to do all afternoon: he took off his boots and dived, fully clothed, into the clear pool beneath the willow. All the children on the Island learned to swim at a very early age, and Silo had the added advantage of webbed feet; now he cleaved through the sparkling shallows with the grace of an otter, and as he did so a dark cloud blossomed in his wake as he shed the accumulated grime of weeks. When he finally surfaced, the air around him was rent with shouts and splashes. The other children were following suit.

"Hooray! Bath time!" cried Daisy. "Remember to wash behind your ears, everyone!"

But for the moment they were more interested in water fights and ducking their friends. The river around them turned black for a moment, and all looked considerably cleaner when they emerged, laughing and dripping, fifteen minutes later.

"We need to get a camp organized," said Ruby. "Look out for a good spot for the fire—somewhere hidden. Some of you get the spuds and bread and sausages. Everyone stick together until we've checked the place for zoo animals, and then we can start collecting firewood."

An hour later a cheerful fire was blazing in the gathering twilight. It was sited in a snug hollow and the trees grew thick about it, shielding its glow from anyone passing on the riverbank. The Bolton brothers had been dispatched to the ends of the island to act as lookouts, and two of the smaller children had been sent after them with supplies of hot sausages. The rest were seated around the fire, having just polished off a gargantuan meal of sausage sandwiches and plum cake. Their clothes steamed gently in the heat of the fire, and Daisy had laid potatoes to bake in the embers. Ruby paced back and forth at the edge of the hollow, her bottom lip thrust out, a look of grim determination on her face.

"Time for a council of war," she said. "Well, we've escaped, which is excellent. Nice work, everyone. Special congratulations to Drusilla for her work on the treadmill, and to Silo for handling the raft and getting Frisk off our backs. That was genius, by the way—wish I'd had time to watch. Also to Orlando for lying to the watchmen—that's a real gift you have there."

Maximillian, seated beside Silo, muttered dark things.

"Now we have to make plans. How many of you have homes to go back to?"

Only Daisy raised her hand.

"How many of you are orphans?"

Maximillian and Orlando raised their hands. Beside them

Silo's hovered for a moment. His father had been a mystery for fully ten years now, and from what little Silo knew of him it seemed he lived a life of relentless action and adventure. Such a man could die in any number of ways, and very likely had, but Silo was not prepared to abandon hope. Not yet. He clasped his hands firmly in his lap.

"How many of you have parents who've been shipped out?" said Ruby, and a forest of hands arose all around the fire.

"Yeah, I thought as much. So right now we need to find help, and that means the Raiders. They're the only ones brave enough to stand up against the Government. Everyone else moans about them all the time, but they're too scared to do anything about it. But not the Raiders. They're always up for a fight. The Government might control the land, but the seas are still up for grabs. And at this rate we'll reach the coast tomorrow. There's a town there, a place called Mudville."

"Is that where the Raiders live?" someone asked hopefully.

"No, and it's finding them that's going to be the hard part. They say they operate from a hidden base off Mainland, but no one knows where exactly. Some say it's in the Northern Isles, some say out west past the Horse Island Straits, but it's all just guesswork. It could be anywhere. They have a Code of Silence—Raiders only tell other Raiders. What we really need is someone with inside contacts."

"I might be able to help you there," said Orlando. "My sister is Valeria the Violent."

Ruby was impressed. "Straight up? That woman's the business. She helped Ingall the Unclean attack the outposts on the southern coast last year. They say she left nothing behind her but scorched earth."

"Doesn't surprise me," said Orlando. "She used to do that when it was her turn to do the gardening."

Daisy spoke up. "The little ones are much too young to fight. We need to find a safe place for them to stay where they'll be properly fed and treated with kindness."

"True," said Ruby. "We'll have to work on that."

"I'm up for joining the Raiders," said Silo, "but I have to go to the Island first, to warn them that the Division is on its way."

"I've been thinking about that," said Ruby. "I think it's high time we got our revenge on the Division."

"I thought the thing with the sewage was pretty good," said Orlando.

"Yeah, but we can do better. I've heard a lot of talk in the Capital about the Division. Apparently the Government's getting a bit fed up with them. They've given them loads of money to dig up ruins and stuff, but they're not coming up with the goods. They still don't know what the power of the Ancients was. And from what I heard, if they don't have a big success soon, they're in trouble—so I think we should find a way to make sure this eastern expedition's a complete disaster."

"How?" said Silo.

"We're going to have to sleep on that one," said Ruby. "Are those spuds done yet?"

—:—

Within the hour they were back on board the raft. The children were clean, dry, and fed to the bursting point. They had made a cabin of sorts by pushing the crates and barrels into a square and rigging the tarpaulin over it. Ruby was supervising the loading of grass-stuffed sacks to act as mattresses.

"Is everyone aboard? Do a head count, Drusilla." She watched as Drusilla counted painfully on her fingers, her face knotted with concentration. "On second thought, you do it, Daisy."

"Thirty-one," said Daisy, after a brief pause.

"We'll be on our way, then. Cast off fore and aft."

Silo turned the steering paddle and the raft glided out into the river. The sky overhead was a deep blue now. A lurid orange sunset flared to the west, and the river ran dark between inky banks.

"See if you can get some sleep, you lot," said Ruby. "And keep it quiet! It's such a still night the sound will carry for miles. Orlando and I'll keep lookout in the bow."

Daisy herded the children into the makeshift cabin and Silo was left alone at the helm. Or thought he was, until something small and bullet-headed blundered into him in the dark.

"Maximillian? Why don't you get some sleep?"

"I want to help you, Silo."

Silo sighed. "All right, then, but sit down. The last thing we need now is you falling overboard. And wrap up in a sack so you don't get cold."

And so began their long and eerie journey. It seemed

strange to be out on the river at night, with only the stars and the owls for company, and navigating an unknown channel in the dark was nerve-racking work. Silo gazed into the blackness ahead, and occasionally Orlando or Ruby gave him whispered messages:

"Floating tree trunk to your left!"

"White water dead ahead."

"Another island coming up—I think the main channel's to the right."

Once, they startled a family of sleeping swans, which flew off into the night with a great flurry and whir of wings and startled the children in their turn. As the long hours passed they began to scan the banks for signs of life with increasing anxiety. Dawn could not be far off now, and they needed to be clear of Parris Port by daybreak. Finally Orlando came creeping to the helm.

"I think I see lights on the left bank, way downriver—that must be it, surely. . . ."

Silo strained his eyes into the gloom and saw, faintly discernible, a few pinpricks of light. There was a brighter glow on the horizon now, and by the time they drew level with the lights it had thickened into a broad pink band. Silhouetted against it, Silo could clearly see the tumbled roofs of Parris Port, and before them a forest of masts. The Government's fleet was assembled and meant business. The ships lay silent as the raft ghosted past, but the streets were deserted and the whole town was wrapped in slumber. The Rampage was broader now, and Silo could feel the tug of the tide beneath them and smell a salt tang in the air.

"Well," said Ruby, yawning mightily, "that's the hard part done. Time to catch some sleep. Can Drusilla be trusted on the helm?"

"No," said Silo firmly. "Put the Bolton brothers in charge. Their family are fishermen—or at least they were before they got shipped out. They know a thing or two about boats."

Silo crawled into the makeshift cabin, towing a sleep-walking Maximillian behind him, and woke them up. Then he stretched out on their still-warm mattress and was asleep within seconds.

‍‌‌‌‍⁓

He awoke hours later. The cabin was packed with children feasting on jam sandwiches, rain was thrumming on the tar-paulin roof, and Drusilla was poking him in the chest.

"Ruby said to wake you up. We're lost."

Dazed with dreams, Silo crawled out on deck. The raft was drifting down a channel between gleaming mud banks. In every direction a flat expanse of marsh spread to the horizon. The wind tugged at his tattered clothes, and the gray skies above him were full of gulls, wheeling and crying above the rain-swept landscape. His long journey had come full circle, and he was back on the Eastern Marshes.

"It's a delta," said Basil, the older Bolton brother. "Once it got light there was a fair bit of shipping in the main channel, so we took a smaller one to stay out of sight. But there are hundreds of islands, and now we're lost. You don't recognize it, do you?" he finished hopefully.

"No."

"Shhh!" said Ruby. "There's some kind of creature up ahead—quite a big one. Are you sure there aren't zoo animals on these marshes, Silo?"

"Yes." Silo peered into the drizzle. Something hunched and hairy was crawling in the mud. Then he saw, to his delight, that it wore a tattered sack. He was nearing home.

"It's an eel trapper," he said. He hailed the figure with the traditional yodeling cry of the Marshlanders, and it rose slowly to its feet, squelching as it did so. They drifted alongside and it revealed itself to be a filthy old man, dripping mud from head to foot. His hair and beard were matted, his eyes were wild, and he was armed with an eel spear. Daisy uttered a small cry of distress, and even Silo was somewhat taken aback. He had been away a long time and had forgotten quite how unusual Marshlanders appeared in the eyes of Uplanders. He was growing worldly and sophisticated, he realized, with a little glow of pride.

Ruby addressed the festering apparition. "Do you know the way to Mudville, please?"

"And why would a bunch of Uplanders be looking for Mudville?" said the old man.

"We're on an urgent mission. We need to find the Raiders," said Ruby.

The man stared at her. "There's always folks who wants to find the Raiders, but the Raiders ain't the kind of folk who want to be found. You have to know the right kinds of people."

Orlando stepped forward. "My sister is Valeria the Violent."

"You say she is, but can your word be trusted?"

There was an awkward silence. The man regarded them all with deep suspicion, then spat a gob of something green into the creek. Daisy winced delicately at Silo's side.

"The Raiders is friends to the common man," he said, "but those who comes from the Uplands to look for them is usually government folk."

"Do we look like government folk?" said Ruby in exasperation.

"They comes in all shapes and sizes," said the man, "and rides on all kinds of craft."

He eyed the raft, which Silo suddenly remembered had GOVERNMENT PROPERTY written all over it in huge letters.

"Look," he said, "we stole the raft, and I'm not from the Uplands. I was born and raised down the coast from here. I'm a Zyco."

"Figures," said the man. "The Zycos always was a light-fingered bunch. Rafts, eel traps, the very eels themselves; nothing was safe from their thieving hands. But they say the gods sent a tidal wave to punish them for their evil ways. They's all dead now, all save one, and him the worst of the lot by all accounts: a dwarfish, ill-tempered child with a powerful stare. They say he practiced dark arts and carried the curse of the seeing. Zyco the Psycho, they called him, but his given name was Silo."

"Nice to meet you too!" snapped Silo.

The man sprang back. "So you've returned!" he cried. "An evil omen for all us marsh folk, and a sign of ill luck to follow! But you must prove to me, beyond a shadow of a doubt, that you are this so-called seer, this Silo Zyco!"

Silo had forgotten just how irritating Marshlanders could be. Scowling, he removed his boots and displayed his webbed feet. "There! I'm the last of the Zycos. Now will you tell us where Mudville is?"

"No! Bad fortune walks with you, webfoot! Go back to whence you came!"

"If I do, you'll be sorry."

"Why?" cried the old man fearfully.

Silo knew his Marshlanders.

"Because I know how to make coffee out of seaweed," he said.

13

HOW AQUINUS
BECAME ACCURSED

That evening Silo, Orlando, Maximillian, Ruby, and the aged eel trapper were seated in a ramshackle hut on the outskirts of Mudville. Silo had just finished explaining how to make coffee out of seaweed.

". . . and whatever you do," he was saying, "don't drink it for at least six weeks. It's not suitable for children and it's poisonous to goats. You can use it for fishing, though. If you pour a jugful into the middle of a shoal, it stuns them. Now where can we find the Raiders?"

"You could try the Ship and Squid," said the eel trapper. "It's by the harbor, next to the gutting sheds. There's all sorts go there."

Silo scowled, for his coffee recipe was a good one, and the old man's vague information seemed a disappointing return. But Ruby seemed content.

"Let's go!" she cried, springing to her feet.

The raft was moored in a quiet backwater. The rain had stopped and the older children were engaged in a lively game of goatball on the marshes. In lieu of a goat Drusilla had assumed the role and was hurling hapless players around with wild abandon. The twelve smallest ones were clustered around Daisy, who was, Silo noticed to his dismay, teaching them a new song.

"Drusilla and Daisy can keep an eye on things here," said Ruby, "and we'll go with Orlando. They're bound to have heard of Valeria the Violent at this Squid place."

"I'm coming too." It was Maximillian. "Something bad will happen here. Something huge and hairy will come from the sea. It makes a roaring noise, and people will run away from it. I heard them screaming. I'm scared. I want to stay with Silo."

Finally Maximillian had had a useful seeing, and they all rather wished he hadn't. Although no one had seen fit to mention it, the town of Mudville had a depressing appearance, and the news that marauding marine creatures ran riot in its streets at night was unwelcome, for twilight was falling. Silently they turned their faces to the fetid warren of streets. A battered sign read WELCOME TO MUDVILLE, BIRTHPLACE OF INGALL THE UNCLEAN, and the smell of rotting fish hung heavy in the air.

"I can see why he left," said Orlando.

Mudville was, as its name suggested, built mostly of mud,

a closely packed warren of houses overshadowed by a soaring lookout tower. The place seemed deserted, and they saw no one until they arrived at the main square, a bleak expanse of churned mud. Here a depressed-looking goat was standing on a dung hill, presumably in a futile effort to keep its hooves dry, and an aged crone was standing before a notice board headed OFFICIAL GOVERNMENT INFORMATION: LATEST BY PIGEON POST. She was pasting a poster to it using, unsurprisingly, a bucket of mud, and Silo was horrified to see his own name in huge letters. Ruby motioned them into the shadows of an alleyway and there they lurked, watching intently as the aged crone pasted a second poster beneath the first. She straightened up slowly, inspected her handiwork, then finally hobbled off into the encroaching gloom.

No sooner had she gone than they hastened over to the notice board and found news of an unwelcome kind. The poster read:

WANTED

SILO ZYCO

also known as **ZYCO THE PSYCHO**,
for Inciting Rebellion, Consorting with Enemies of the State,
Vicious and Unprovoked Assault on a Government Official,
Stealing Government Property,
and the Kidnapping of Maximillian Crow.
A Reward of Thirty Silver Crowns
for Information Leading to his Capture.

Silo was outraged. "None of this is true! I didn't kidnap anyone, and no one calls me Zyco the Psycho!"

"Everyone at the Academy did," said Orlando. "All the other students anyhow."

The description below did nothing to cool Silo's temper.

A Thin Boy of Dwarfish Stature,

Black Hair, Pallid Complexion,

Wild Staring Blue Eyes, Webbed Feet,

Ten Years of Age.

"It's all lies," he said furiously. "And anyway, no one will know me from that stupid description."

But Orlando and Ruby were silent. Then Ruby pointed to the notice pasted below. It was headed STOLEN PROPERTY.

"That's a description of our raft," she said grimly. "We'll have to ditch it. Me and Orlando best go back and warn the others, and as for you two, you need to get off the streets. Go to the Ship and Squid and stay there. We'll meet you later."

She and Orlando slipped off into the dusk, and Silo swiftly peeled off the posters. He approached the depressed goat and held them temptingly beneath its nose, in the hope that it might eat them and so destroy the evidence, but it merely shot him a contemptuous look. And then a bell began to toll from somewhere high overhead and a voice cried from the lookout tower: "The *Sea Pig*! The *Sea Pig* is coming!"

Cursing, Silo stuffed the muddy posters under his cloak.

"What's a sea pig, Silo?" said Maximillian.

"I don't know," said Silo, "but whatever it is, it's bad news."

For finally the inhabitants of Mudville were to be seen. All around them doors were opening and anxious people were emerging into the square, all peering apprehensively in the direction of the harbor. Silo pulled Maximillian back into the alleyway and watched as the householders set to work barring their shutters. They worked fast, and within moments doors were slamming shut the length and breadth of the square. There followed the sound of keys being turned in locks, the rattle of chains, and the snick of bolts sliding home. Silo recalled Maximillian's vision of something huge and hairy that came from the sea. He trusted Maximillian's gift, and in the circumstances it seemed foolish to head for the harbor lest they come face to face with the unknown horror that was the *Sea Pig*.

"We'd better find somewhere to lie low for a while," he said. He set off up the alleyway, and as they squelched their way up its murky length a familiar scent drifted into Silo's nostrils, one that reminded him of happier days when he had traveled with Ruddle and Blossom: the smell of hay and horses. They had arrived at a stable yard and could hear soft stirrings in the darkness and the steady munching of unseen jaws, sounds at once familiar and comforting.

"In here," said Silo.

There was a shed inside the gateway. Harnesses hung from pegs and the floor was stacked high with hay. Gratefully they slipped into its shadows.

"Will we be safe here?" said Maximillian.

"Yes," said Silo firmly. "See if you can get some sleep. I'll keep watch."

And so he did for a while, propped stiffly against the wall and listening intently to the distant sounds from the streets. He gloomily considered his new status as a boy with a price on his head, and then his thoughts turned to Ruby and Orlando. Where would they find to hide the raft? he wondered. Or a horde of children, come to that? But he had been up most of the previous night and was deathly tired, and gradually his thoughts began to drift. Presently his heavy eyelids closed and his breath lengthened, until finally he slept as deeply as Maximillian, who lay curled up beside him. And so it was that, an hour or so later, when a distant roaring could be heard from the sea, he slept on unheeding, for by then he was far, far away, dreaming that he stood on the deck of a ship that sailed beneath a star-spangled sky. The full moon laid a glittering path upon the water, and a shadowy figure stood beside him at the wheel, steering for unknown lands beyond the dark horizon. Silo knew, with a sudden joyful certainty, that it was his father. Eagerly he looked up to see his face . . . and saw a furious bald man, his cheeks glowing orange in the light of the lantern he held.

"That's right!" he cried. "Very clever! Sleep right inside the doorway just where I'll trip over you!"

Silo shook himself awake. The man fumbled in the gloom for his saddle, then stomped off across the stable yard; all around him the horses were stirring uneasily in their stalls. Night had fallen while Silo slept, and he could hear wild cries from the streets beyond. Cursing under his breath, he dragged himself to his feet and approached the man, who was now tugging a reluctant pony from its stable.

"What's the sea pig?" he said. "Why's everyone so afraid of it?"

The man glared at him. "The *Sea Pig*'s just a ship. It's her captain that's the problem. Black Tom, they call him. He turns up every few months, and he arrives with a powerful thirst. He's a monster of a man, and when he's got a few gallons of booze inside him he grows frisky. Last time he tore up half of Goat Street. *And* he threw me in the harbor, so this time I'm leaving town."

"Can't anyone stop him?" asked Silo.

"There's none brave enough. Besides, he says he's a Raider, and folk around here have a soft spot for Raiders."

A Raider! Here at last was the opportunity Silo had been seeking. Resolutely he turned his face to the harbor, where he could hear the distant sound of running feet, screaming, and breaking glass. He had imagined the Raiders to be a noble race, friends to the common man, but it seemed he was mistaken. But it was the Raiders and the Raiders alone who could help him in his present predicament, and so he screwed up his courage and stepped out into the alley.

"Is it safe, Silo?" said Maximillian, who had shaken himself awake and now trotted faithfully by his side.

"Yeah," said Silo shortly, "but just stay behind me, OK?"

—:—

Black Tom was not a hard man to find, for when they reached the harbor they heard a peal of hideous laughter, one that grated horribly on the ears: "Huurgh! Huurgh! Huur-ugh!" Black Tom was evidently in a cheerful mood. He stood outside the Ship and Squid; the landlord appeared to be begging him not to enter, while his customers scrambled out the windows in a desperate attempt to escape. But the braver among them had taken up a large fishing net and seemed to be having a whispered discussion as to the wisdom of trying to entrap Black Tom in it. Silo understood their hesitation, for Black Tom was a mountain of a man. He wore a tattered coat decorated with tarnished gold braid, and a row of rusty medals, and a tricorner hat sat on his matted locks. He had a gigantic black beard with bits of dinner stuck in it and a single bristling eyebrow that slashed across his forehead, sheltering two mismatched eyes, one small and piggy and the other a great glowing brown orb. His mouth, the source of the horrible laughter, was open to show a set of gleaming gold teeth. He held aloft the goat that Silo had seen earlier, and as they watched he tossed it playfully at the landlord of the Ship and Squid, striking him full in the stomach. The goat seemed unhurt, if somewhat sulky, but the landlord collapsed moaning to the ground, his legs kicking feebly.

And then Black Tom paused, looking about as though in search of a new assailant. The men with the net melted back into the shadows, and his eye fell on Silo. An evil smile spread over his face and he strode toward him on huge booted feet that struck sparks from the cobbles. As his great shadow fell across him Silo opened his mouth to speak but found himself being swept up by a powerful hand and brandished aloft. It seemed that Black Tom considered the smaller of Earth's creatures— goats, children, and the like—simply as ammunition. Like most small people, Silo hated to be manhandled. Suspended upside down at the end of Black Tom's brawny arm, he swallowed his fear and fixed him with his most powerful stare.

"Stop!" he said. "I need your help. I—"

But Black Tom uttered an astonished grunt. He lowered Silo to eye level and scrutinized him with a squint-eyed, drunken stare. Then a look of wonder crossed his brutish features. "You must be Aquinus's boy," he said. "You're the spitting image of the man!"

Silo was flooded with astonishment. Here, finally, was someone who could tell him about his long-lost father! "Where . . . ?" he began eagerly.

But at that instant a bucket of mud, thrown with astonishing force and accuracy, came hurtling out of the gloom and struck Black Tom square on the back of the head. A look of bemusement crossed his face, his eyes rolled up, and he fell back unconscious, his great bulk crashing down to lie motionless in the mud. Ruby—who else?—stepped into the pool of light that spilled out of the Ship and Squid, with Orlando at her side. She received a spontaneous round of applause from the bystanders, a smattering of cheers, and three cries of "Good shot!"

"Are you all right?" she said, hauling Silo to his feet. "I saw him lobbing goats around and I thought you'd be next."

"I'm fine," said Silo, his mind reeling with shock. He

gazed down at the comatose form of Black Tom. "He knows my dad."

"Your dad keeps weird company," she said, and then, turning to the inhabitants of Mudville who were clustering around to offer her their congratulations, "Thank you. Really, it was nothing. Glad to be of help."

But a beaming woman was shaking her by the hand. "I'm Edna, landlady of the Ship and Squid, and I'm very much obliged to you. Last time he was here he wrecked the place, and we've only just had it redecorated. If you and your little friends"—she smiled down at Silo and Orlando and Maximillian—"need somewhere to stay for the night—free of charge, of course—you're very welcome."

"Thanks!" Ruby turned and gave an ear-piercing whistle.

Drusilla materialized out of the darkness, tailed by twenty-six ragged children.

"Come on, everyone!" said Ruby. "We're staying here tonight."

A small, shock-headed tide flowed up to the Ship and Squid. Daisy was the last of them, and she addressed the astonished Edna with the utmost politeness.

"Thank you *so* much for taking us in! It's well past the little ones' bedtime." She smiled down at the smallest children, who stood crowded about her. "What do we say to the kind lady, everyone?"

"Thank you!" they chorused.

A little curly-haired moppet went one better. "Can we sing her our song, Daisy?"

"Would you like that?" said Daisy, giving Edna a winning smile.

They took her stunned silence for assent and launched boldly into a song about elves. Silo was appalled. They had, against all the odds, found a safe haven for the night, but surely this would ruin everything. But he was mistaken. It seemed that there was no accounting for taste, for Edna smiled down at Daisy's little choir as they worked their way through verse after verse, and when they finally finished and beamed proudly up at her, she wiped a tear from her eye.

"Bless you, dears!" she said. "Such a pretty song! But come on in out of the cold. I expect you'd like something to eat."

They nodded eagerly and filed inside. Edna turned to Silo, Ruby, and Orlando. "They're so sweet at that age!"

Dumbly they nodded, well aware that it was some years since anyone had considered them sweet—if indeed they ever had.

"What about him?" Silo pointed to Black Tom.

"I'll get some of the men to carry him inside. Looks like he's out for the night; he'll be a different man in the morning."

Silo spent a restless night. Edna had been true to her word, and he lay in a little attic bedroom in the Ship and Squid, but it was a bit of a squash. Silo was sharing a bed with Orlando, the Bolton brothers, and Maximillian, and the latter, true to his word, tended to scream in the night. Besides, Silo was in a fever of impatience to find out more about his father—

which was why, when dawn was still pink in the sky, he got dressed and crept downstairs to the bar, where Black Tom lay sleeping.

Edna had said he would be a different man in the morning, but to Silo, as he gazed down at the great snoring length of him, he looked very much the same as he had the previous night—large and scary. He turned and studied the array of bottles behind the bar, carefully scanning the labels. There was BOOZE, BEST BOOZE, and BARGAIN BOOZE, but his gaze fell upon a squat black bottle inscribed DOCTOR PYTHON'S PICK-ME-UP POTION: *Add three drops to your morning tea and say good-bye to Fatigue, Headaches, and Nervous Irritability!* Black Tom had had a lively evening the night before, besides being knocked unconscious by a bucket of mud, and Silo calculated that he would be suffering from all of the above. He doubted he was a tea drinker, though, so he simply emptied the contents of the bottle into the largest tankard he could find and topped it up with Bargain Booze. It steamed and bubbled in an alarming manner, but the smell was really rather pleasant. He placed it by Black Tom's side and poked him with a broom. Then he hid behind the door and listened. He heard firstly faint stirrings, then groaning, and then a pleased grunt followed by prolonged slurping noises. Then a profound silence fell.

Silo waited for a full minute, his heart pounding in his chest, then stepped boldly out from behind the door. Black Tom had heaved himself into a nearby chair and glared at him with bleary, red-rimmed eyes. He raised his hairy black eyebrow in a mute question, and Silo pulled his wanted poster from his pocket and presented it with a flourish. Black Tom smoothed the crumpled document and read. It seemed to take him a very long time, but by the time he had finished his mood had visibly improved. He smiled, and Silo winced inwardly as his horrible laughter rang out.

"Huurgh! Huur-ugh! Huur-urgh! Inciting rebellion, kidnapping, assault—and you only ten! And they've described you down to a T—'wild staring blue eyes'! I remember you now from last night. You're Aquinus the Accursed's boy. We was talking, and then . . ." Black Tom looked puzzled and touched the lump on his head.

"Do you know where he is?" said Silo. For one glorious moment he had a vision of himself sailing to the rescue of the Islanders at the head of a fleet of Raiders' ships, his father at the helm, but Black Tom's next words snuffed out all his hopes.

"He set sail for the Us of Ay five years back. The Bucket Heads was on his trail and he'd just found out your ma was dead—there didn't seem no point in his hanging about."

"Do you know how he met my mother?" said Silo.

"There's not much I don't know about the Raiders," said Black Tom proudly. "He met her when he was on the run. They say he was shipwrecked on the Walrus Sands and drifted for days on a raft he'd made of booze barrels. He was plagued by sharks but he turned the tables on them, clubbed one to death and ate it. And luckily he had plenty of booze to drink. And speaking of which . . ."

Silo picked up the empty tankard and topped it up at the bar. Black Tom drank deep, then settled himself back comfortably in his chair and continued his story.

"He was a hardy man, was your dad, and finally he washed up on a lonely marsh. And who should he meet there but your ma. A fine, handsome woman, they say, and handy with an eel spear. Well, seems she took pity on him and let him hide out at a place called Mud Island, and that's where he told her of his long fight against the Government. And it seems she was struck by the dash of the man, and the pair of them fell in love. A strange thing, that, but the ladies was always taken with Aquinus, despite him being such a runtish little bloke."

Silo's heart sank. He had hoped that he was one of those small boys who suddenly shot up in their teens, but it seemed that in this, as in so many things, he was doomed to disappointment.

Black Tom was shaking his head, his monobrow creased in thought. "There's no accounting for it," he said. "You'd expect them to favor a fine figure of a man. Maybe a man more like meself."

But Silo had no interest in Black Tom's love life, or lack of it. "And then what happened?" he said.

"They got married—a secret wedding, it was, in the tradition of the Raiders. They spoke their vows, exchanged written testimonials, and received the blessing of a tribal elder."

"What tribal elder was that?"

"A woman by the name of Mudford."

Now Silo had the answer to a question that had long troubled him. His mother had not been a simple marsh girl. She had formed a romantic attachment to a notorious outlaw, and getting Miss Mudford to bless their marriage had been a seriously smart move. Miss Mudford had never made sense since the mud fever had settled on her brain, and no one would have been surprised if she told them that Zenda Zyco had married a Raider—or believed her either.

"This written testimonial . . . was it my father's wanted poster?"

"As like as not," said Black Tom. "Anyway, your dad regained his strength and left the marsh, said he'd return with a ship and take your ma away with him. But he had a price on his head, and they chased him the length of the land. They captured him and imprisoned him, but still he didn't forget his promise. Finally he managed to escape, but he was a sight too late. Your ma had died of marsh sickness only months before."

"How did he find out?"

"Man called Ruddle," said Black Tom. "Seems that the Raiders had promised Aquinus they'd keep their ears open for news of your mother, and this Ruddle was a guide for the inspectors. A chatty man, they say, and one who liked a drink. Anyway, a friendly stranger bought him a few one evening, and asked him about the Island and how things did there. He said it was a festering bog of a place where food was short and folks could scarce read or write. And the stranger found out that your ma had died and you were left with no one to take proper care of you. Well, Aquinus was revered among the Raiders, and they'd let no child of his die of hunger or neglect, so they sent Mungo Ryker to keep an eye on you. He was tired of living on the run and needed somewhere to hide out for a spell, so it all worked out very handy."

So that was why Ryker had come to the Island! And his first name was Mungo. No wonder he had kept it a secret.

"Why was he on the run?" asked Silo.

"Seems like he was a teacher once, and a good one at that, but the Government didn't hold with some of the stuff he taught. He didn't see eye to eye with them on the Ancients, so they decided he was an enemy of service and obedience and all the rest of it, and they branded him and got him chucked out of his job. People was afraid to employ him after that and he fell on hard times. And that's when he met up with the Raiders."

"He was a Raider, then?"

"No," said Tom emphatically. "The man was a menace aboard a ship. If he wasn't hauling on the wrong rope, he was falling over the side. More a thinker than a man of action, I reckon. And as to how he came to be a wanted man, it came about like this. The Bucket Heads was collecting taxes just up the coast from here, and those who couldn't pay were rounded up and held at a fort called Deadwell. Well, the Raiders thought to put a stop to it, and it so happened that Ryker had discovered that one Captain Block from the Southern Shires was on his way to take command of this tax squad. Word was out that he was a holy terror—a little man, they said, but a mean 'un and bloodthirsty besides. So Ryker came up with a plan. They ambushed a gang of Bucket Heads. It was a fine punch-up by all accounts, and they took them completely by surprise, nicked their horses, their weapons, their dogs—"

"Why did they have dogs?" asked Silo.

"To hunt folk down," said Black Tom. "So anyway, they left the Bucket Heads locked in a lonely pigsty and rode off on their horses. They wore their uniforms and carried their weapons, and your father rode out in front. He was the smallest man among them but he had an imposing way about him, so it seemed fitting that he should play the part of Captain Block. And they carried the banner and beat the drums and everything. Well, Deadwell was a great wooden fortress and they arrived there just before nightfall. The Bucket Heads came out to meet them, all keen to make a good showing for the great Captain Block. But they say your father gave them hell! He fixed them with his most powerful stare and told them that they was a disgrace to the nation. He said they was too soft on tax evaders, that they should make an example of them. Fact is, he told them to burn down the whole fort with everyone in it. Well, they were hesitant at first, but your dad has what you might call a powerful personality. So finally they fired up the fort. And Aquinus sent his men around to guard the back door—so none should escape the flames, he said. But of course they opened it and let all the prisoners out into the night, and they gave them the tax money for good measure. It was smart work and no mistake."

Black Tom uttered a faint "Huurgh, huur-ugh" and drained his tankard to the dregs.

Silo was enthralled. It seemed his father was everything he could have hoped for. "Go on!" he said. "What happened next?"

"Way I heard it was this: Aquinus rides out before the blazing fort. His horse rears up beneath him and he raises his sword high above his head and cries out, 'Justice never sleeps!' then gallops off into the night, his friends hard on his heels. The Bucket Heads thought they was going to hunt down more tax evaders, but of course they was making their getaway. And from that day on your father was known among the Raiders by the name his enemies called him, Aquinus the Accursed. Anyway, the very next morning the real Captain Block turned up and found the fort a smoking ruin and the prisoners and taxes missing. They say angry barely describes his feelings! So that's how Ryker came to be a wanted man, and your dad besides."

Glowing with pride, Silo swiftly reviewed the charges on his father's wanted poster: dog theft, horse theft, tax theft, fire raising, impersonating a member of the armed forces, obtaining weapons by unlawful means, consorting with enemies of the state, and the destruction of government property. That seemed to cover it all nicely.

"So the Raiders took to the high seas," continued Black Tom. "Ryker sailed with them for a while, but he missed his old teaching job, so when the Raiders heard about you being in need of care they thought he'd be happier on the Island,

and safer besides. Seems like they were mistaken about that, though."

"Why didn't he tell me all this? About my dad and everything?"

"To protect you, is my guess. What if he'd been captured? The less you knew, the better. But the time was coming. The Raiders knew that the inspector was due back on the Island this year, and they'd be bound to ask questions about an Uplander. So they sent a ship to collect the pair of you. It was meant to pick you up from a place called Seal Point, but when it arrived there was no answer to its signals."

Silo remembered with wonder a ship that had sailed past a few weeks after Ryker's death, and Ben Mudford sounding the horn to warn of its approach.

"They guessed then that Ryker must be dead. What became of him?"

"He was mistaken for a muskrat and shot," said Silo sadly. It seemed that Ryker had given up a great deal to be of service to him, and he wished above all things that he had survived to be united with his friends again.

"A muskrat?" Black Tom was thunderstruck. "No one could mistake a grown man for a muskrat!"

"You don't know Vernon Bean," said Silo. "He's an idiot."

Black Tom nodded. "Maybe. I've heard that Island of yours is alive with them."

Silo had discovered much, but there was one last thing he must know. "My mother left me a message. She said I was to complete the great work my father started. What was it exactly?"

"To restore a right-thinking government to the Kingdom Isles, is my guess. That's why Aquinus sailed to the Us of Ay. Some say it's just a legend, but your dad thought he knew better. Said he'd found out a thing or two about the place. He said in Ancient times they called it the land of the brave and the home of the free. Well, that got him thinking. Aquinus is a brave man himself, and it struck him that if the folk as lived there was all brave and free, chances are they'd be a bit bored as well. Stands to reason—if they're free, they'd have no one to fight, and if you're brave, it's nice to have a scrap to prove it every now and then. So he thought he'd sail over there and recruit them to the cause, see if he could get some of them to come back with him and help free the Kingdom Isles. But he's been gone a long time now, so maybe he was mistaken."

Silo was silent. Finally he had found out his father's history and something of his character: a brave man with a wild and reckless streak, and a rebel to his heart's core. And his mother had known this and loved him for it—no simple marsh girl she. He remembered her standing on the lookout tower staring out to sea, waiting year after year for her husband's return until death put an end to her lonely vigil. He felt a sudden, terrible pity for her—for her and his father and himself besides. Aquinus the Accursed had chosen to fight the might of the Government, and as a result he and his little family had never known a moment's happiness together. Silo knew that his mother was lost to him forever, and now he dreaded that his father was too, for he remembered Orlando's words about the Us of Ay—"Most people think it doesn't exist"—and had a terrible vision of a ship sailing on and on across a boundless ocean, searching in vain for a landfall that never came.

14

THE *SEA PIG*

Parris Port was an altogether more elegant town than Mudville. The shops and inns that ringed the harbor were doing a roaring trade, and there was a great bustle of traffic as cart after cart loaded high with provisions came down to the quay to unload. The Government's fleet was being made ready and the whole town was in turmoil. Several squadrons of collectors had arrived the previous evening and were busy rounding up seamen to crew the ships. The Government paid no wages and so the sailors were understandably reluctant; thus the streets rang to the sound of running feet, bellowed orders of command, and occasional cries of "Got one!"

Elgarth was in a shop called Marine Supplies trying on pair after pair of sea boots. He was fussy about his footwear and was debating the relative merits of leather versus canvas when Rankly materialized discreetly at his side.

"There's a man as wants to speak to you, master."

He indicated a disreputable-looking figure thickly covered in mud and hair and dressed in a filthy sack. Silo would have recognized him, for it was the eel trapper who had acted as his guide the previous day. Now he groped around in his sack and produced a muddy poster.

"They stuck these up all over Mudville," he said to Elgarth. "Says there's a reward for Silo Zyco. Happens I saw him yesterday. This bloke here"—he nodded to Rankly—"said you'd be interested. Zyco and a bunch of other kids was riding on a raft in the Gutfleet Backwaters. He admitted that he stole it, bold as brass, but then the Zycos always was a shameless crew."

Elgarth sprang to his feet. "Do you know where he is now?"

The old man held out a filthy hand. Elgarth counted out ten crowns from his purse and handed them over. It was expensive, but he suspected it would be worth it.

"He's at the Ship and Squid in Mudville. That's where I sent him, anyway. He said he was looking for the Raiders."

"Are the Raiders at Mudville?" said Elgarth eagerly.

The old man shrugged. "Doubt it. It's been years since they berthed there. But the *Sea Pig*'s in the harbor—I heard them all shouting about it as I was leaving."

"What's special about the *Sea Pig*? Is her captain a Raider?"

The old man snorted derisively. "Her captain's a drunken fool," he said, "but he puts it about that he's a Raider. Could be Silo Zyco believes him."

"Go back to the start," said Elgarth. "I want all the details—

what he said, who he was with, everything." He listened intently to the narrative that followed, and when the old man was done he said, "Does anyone else know about this?"

"Not a soul. I left Mudville as soon as I found out about the reward, and I've been rowing all night. You're the only ones I've spoken to."

"Well, keep it that way," said Elgarth.

For Elgarth had a plan. He set off along the quay toward the Division's flagship, the *Unbeatable*, with the faithful Rankly padding at his side.

"Do I keep quiet about this, master?" he said. "Could be a problem if they catch the little Crow boy, him being so gifted and all."

"I've been thinking about that," said Elgarth, "and I'm not so sure now. I don't think he's as big a threat as I first thought. Superintendent Frisk has a very low opinion of him—he said the only thing he seemed good at was projectile vomiting."

"Not a happy gift," said Rankly thoughtfully.

"No. So I'm beginning to think it might be better to have Maximillian somewhere I can keep an eye on him. If he turns out to be a problem, I'm sure I can work out some way of getting rid of him."

And Elgarth was motivated by another reason, one that remained unspoken. In truth he had no desire to compete against the greatest seer in all Mainland, but if Silo was captured, it seemed inevitable that Maximillian would be too, and that was a price that Elgarth was willing to pay—for he wanted his revenge, and badly. Word of the incident in the Unicorn Tower had spread like wildfire: Elgarth had noticed that complete strangers whispered and sniggered behind his back, and unspeakable brown tides surged to and fro through his dreams—or rather his nightmares. This was Silo's doing, and Elgarth meant him to pay dearly for it. As he brooded they passed a tavern, and his ears were assailed by the sound of coarse voices upraised in song:

Silo Zyco was a seer, an honor to our nation!
The Division set him working on an Ancient excavation!
They made him do their digging, but Silo set a trap
And tried to drown old Frisky in a steaming sea of—

Enraged beyond measure, Elgarth stooped, picked up a passing piglet, and hurled it through the open doorway. But the clientele was evidently accustomed to flying livestock, for the singing continued unabated.

He isn't tall, he's rather small, some say he is a psycho,
But if you care for freedom, drink a toast to Silo Zyco!

In his current mood Elgarth would gladly have toasted Silo Zyco, but only if it could be very, very slowly and over an open fire. But he brightened a little when he arrived at the *Unbeatable*, for she was a splendid ship, the largest and swiftest in the fleet, and soon he would be sailing on her. Mrs. Morgan stood on her quarterdeck, watching as some collectors prodded a herd of disgruntled seamen aboard at swordpoint.

"Mrs. Morgan!" cried Elgarth. "I've just had a seeing that may prove useful. Silo Zyco is at the Ship and Squid in Mudville. He's looking for the Raiders, and Maximillian Crow is with him."

Elgarth, like Silo, didn't have very many seeings and was aware that the Division might find this something of a disappointment. Taking this into consideration, it seemed foolish not to use the eel trapper's news to his advantage.

"It is as I thought, then," said Mrs. Morgan. "A plot, and with the Raiders at the root of it! Congratulations, Elgarth—your seeing is very timely. We will apprehend Maximillian Crow and the wretched Zyco boy before we begin our island mission. Rankly! Find the admiral immediately and tell him the fleet sails upon the tide!"

A leisurely breakfast was underway at the Ship and Squid. The tables were crowded with eager children, and Daisy and Edna were bustling about the place serving bacon and eggs, while Black Tom was polishing off a gargantuan plate of sausages. Ruby shot a dubious glance at him and said to Silo and Orlando, "Is he really a Raider? I mean, from the way he was carrying on last night, he seems a bit . . ."

"Deranged?" suggested Orlando.

"He must be a Raider," said Silo. "He knows all about them."

Ruby looked doubtful. "We'll talk to him when he's finished his breakfast, then see if he can help us out."

"Speaking of breakfast," said Silo, "how are we going to pay for it? Edna said we could sleep here, but she never said anything about food. Drusilla's on her third helping already."

"No problem," said Orlando. "We're loaded. I sold the raft for timber and auctioned off the rest of the cargo. The booze alone fetched fifteen crowns. Then I flogged the Ancient manuscripts to a book dealer—got a really good price for them. I could've done better, but everyone had seen those 'Stolen Property' notices and they knew the stuff was hot. But even so . . ." He grinned and laid a weighty money bag on the table.

"Orlando's really smart with money," said Ruby with grudging admiration.

And so he was, thought Silo—especially other people's.

Black Tom emitted a mighty belch and rose to his feet.

"I'll settle the bill," said Ruby. "You two—three"—for Maximillian was hovering at Silo's side—"go and explain the situation to him."

She took up the money and approached the landlady. "How much do we owe you?"

Edna smiled kindly down at her. "It's on the house, dear. Truth to tell, I enjoy having you here. It's a treat to see so many young faces about the place. And that Daisy! She was up with the lark this morning to help me out in the kitchen. Such pretty ways she has about her, and so kindly to the little ones!"

Ruby maintained a diplomatic silence. Daisy had turned out to be surprisingly useful, but Ruby still found her a bit on the soppy side.

Edna regarded the crowded tables with a misty smile. "Albert and I planned to have a big family, but it wasn't to be," she said. "I always wanted to have kids."

Ruby looked thoughtful. "How many did you want?" she said.

Silo, Orlando, and Maximillian followed Black Tom out onto the quay.

"Can we talk to you for a moment?" asked Silo.

Black Tom paused in midstride, looked all around him, and then down. His eyes settled on Silo and he smiled his sinister gold smile. "You again—little Zyco the Psycho! Step aboard, why don't you? I'll talk more comfortable over a drop of something." He nodded to the *Sea Pig*.

She was moored just opposite the Ship and Squid and her crew were lounging about the deck. Silo's heart sank somewhat when he saw her, for she was a broad, stubby-looking vessel and had the look of a ship that was coming to the end of a long and difficult life. Her planking was battered, her masts were reinforced with bands of rusty iron, and her sails were patched. But the figurehead was nice. A little merpig sat perched upon the bows. It had the nether parts of a dolphin and the front part of a pig, and it sat with its tail lashing and its snout proudly raised. They stepped aboard, and twenty minutes later they were to be found seated in Black Tom's cabin. It was furnished with masculine simplicity: a table, a few stools, and a lot of dirt. The ship's dog, Growler, a small beast with coarse black fur and fleas, lay slumbering on a pile of rags in the corner, adding a homely touch to the otherwise spartan interior. Black Tom had just finished a tankard of dark liquid, and Silo had just finished relating their adventures.

". . . so it's really important we get to the Island and warn them before the Division arrives. We were hoping the Raiders could help us."

Black Tom stroked his fetid beard. "They operate from a secret base off Mainland."

"Yes, but where?"

"There's a Code of Silence. Only the Raiders know that."

"But you are a Raider, aren't you?"

"Not exactly, no."

They stared at him in consternation, and as they did so Black Tom seemed to shrink a little before their eyes. He slumped over his tankard, and a sulky, hard-done-by expression fixed itself on his face.

"It's not for lack of trying!" he growled. "I've always wanted to be one—found myself a ship and a crew and everything—but seems they're kind of fussy as to who they sail with. But I've met with them many a time. Why, the hours I've spent in taverns listening to them talk of their battles and adventures! 'Tis a fine life they lead, and one that made me wish to be among their number. Yes, I've listened to their yarns until the dawn was pale in the sky, and I've drunk with them many a time!"

Silo had a sudden sense of foreboding. "How much did you drink?" he said.

Black Tom looked shamefaced.

"Have you ever thrown a Raider at a pub landlord?" asked Silo. "Or in the harbor perhaps?"

"Well, I did throw Ingall the Unclean at a tax inspector once."

They stared at him accusingly, and Black Tom had the grace to look embarrassed.

"A simple enough mistake!" he cried. "He's a small man, and hairy—I thought he was a goat. It was high spirits, is all, but seems he's the unforgiving kind. He's not spoken to me since, him or any of the others. This Island of yours, though"—a thoughtful gleam was dawning in his mismatched eyes—"that would be a rescue mission, helping save innocent folk from the evils of the Division. That's the kind of thing the Raiders appreciate. If I help you out now, and the Raiders get to hear of it, chances are they'll think me worthy to join their band! It's a fine plan, is it not?"

Silo nodded, but he was bitterly disappointed. Black Tom was not the man he had supposed him to be. But he would take them to the Island, and if his medals were anything to go by, he was brave at least. For the first time he read their inscriptions—SYNCHRONIZED SWIMMING, LONDON OLYMPICS 2012; EMPLOYEE OF THE MONTH; PRIZE VEGETABLE: MEADOW-SIDE AGRICULTURAL FAIR—and suddenly found himself doubting whether Black Tom had been their original recipient. He scowled. He had hoped to find the Raiders, that bold and selfless band who fought tirelessly for the cause of liberty, but instead had found a drunken, goat-throwing liar. It was better than nothing, he supposed, but not much.

However, Black Tom had cheered up no end. His horrible laughter rang out: "Huurgh! Huur-ugh! Well, here's a fine chance to wind up the Division! They're a wrongheaded set, to my mind, forever trying to grub up a world that's dead and gone. The Ancients have had their day, and I say good riddance to them—them and all their freakish powers! 'Tis said they could fly, and the last thing we need is a bunch of winged sorcerers swooping about the place."

"They didn't have wings," said Maximillian. "They sat in things that flew."

"What manner of things?" asked Black Tom.

Maximillian considered. "They looked a bit like giant cucumbers, only they were white and had wings. The Ancients got in and lit fires in their tails—or at least, I think they did. They left trails of smoke behind them in the sky."

They stared at him in amazement, their minds reeling at the thought of the Ancients hurtling about the sky in blazing albino cucumbers. Black Tom looked knowingly at Silo, crossed his eyes, and whirled a forefinger at the side of his head. Then he swept a selection of bones and bottles off the table and unrolled a crumpled chart.

"This Island of yours," he said, "is about fifteen miles to our south. This here's our best route—across the Gutfleet

Sound." He traced a great U-shape with a grubby forefinger, a course that took them far out to sea.

"Wouldn't it be quicker if we just sailed down the coast?" said Silo.

"Quicker, yes, but we'd have to navigate the Sea of Souls."

"What's that?" asked Orlando.

"The site of a sunken city," said Black Tom. "They say that back in Ancient times it was the greatest city in all the Kingdom Isles—only they weren't the Kingdom Isles back then, just one big island called the United Kingdom. Seems that the Great Catastrophe shifted things around a little, though, and now this city lies out to sea. There's things that lies unseen beneath the waves there, things that would rip the bottom out of a ship and send her to the seabed."

"Is that why it's called the Sea of Souls?" said Orlando.

"No!"

A quavering voice cried out from the corner of the cabin. The dog, Growler, looked grumpy as the pile of rags he was sleeping on stood up, revealing itself to be a doddering old man of confused appearance.

Black Tom looked depressed. "This is Old Elijah," he said. "He's not crew exactly. He came with the ship. We've encouraged him to settle ashore many a time, but he won't have it."

There was no need to ask why Black Tom wanted him to settle ashore. As Old Elijah arose, so too did a remarkable stench, a noxious compound of seaweed and old socks, and the children reeled back as he advanced toward them. He fixed them with his burning eyes and raised a warning forefinger.

"They call it the Sea of Souls because 'tis haunted by the spirits of the Ancient dead!" he cried. "Even now their great towers rise high above the waves, although the folk that built them have been dead for many a long year. Dead, yes, but not at peace, for sometimes, on still nights, passing sailors see ghostly lights across the water and hear a fearful howling, like the sound of souls in torment. And those who see or hear these things are likewise doomed, for never again do they return safe to their native shores!"

"So how come anyone knows about it?" asked Silo.

Old Elijah was silenced.

Just then the great bell began to toll from the lookout tower. Black Tom cocked his head. "Seems like we might have company," he said. "But whose?"

It was the worst kind. When they reached the deck a voice was calling from the tower: "The Division's fleet is putting out to sea!"

"How many ships?" roared Black Tom. There was a pause, then: "Dunno—too far off to count. But lots."

Black Tom turned to his crew. "Make ready to sail! We've still time to outrun the vermin!"

The inhabitants of Mudville were peering tentatively around their doors, and there was a great thunder of feet as Ruby came charging across from the Ship and Squid, a crowd of children at her heels.

"Can our friends come too?" said Silo.

"Hell's bells! How many?"

"Twenty-eight." It did seem a lot.

"Fifteen," said Ruby, springing lightly onto the deck. "I told Edna we wanted to sail with you, but she said the little ones were too young for seafaring. She said to leave them behind for her to take care of."

"What about the big ones?" said Black Tom hopefully as he watched Drusilla heft herself aboard. She was eating a bacon sandwich and carrying a large club, and looked particularly charmless.

Ruby shook her head. "We want to join the Raiders. That is where we're going, isn't it? To find them?"

Orlando poked her sharply in the ribs. "We'll explain later," he hissed.

"What about you, Daisy?" asked Silo, for Daisy was still standing on the quay, a wistful expression in her eyes.

"Edna's been ever so kind! She's invited me to stay with her," she said.

"But you've got parents, haven't you, and a home to go back to?"

"Yes, but I escaped from the Division, same as you. They may go looking for me there. I'd only cause trouble for my mum and dad."

At the mention of her parents Daisy's eyes filled with tears and she said, with a brave smile, "It's much better I stay here. And maybe someday things will change. Maybe those who've been shipped out will come home, and the little ones will have parents to go back to as well. Until then I'll stay here and help Edna take care of them."

Then she blew her nose and said, "Just don't let the Division catch you, right? And make jolly well sure you stuff up their plans for the Island!"

Silo regarded her with astonishment. The Division had a gift for making rebels of the most unlikely people. "Good luck with it, Daisy," he said.

"And to you too, Silo. I think good fortune sails with you—I had a seeing about you last night. You were sailing to a beautiful white palace that rose high above the waves, and there was a rainbow shining overhead. My seeings are always happy ones, and I feel sure that some joyous surprise awaits you there!"

Silo didn't—but he let it pass, for Black Tom was taking his place behind the wheel.

"Cast off!" he roared. "Man the rigging!"

The crew of the *Sea Pig* bestirred themselves. The Bolton brothers, old hands at the seafaring life, swarmed up the rigging like rats and Silo busied himself with warps and fenders, occasionally tripping over the ever-helpful Maximillian. Ruby laid a tentative hand on a rope while Orlando found himself a comfortable seat and watched the activity with an air of lively interest.

A crowd had gathered to see them off, and Edna and the twelve smallest children were among them. Silo looked back as the *Sea Pig* drifted away from the quay. They were waving to him, and he heard Daisy's bright voice ringing over the water.

"Let's sing Silo our new song!"

He winced inwardly, but Daisy was full of surprises that day.

Silo Zyco was a seer, a seer of awesome power,
And he was held a prisoner inside an ancient tower.
But Silo wouldn't stand for it, so what did Silo do?
He struck a pipe with all his might and filled the place
with—

"Someone's written a song about you, Silo!" Maximillian gazed up at him with rapt admiration. His face had taken on a greenish pallor and Silo recalled, with some trepidation, that he was a poor sailor. He resolved to sleep in a separate cabin.

Above them the *Sea Pig's* tattered sails took the wind, and the water crested beneath her bows as she headed out into the Gutfleet Sound.

His eyes are mad, his temper's bad, some say he is a
psycho,
But if you care for freedom, give three cheers for Silo Zyco!

The children's voices grew fainter as Mudville slipped astern, to be finally drowned out by the slap of the waves and the creak of canvas. Silo gave the little choir a final wave and turned his face to the open sea.

The sunlight glittered on the waves and the sky was full of towering white cumulus clouds. Black Tom might not be the most reliable of captains, but he cut an impressive figure behind the wheel. His peaked cap sat on his matted locks, his gold braid and teeth shone in the sunlight, and his beard whipped in the wind like the tentacles of an angry octopus.

"Hoist the flag," he roared, and a moment later the flag of the Raiders unfurled at the masthead, a long sky-blue pennant that streamed in the wind.

Silo felt a sudden thrill of excitement. The enemy fleet were close behind them, it was true, but Black Tom said they could outrun them. He was sailing to save his island home from the evils of the Division, and before him lay the high seas and adventure. At last he was fulfilling his destiny, following in his father's footsteps just as his dying mother had wished. He was Silo Zyco, last of the Zycos, son of Zenda, son of Aquinus the Accursed, a rebel born of rebel blood, and he would prove himself worthy of his illustrious ancestry. A glow of pride suffused him, warming him right down to his toes. Maximillian had just been sick on his boots.

15

THE SEA OF SOULS

The Government's fleet sailed majestically out from the mouth of the Rampage: seven tall ships, each bearing aloft a mass of snowy canvas, the sign of the red hand streaming at their mastheads. The first and greatest was their flagship, the *Unbeatable*, and behind her followed the *Unsinkable*, the *Undefeatable*, the *Unstoppable*, the *Unavoidable*, the *Unvanquished*, and the *Unwelcome*. They were a fine sight as they headed out into the Gutfleet Sound.

Elgarth was new to seafaring, but as he stood on the quarterdeck of the *Unbeatable* it all seemed pleasant enough, for he was in an excellent mood. He had just had time to dash off a letter to his father before they sailed. It had perhaps been rather a boastful one, but the circumstances seemed to demand it. The cream of the Government's navy had put to sea and all because he, Elgarth Early, had willed it to be so. Surveying the progress of the great fleet, he was secretly thrilled by the majesty he had set in motion: so many ships and soldiers and sailors on the move, and all because he had had a seeing—well, maybe not a seeing exactly, but as good as one. Certainly he had described it to his father as such, and then gone on to describe its happy consequences: the apprehension of the one person the Division wanted above all others, and the capture of a gang of criminals besides. He mentioned too the important discoveries that awaited them at the Island, and the triumphant return the fleet would soon be making to Parris Port; finally he dwelt on how favorably the Government would view his role in all this, and the honor it would bring to the family name. His brother was still busy burning villages, and Elgarth thought it time to steal a little of his thunder.

It seemed that the first part of their mission would very soon be accomplished. The admiral was passing his telescope to Mrs. Morgan, who was pacing the quarterdeck in a fever of impatience.

"Enemy ship to starboard—it's the *Sea Pig* right enough. Looks like she's making a run for it. She's under full canvas and flying the flag of the Raiders."

The *Sea Pig* was a dark speck on the horizon, but even to Elgarth's untrained eyes, she was a speck that seemed to be growing larger by the minute.

"Are you sure we can apprehend them?" said Mrs. Morgan.

"I'm certain. The *Sea Pig*'s the slowest ship on the coast

and riddled with worm besides. Her captain's a drunken fool—they say he stole her from a breaker's yard."

Mrs. Morgan smiled. "I only wonder they chose so ill. No doubt Silo Zyco is the cause—he seems to have a taste for low company."

Elgarth saw his opportunity. "I've noticed that myself. In fact I have wondered . . ." He paused, his face at once hesitant and sorrowful. "It's just that I can't help wondering what kind of boy Maximillian must be, to take up with the likes of Silo. I know he's very young, but even so I would have expected him to show better judgment in his choice of friends."

"I have thought as much myself," said Mrs. Morgan grimly, "but he will be in our hands before the day is out, and I mean to give him a very serious talking-to."

Maximillian was blissfully unaware of the threat that lay in store for him, but Silo, standing beside him at the rail of the *Sea Pig,* was watching the rapid progress of the fleet with growing alarm. Black Tom was unrolling a chart, and then he rummaged in a sea chest to produce a fistful of rusty navigational instruments.

"Let's see now—we've an easterly blowing, and taking into account the run of the tide . . ." He did some sums, scowled, crossed them out, did them again, and again, then said, "I can't see them catching up with us for at least an hour." He frowned darkly at the chart. "Bit of a problem, that."

To Silo this seemed an understatement of epic proportions. The Division had sentenced him to ten years merely for warning the villagers of Baldock, and when he thought of the long list of crimes on his wanted poster, his blood ran cold within him. If he fell into their hands for a second time, he doubted he'd ever see the light of day again.

But Black Tom was deep in thought. He creased his bristling monobrow, and slowly, very slowly, a look of dim comprehension dawned in his bloodshot eyes. Then, inexplicably, he began to shake with laughter.

"Huur-ugh! Huur-ugh! We're not done yet, though—they think they'll catch us, but they'll not! We'll stop the creeping cowards! We'll sail the Sea of Souls, and they'll not dare to follow, for in all the Kingdom Isles there's no man bold enough to cross that accursed sea but I!"

It seemed he was right, for his crew stopped dead in their tracks.

"Well, what are you waiting for?" he bellowed at them. "Ready about!"

The crew looked at him with stricken faces, and then at each other, and then at the white sails of the Government fleet, creeping ever closer across the Gutfleet Sound.

"NOW!"

Black Tom swung the wheel, and with extreme reluctance the sailors crept to their posts, muttering darkly as they did so. The very *Sea Pig* herself seemed unwilling, heeling about with an ominous creaking of timbers. And her reluctance seemed justified, for the sea that spread before them looked perilous indeed. It was studded with roofs and chimneys, and foaming white waters marked the site of other obstacles, all the more deadly for being submerged beneath the waves. On the horizon still greater hazards loomed, for there, silhouetted against a brooding sky, the tall towers of the Ancients stood in wait, and maybe too the unquiet spirits of those who had once dwelt there. Children and crew alike turned to their captain for words of courage and comfort, but he was staring astern, watching the enemy fleet with blazing eyes.

Still the *Unbeatable* held the line, the white water surging beneath her prow. She was close enough now for Silo to see rows of gleaming bald heads lining the bows as the collectors tracked their quarry, and the sunlight glittering on their weapons. But something was wrong. Suddenly her momentum was checked, and her sails shivered and slackened as she lost the wind. She was turning, she and all the others who followed in her wake. There was confusion in the Government's fleet. Shouted commands and shrill cries were borne faintly across the water, and then, with a great grinding of timbers, the *Unstoppable* collided with the *Unavoidable*.

"Huurgh! Huurgh! Huuur-ugh!" Black Tom heaved with laughter. "Cowards!" he roared. "Baldy, baldy Bucket Heads! Run back to your mummies, you sniveling slap heads, and may you die unloved in embarrassing circumstances!"

Then he turned to his crew, his eyes alight with triumph. "Well, we've rid ourselves of those vermin! Now for the Sea of Souls!"

The *Sea Pig* crept forth, and as she did so the clouds darkened overhead and a sweeping squall of rain engulfed her.

"Is it safe, Silo?" asked Maximillian in a small voice.

"How would I know? You're the one who has a dozen seeings a day." Silo was a little acerbic, but the sudden and unexpected turn of events had unnerved him. It wasn't that he was afraid of the ghosts of the Ancient dead—not exactly—but sailing over a submerged and uncharted city with Black Tom at the helm seemed like a breathtakingly reckless undertaking.

Ruby was evidently thinking along the same lines. "Won't we run aground?" she said.

"I've a chart," said Black Tom proudly. He rummaged in his sea chest. "Here!"

The chart was drawn on a sheet of parchment, tattered and brittle now with age, and titled *Tourist Map of Sentral Lundun*. Below was a tangled web of inky lines; a positive rat's nest of winding streets.

"'Tis a copy of a copy of a copy," said Black Tom proudly. Silo had suspected as much, for some of the spellings seemed rather strange.

"This is before it flooded!" said Ruby. "There's nothing here but roads."

"But there's a river," said Silo, tracing its serpentine path with his forefinger.

"That's right!" cried Black Tom. "And we'll follow its course! That way we can be sure of deep water beneath our keel."

"How do we know where it is, though?" said Orlando.

"I'm not entirely sure," said Black Tom as he scanned the

turbulent waters ahead, "but seems like our best bet is to steer for that big gap between the chimney pots."

"What if it's a goatball stadium or something?" said Orlando. "And won't there be bridges over the river?"

"No!" A powerful stench assailed their nostrils. Old Elijah had emerged from the bowels of the ship and was watching them with feverish eyes. "No bridges! All was destroyed, way back at the time of the Great Catastrophe."

Seeing he had their attention, he drew himself up to his full height, then pointed a trembling hand to the heavens. "Hard times, they were then—a time of terror and a time of reckoning! The specter of plague stalked the land, sweeping through the Southern Shires and dealing death to all it touched! And here in this city, folk resolved to destroy the bridges lest those from the south crossed over, for they feared that they might carry disease among them, and so doom all alike to a long, lingering, and loathsome death."

"How do you know all this?" asked Ruby.

"I'm an old, old man," said Old Elijah. "I've seen and heard much, and there's many a strange thing I've learned in my long years on this Earth."

It was a pity that the habit of bathing was not among them, but otherwise they were impressed by his words, for it seemed that he was right about the bridges and Orlando was wrong about the goatball stadium. Black Tom maintained his course between the chimneys, and a broad stretch of open water lay before them. Strange currents and riptides rippled its murky surface and all stood with bated breath, expecting at any moment to run aground on some unseen obstacle lurking beneath the dark waters, but their course ran unchecked. Black Tom had found the old river and the *Sea Pig* sailed on beneath the weeping skies, across the Sea of Souls, and into the heart of the drowned city of the Ancients.

It was a horrible journey. Old Elijah's tales of the restless dead obviously held credence among seafarers, for the crew went about their work like sleepwalkers, anxiously scanning the buildings that marked the river's edge: rank upon rank of blocks and towers and terraces all going to ruin, washed by the waves for centuries past. As they progressed, the vast extent of the city was revealed to them, and Silo could not help imagining it as it had been in the days of its glory with its streets and buildings bustling with human life, loud with the hubbub of trade and traffic. But now the only sound was that of the wind sighing in the rigging and the mournful cry of the gulls, and his thoughts turned inexorably to what lay beneath the waters: to silent streets where forests of rippling seaweed grew, to barnacle-encrusted houses where eels twined through the banisters, and shoals of fish flitted through endless empty rooms—and to the relentless tides stirring the bones of the ancient dead.

And then the lookout called from the crow's nest. "It's the fleet! They're following!"

The children ran to the stern and stared back down the rain-swept river—and there, sure enough, were the dim silhouettes of the Government's fleet, distant yet remorseless as they tracked their prey through the great watery wasteland that was Sentral Lundun.

"Damnation!" snarled Black Tom. "Who'd of thought it? Seamen fear this place worse than catching crab pox in a cyclone. What's got into the fools?"

The answer was a simple one. It was true that seamen feared the Sea of Souls, but the Bucket Heads were landsmen and the admiral, perhaps wisely, feared the wrath of Mrs. Morgan more than that of the undead. After the first flurry of panic among his crews he had ordered them, and in no uncertain terms, to put the fleet back on course, and to ensure that his commands were obeyed he had ordered the collectors to back him up with force. The reluctant seamen who had been press-ganged at Parris Port were sailing at swordpoint, but even so they were sailing considerably faster than the *Sea Pig*.

Black Tom tugged at his beard and ruminated. "She's a touch slow, is the *Sea Pig*—could be they'll catch up."

Old Elijah chose this moment to share his thoughts with them: "Be thankful for it, for it be a mercy! Better by far to die at the point of a sword than to face the heartless hordes of the undead! For though long centuries have passed since they met their frightful fates they envy the living yet, and all those who fall into their rotting, skeletal hands— Ow!"

Black Tom had rapped him smartly on the head. "We've the chart, though," he said. "Best we take to the streets and lose them among the buildings. What's up ahead?"

Ruby consulted the chart. "There's something called the Bank of England."

"Don't like the sound of that," said Black Tom. "Could be a sand bank or a mud bank, but either way it's a menace. This street here will do as well as any." He swung the wheel to port. "Going about!" he bellowed to his crew. "Sort those sails, and sharpish." He peered at the chart. "Now where the hell are we?"

The *Sea Pig* was drifting down a street so narrow that her yardarms almost touched the buildings on either side. The wind died in her sails and they hung lifeless, for the tall façades shielded her from even a breath of breeze.

"Looks like we'll have to tow her a step of the way," said Black Tom. "Lower the ship's boat! Man the oars!"

The boat was duly lowered. Drusilla jumped in with a thud that made it tremble from stem to stern, but none of the crew seemed in a rush to join her.

"Cowards!" roared Black Tom. "Are you afraid to follow where a little girl leads?"

Drusilla was hardly little, but Black Tom carried his point. A dozen unwilling crew members clambered in beside her and unshipped the oars. The towrope grew taut as they bent their backs to their task, and the *Sea Pig* glided deeper into the maze of streets. Black Tom watched the dripping buildings slip by on either hand.

"Reckon they're flooded up to the third story or so," he said. "That should give us a couple of fathoms beneath us."

He squinted over Ruby's shoulder at the chart. "Looks like we're coming up to Whitefriars Street. If we hang a right at the top, we'll be headed down Fleet Street. It runs due east, so we can pick up the wind and get her sailing again."

For Silo that moment couldn't come too soon. He found the Ancient capital deeply oppressive. He longed to regain the safety of the open sea and leave this vast and rotting metropolis far behind him, for it was impossible to sail amid its ruins without thinking of the countless thousands who had died here, and he found his imagination dwelling unpleasantly on the manner of their deaths. The rows of shattered windows seemed to stare down on him as they passed, and once the main yard scraped along a length of crumbling cornice, dislodging it and sending it plunging into the dark waters below. Its wash sent the waves slopping and sloshing through the dark interiors with a greedy, sucking sound. Great streamers of seaweed blossomed from the windows, and staring in, Silo saw a seemingly endless procession of dark rooms and doorways and corridors, scoured for centuries by the restless waves. The stench of damp and decay hung heavy in the air.

The atmosphere of the place seemed somehow charged and expectant, and he felt the hairs rise on the back of his neck as he fell prey to a sudden, horrible conviction that they were being watched. Unseen eyes were upon them—but in what heads those eyes were set was a thought too terrifying to contemplate.

Maximillian, huddled at his side, seemed to share his fears. "I saw something nasty in one of those buildings," he whispered.

"What?" said Silo, fighting back a note of panic in his voice.

"I'm not sure, but it was big. And it had tentacles."

"Probably just a giant squid."

Silo spoke with a nonchalance he didn't feel. And then he heard, or thought he heard, the distant rattle of chains. He froze where he stood, his ears straining to hear above the creak and drip of the oars, and then he caught, very faint and far away, the sound of laughter drifting through the deserted streets. It was a sound that made his flesh crawl, for it seemed impossible that any living thing within all this great drowned necropolis could find cause for mirth. Then Growler began to howl, and a moment later Old Elijah joined him: "'Tis the Ancients! The Ancients are stirring! I feel their dark presence all about us, and hear the joyless laughter of the undead!"

"Thing on the rooftops!" cried the lookout in a trembling voice.

"A *thing*?" roared Black Tom. "What manner of thing?"

"Not sure—I only saw it out of the corner of my eye."

"Well, it can go to hell!" growled Black Tom. "This must be Fleet Street."

They were gliding into more open waters, and once again the wind sighed in the rigging. The exhausted rowers shipped their oars and scrambled back on board at record speed as Black Tom brought the *Sea Pig* about. The water creamed under her bows as her sails filled, and a moment later they were sailing down the center of the thoroughfare that the Ancients had known as Fleet Street.

This was much better, thought Silo. For one thing the street was wider, and before it had flooded it had evidently run downhill, for the line of buildings on either side dipped downward. Soon they were sailing on the level of their upper stories, and with a broad sweep of sky above him his feeling of dread lifted a little. He scanned the rotting roofscape of turrets and chimneys and spires but could see no one stirring there, living or dead. A crossroads lay ahead of them, or what had been a crossroads once, but now it was a broad channel of choppy gray water. In the time of the Ancients it must have lain in a valley, for beyond it the roofs began to rise up again, the dripping buildings poking higher and higher out of the water until they terminated in a cluster of spires and an enormous dome.

Ruby was navigating. "We're coming up to Ludgate Circus—Farringdon Street's to the left, Bridge Street to the right, and Ludgate Hill is straight ahead."

Black Tom considered. "I wonder, should we go down Farringdon Street or straight ahead?"

His question was answered with startling suddenness. As the *Sea Pig* sailed out into the wide waters of Ludgate Circus a great commotion broke out to their right: the sound of raucous cheering and the sudden, deafening clash of swords on shields. It was the fleet. They had abandoned the course of the old river and were advancing up Bridge Street at terrifying speed. Crews of collectors manned the ships' boats, rowing furiously and with a machinelike precision, and behind them glided the seven great ships of the fleet: towering, remorseless, and with the sign of the bloodred hand streaming from their mastheads. No sooner had they sighted their quarry than the drums began to beat out—*bam-BAM, bam-BAM, bam-BAM*—menacing and insistent, and crowds of whooping collectors lined the decks. It seemed that they scented victory, for they urged the rowers on with roars of encouragement and brandished a terrifying array of weaponry. Insults and bloodthirsty cries came flying across the rapidly diminishing stretch of water that lay between them and the *Sea Pig* while Black Tom stood thunderstruck at the helm, absently pawing at his beard.

"Hell! Who'd have thought it?" he finally said. "Best we go straight ahead, then. You said it was marked as Ludgate Hill, so we're in with a chance still. The *Sea Pig* draws less water than the Government's ships and we'll be heading into shallow water at the top of the hill. Could be their fleet will run aground."

Silo hoped upon hope that he was right, for the foremost of the ships, the *Unbeatable*, was alarmingly close behind. The collectors jeered as the *Sea Pig* steered across their bows and into the uncertain safety of Ludgate Hill and fired off a volley of arrows. They splashed harmlessly into the water, but soon it would be a different story, for already the *Unbeatable* was turning into the wind. Her sails were filling again, and they all knew that she sailed a great deal faster than the *Sea Pig*.

"Children and animals to the forepeak!" cried Black Tom.

The children and Growler obeyed, and once he had reached the bows Silo stared resolutely ahead, willing the *Sea Pig* forward. She was doing her best, but even so the buildings on either side seemed to drift by at a funeral pace, rising higher and higher above the water as the seabed rose beneath them. The cries of their pursuers rang loud in his ears, together with the whiz and thunk of arrows. For they were within range now, and although most buried themselves harmlessly in the *Sea Pig*'s stern, some were fired higher and to better effect: holes were beginning to appear in the straining canvas of their sails. Silo fixed his eyes on the huge building that stood at the top of Ludgate Hill, watching as it drew slowly nearer. And then it was looming over them: gargantuan in size and impossibly grand, with twin towers of pale stone and a massive, soaring dome between. A row of columns, thicker than the trunks of the mightiest trees, rose from the waves. They supported a balcony, from which sprang yet another row of columns that supported a vast portico. At the very apex stood a gigantic statue of a stern bearded man, glaring out from his lofty eminence. The scale of the place was so breathtaking that for a moment the children forgot their danger and gazed up at it in simple wonderment.

"Now, that," said Orlando, "is big. I wonder what the Ancients used it for."

"It's marked on the chart as a restaurant," said Ruby.

Silo was staggered. "A restaurant? That size?"

"That's what it said—St. Paul's Café and Grill. I see what you mean, though. They must have been a right bunch of pigs."

Silo stared up at its mighty bulk, and as he did so the rain stopped and a rainbow shimmered overhead, its colors jewel-bright against the leaden skies. And then he remembered Daisy's words: the beautiful white palace rising out of the waves.

"Daisy had a seeing! She said I was going to have a surprise here!"

"I expect she meant about the ship sinking," said Maximillian.

They stared at him in horror. Orlando's voice trembled slightly as he said, "Have you had a seeing too?"

Maximillian shook his head. "No. But we're going to hit that stone lady."

Silo looked down and saw a head rising out of the water immediately beneath their bows. It wore a crown and a look of dignified contempt.

"Look out!" he yelled to Black Tom. "There's a statue dead ahead!"

Too late—the *Sea Pig* checked, then shuddered all along her length, and there was a horrible rending, scraping noise from somewhere deep in her bilges.

"'Tis the dead rising up against the living!" cried Old Elijah.

"No, it's Queen Anne," said Ruby. "She's marked on the chart."

"Well, to hell with the wretched woman!" growled Black Tom. "She's holed us beneath the waterline!"

He cursed and swung the wheel, and the stricken *Sea Pig* made one last valiant effort. She turned to port with infinite slowness, creeping along the length of the great building, but as she did so she settled lower and lower in the water. Then she listed sideways and lodged against the towering columns of St. Paul's Café and Grill, her shattered timbers coming to their final rest on some unseen obstruction beneath the waves. The *Sea Pig* would sail no more.

16

THE BATTLE OF LUNDUN

A cheer of triumph went up from the fleet, one that echoed from ship to ship the length of Ludgate Hill. Already the *Unbeatable* was almost upon them, coasting up the street at an impressive rate. She was traveling at such a speed that for one glorious moment Silo thought her momentum would send her crashing straight into St. Paul's, but at the last moment she went about with a great commotion of flapping canvas, turning broadside on to the great building.

"Take her alongside!" cried the admiral. "Prepare to board!"

But then she ran aground, stopping with a suddenness that sent her crew sprawling on the decks. The collectors picked themselves up and glared across the narrow strip of water that separated the two ships. A crisis was at hand, and aboard the *Sea Pig* all eyes turned to Black Tom. As they watched he drained a bottle of dark liquid, then seized a harpoon and brandished it high above his head. He seemed a little unsteady on his feet but otherwise cut an impressive figure, with his flashing eyes and teeth, his beard billowing in the breeze. Defiantly he hurled his empty bottle at the *Unbeatable*.

"Children, abandon ship!" he roared. "And as for the rest of you, we fight to the last man—death to the Bucket Heads!" He turned to face the foe, and as he did so Silo felt a sudden wave of affection for him. He had misjudged Black Tom. His medals might not be his own, but no one could question his bravery.

Ruby was tugging at his arm. "We need to get Maximillian out of here—fast! Drusilla! Man the ship's boat!"

"No go." Drusilla was peering over the side at a little flotilla of matchwood and oars. "It got squashed against the pillars."

"We'll have to swim, then."

"Is that a good idea?" said Orlando. "It's just that there may be weird things under the water—currents and stuff."

The children who stood around him were not deceived by his words. They knew it was not the currents that worried him but the weird things—maybe the undead things: slimy skeletal things that had stalked the flooded streets for centuries past, awaiting their chance to wreak vengeance on the living. And the children, like Orlando, were in no hurry to find out if these existed only in their imaginations or in some form infinitely more horrible.

"Up the mast!" said Silo. "We can climb onto that balcony there."

They looked up at the Café and Grill. It reared above them like a cliff face, but the *Sea Pig*'s yardarms were conveniently level with its balcony.

"Good thinking," said Ruby. "You two!" She turned to the Bolton brothers. "Get going, and take Maximillian with you."

"I want to stay with . . . ," said Maximillian, but he was already halfway up the mast. Basil Bolton had slung him over his shoulder and was swarming up the rigging at lightning speed.

The other children were following, but Silo hung back. This was all his fault, he realized. It was he and he alone who had set this whole catastrophe in motion: he and his gift of the seeing. It was his vision of the vanished Island that had brought them here. He had hoped to avert a disaster but he had failed, and failed miserably, and now it seemed it was not just the Islanders who were doomed but his friends as well, for he had placed them all in deadly danger: Orlando, Maximillian, Ruby, the children they had led from the Unicorn Tower, and Black Tom and his luckless crew. It was a crushing realization; for one terrible moment Silo saw himself as the Marshlanders had seen him—as an accursed and unnatural child, born under a dark star, forever fated to bring misery and ill fortune to all who crossed his path. His friends were in danger because of him, and somehow he must make amends.

His voice shook a little as he addressed Orlando. "We should stay and fight."

He turned to him—or rather to where he had stood a moment past, for Orlando had vanished. Looking up, Silo saw the seat of his breeches rapidly diminishing as he scuttled up the rigging. Orlando had many fine qualities, but noble self-sacrifice was not among them.

Silo acted quickly before his resolve could fail him. He ran over to where Black Tom stood. The faithful Growler accompanied him, springing into his master's arms with a mighty bound.

"I want to fight!" cried Silo.

"Little Zyco the Psycho—you're just like your dad! But a battle's no place for a boy. Go and join your friends." Tom nodded up aloft, to the children scrambling along the yardarm to the safety of the balcony. "That's an order! Besides, I've a mission for you, and one I'd not trust to many."

"What?"

"Look after Growler for me, would you?"

Growler was nestled in his arms, his tail beating furiously, and Black Tom stroked the little dog with an unexpected tenderness.

"Get him to someplace safe. And there's something you should know before we part, Silo: something important. If anything should happen to me . . ."

Silo, moved in spite of himself, awaited his final words.

". . . he's very partial to lamb bones. Farewell, little friend. And you too, Silo."

And he thrust Growler into Silo's arms and turned to his crew. "To arms! Prepare to repel boarders!" he roared.

And this was a real danger. Aboard the *Unbeatable* Mrs.

Morgan was glowering across the narrow strip of water that separated the two ships and uttering shrill cries of rage.

"We must board the enemy! Have this gap bridged immediately!"

The admiral turned to his crew. "You heard what the lady said! See to it!"

And then the collectors were seething about the ship, gathering together anything that could be used to form a gangplank. Silo had seen enough. Growler was struggling in his arms, and with some difficulty he stuffed him down the front of his jacket, ran for the mast, and began to climb the rope ladder that led up to the yardarm. He made slow work of it, for it swayed beneath his feet and Growler, sensing his master's danger, squirmed and whimpered against his chest. Cursing under his breath, he heaved himself ever upward until, after what seemed like an eternity, a familiar pair of boots appeared in his line of vision.

"Orlando? What are you doing here?"

"I thought you might need a hand."

Orlando was seated astride the yardarm, reaching down to haul him up. And just as he did so something thudded into the mast beside them, missing them by inches and sending out a shower of splinters. A grappling hook had embedded itself deep into the timbers: a hook with a length of stout rope attached. Silo traced it back to its source and his heart lurched within him, for they had company up aloft—unwelcome company. Rankly stood high in the rigging of the *Unbeatable* with a coil of rope in his hands, and as they watched he passed it around the mast and cast it down onto the deck. It unwound in a long, lazy spiral, finally striking a group of collectors loitering far below. They stared up with bovine suspicion, only to be rewarded by the sight of Elgarth yelling at them. He was perched in the rigging alongside Rankly and seemed to be in excellent spirits.

"You lot!" he cried. "Don't just stand there! Pull on the rope!"

"God, he's *such* a scumbag!" said Orlando. "What's he up to now?"

Silo wasn't sure, but experience suggested it would be something unpleasant. He watched intently as the collectors gathered up the rope, then engaged in an animated discussion. And then he understood.

"They're going to try to pull the two ships together."

"Fat chance!" said Orlando. "They're aground."

"Yeah, but if they pull hard enough, the masts will be drawn closer together, and then maybe they can climb across the yardarms and board the *Sea Pig*."

Orlando snorted derisively. "It's going to take a hell of a lot of them . . ."

By now the collectors were calling for reinforcements. Dozens upon dozens of them were massing at the foot of the mast, uttering excited cries and flexing their biceps.

". . . but it might be worth us getting a move on."

Silo thought likewise. "You go first," he said. "And hurry!"

And they tried to. The Bolton brothers, with the advantage of their nautical past, had gone striding along the yardarm with the easy confidence of tightrope walkers, but Orlando and Silo preferred to shuffle along on their bottoms, inching their way across and trying—albeit unsuccessfully—to ignore the hideous drop beneath their feet. Silo kept his eyes fixed firmly on the balcony, and on the row of anxious children who awaited them there. Foremost among them was Ruby. There was a gap of some feet between the tip of the yardarm and the balcony, and she was waiting there to receive them, leaning boldly out into space with Drusilla holding firmly onto the seat of her breeches.

"Give me your hand, Orlando," she cried. "Now put your foot there—no, not there, you idiot! Bleeding hell! Well held, Drusilla! Your turn, Silo—easy does it. You'd better pass me that dog."

But there was no need. Growler burst from Silo's jacket in a shower of buttons and sprang into her waiting arms. Silo breathed a sigh of relief, for he was within a whisker of safety.

The children were urging him on with cries of encourage-ment. "Come on, Silo! Nearly there!"

Ruby stretched out a hand, but just as Silo reached across to grasp it a great cry broke from the *Unbeatable*: "Heave!"

And suddenly the yardarm lurched beneath him. He clung on for dear life, casting a terrified glance over his shoul-der, and what he saw there made his blood run cold. The rope that ran between the two ships was stretched taut, one end attached firmly to the grappling hook and the other wrapped around the *Unbeatable*'s mast and then stretching down, down, down—Silo's head swam as he contemplated the drop—to the deck below. A long line of collectors were hauling on the rope that bound the two ships together—and to good effect. The yardarm was moving, sloping back and away from the blessed safety of the balcony; slowly but inexorably the two masts were being drawn together.

"Heave! Heave! Heave!"

The ships' timbers creaked and groaned under the strain, and the collectors redoubled their efforts.

"Heave! Heave! Heave!"

Silo heard cries of consternation from below as the decks of the *Sea Pig* and the *Unbeatable* began to tilt toward each other—and tilt, and tilt, and tilt, sending their startled crews sprawling.

"Heave! Heave! Heave!"

And he himself was sliding backward—slowly at first but then with increasing speed—sliding back down the sloping yardarm that he had just so painfully traversed. He slammed back into the mast, his heart racing, and grabbed a steadying hold on the rigging.

"Heave! Heave! HEAVE!"

And then there was a great screeching and a splintering as the two topmasts finally met, leaving the two ships locked together at a crazy angle, like a great inverted V.

The gap between the *Sea Pig* and the *Unbeatable* had been bridged—up aloft, at least—and now collectors were swarming into the rigging, eager to board the enemy. And at their head was Rankly, inching his way across the interlocked spars with an ax tucked into his belt.

Elgarth was urging him on. "Go get him, Rankly!"

Swiftly Silo contemplated his options, but they were none of them good. Below him Black Tom was rallying the crew of the *Sea Pig*, but they looked desperately few against the hordes pitted against them. The galley had evidently been ransacked for weapons: Silo saw, mixed in among the clubs they wielded, skewers, a toasting fork, and a humble frying pan. By comparison the *Unbeatable* positively bristled with weaponry, her rails thick with collectors brandishing swords and clubs. They had almost completed their work on the gangplank, and it could only be a matter of minutes before they boarded the *Sea Pig* in overwhelming numbers. And Rankly would be at the forefront, for even as Silo stood irresolute he was stepping across onto the *Sea Pig*'s yardarm. Cursing, Silo took to the rope ladder that ran up to the masthead. He fixed his eyes on the fluttering sky-blue pennant of the Raiders that flew high above and willed himself upward, for it seemed he was fated to make a desperate last stand in the crow's nest. It was not, however, the secure haven he had hoped; like everything on the *Sea Pig* it had seen better days, and when he reached it he found it to be a ramshackle construction with worm-eaten timbers. And then the precarious rope rungs quivered beneath his hands, for Rankly was hot in pursuit, and the ladder was dancing under his weight. Silo made a desperate effort and heaved himself over the rim of the crow's nest. He landed on something small and bullet-headed, something that squeaked.

"Maximillian! Why aren't you on the balcony?"

"I wanted to help you, Silo."

Maximillian looked very small and scared. His loyalty was touching, but in the circumstances Silo would have preferred the company of Drusilla and her club. He crouched down beside Maximillian, desperately pondering his next move, and as he did so Elgarth's voice rang out, a voice full of happy anticipation.

"Go on, Rankly! You're nearly there!"

And then the flimsy floor beneath them shuddered under a savage blow, and Silo grabbed Maximillian just in time to stop him from falling through the huge hole that had appeared at their feet. Rankly had arrived. He had used such violence that his ax had embedded itself deep in the timbers of the crow's nest, and as he struggled to free it he smiled up at Silo, but it was a smile that boded nothing but ill. Silo's heart froze within him—for all, it seemed, was lost.

But then, with a delightful and unexpected suddenness, Maximillian did something extremely helpful. He leaned over the hole and vomited a stream of buff-colored puke. Silo had seen this scene enacted many times in the course of their brief acquaintance, but this was one of Maximillian's most impressive efforts, ejected with a propulsive force surprising for so small a child. The hapless Rankly took it full in the face. He uttered a muffled cry of horror and revulsion, swiping blindly at the steaming mask that obscured his features. And as he did so he lost his grip on the rigging. His hands were clawing at empty air, and then he was falling. Silo, incredulous with amazement, was watching the soles of Rankly's boots rapidly receding—watching as he bounced first off one spar, and then another and another, howling as he went, to finally crash down onto the deck of the *Sea Pig* way below, causing astonishment among Black Tom and his beleaguered crew. But Silo's joy was short-lived, for even as the thud of Rankly's landing was yet ringing in his ears, Elgarth's voice was calling from far closer to hand.

"I'll get you for that, Zyco!"

Silo peered over the rim of the crow's nest and saw his enemy at close quarters, for Elgarth had climbed high into the rigging of the *Unbeatable*, the better to view Silo's bloody demise. And now he was yelling down at the collectors.

"You lot! Get up there and sort him out!"

But by now they were swarming up the rigging in their scores and needed no encouragement from Elgarth: already a line of men were following in Rankly's footsteps, edging their way across the tangle of spars that bridged the two ships. And then Ruby's voice rang out, and her words were music to Silo's ears.

"Not so fast, you festering turds! Ammo at the ready! Take aim! Fire!"

A volley of rocks came hurtling from the balcony. The children had armed themselves with lumps of stone and rubble, and now they hurled them into the fray, Ruby with her customary accuracy and the others with more variable results. Silo and Maximillian cowered in the wreckage of the crow's nest as rocks whistled all around them. There was a melodic chime as one of Ruby's shots struck the leading collector square between the eyes, knocking off his helmet and sending him staggering back. His troubles were not at an end, for Drusilla was whirling her club around and around her head until finally, with a fearsome grunt, she unleashed it with mighty force. It hurtled through the air to strike him full in the chest, knocking him clean off the yardarm to plunge down into the chaos below. His followers faltered, and as they did so Elgarth rained curses down upon them.

"Morons! Do I have to do everything myself?"

And to Silo's horror he unslung a bow. He stood braced against the mast as he reached for an arrow; his eyes, alive with malice, were intent on Silo—who saw death staring him in the face, for it seemed impossible that Elgarth could miss from such close range. But then, suddenly and mysteriously, the knowledge worked a fierce change in him. His fear was gone and in its place came a raging tide of fury, for was he not Silo Zyco, son of Zenda, son of Aquinus the Accursed? And he had been unjustly accused; he had been hunted and threatened and persecuted, and he would stand for it no more. His fists clenched and his blood boiled within him. He fixed Elgarth with his most powerful stare, and with his rage came a brain wave, one of glorious, fiendish, malevolent brilliance.

"Stay here, Maximillian," he said. "And hang on tight—really, really tight."

Silo seized the ax that Rankly had left embedded in the timbers. His rage seemed to fill him with a superhuman strength, and he wrenched it free and tucked it under his belt. He sprang from the shelter of the crow's nest and then he was scrambling down the rigging, barely conscious of the nauseating drop beneath him, blind to the arrows that whistled past his head, intent only on reaching his goal—the grappling hook that lay lodged in the mast. He arrived, then grabbed at a length of dangling rigging, looping it through his belt and knotting it tight. And thus secured, he turned his attention to the rope attached to the grappling hook—the straining rope that held the two ships bound together.

And Elgarth, busy fitting his next arrow, suddenly realized what he was about to do. "No!" he cried. "Don't! I won't shoot again, I promise!"

Too late. Silo was swinging the ax with all the strength at his command, and the blade bit deep. The rope parted, and as it did so the two ships sprang apart with the force of a coiled spring, dislodging a shower of Bucket Heads from the rigging. And Elgarth, who had climbed the highest, traveled the farthest. As the masts whipped apart he was hurled from the rigging as though from a catapult: high, high into the air, revolving as he went, startling seagulls with his passing. Elgarth was flying. He was soaring up into a blue sky beneath the arch of the rainbow—and there he seemed to hang for a second, a tiny figure spread eagle against the sky. Beneath him lay the city, bigger than any he had ever seen or imagined, surrounded by its glittering network of canals—and then suddenly it was hurtling toward him at terrifying speed. Elgarth was screaming, and his howls of terror were abruptly cut short as he plummeted into the waters of Ludgate Hill with an almighty splash.

Silo had no time to enjoy the spectacle; he too had been

jerked from his foothold, and for a few terrible seconds he found himself falling headfirst, but then there was a wrench around his midriff that knocked all the wind out of him, and he found himself swinging above the deck of the *Sea Pig* like a pendulum. The rope tied to his belt had held, and he was looking down onto a mass of struggling, upended bodies—for as the two ships righted themselves everyone aboard had been sent reeling and tumbling about the decks. Cries of pain and astonishment could be heard, together with some very bad language. And into this scene of pandemonium came enemy reinforcements. The *Unsinkable*, next in the line of battle, was bearing down on them at a spanking pace, and her captain steered her dead at the *Sea Pig*.

"Brace yourselves!" cried Black Tom as he staggered to his feet. "Arms at the ready!"

The *Sea Pig* shook from end to end as the *Unsinkable* crashed into her stern, smashing the steering wheel and a barrel of booze Black Tom kept beside it for emergencies. And he had one on his hands now, for the collectors aboard the *Unsinkable* were massing for attack, donning their helmets and shouldering their clubs, readying themselves for battle. Already their leader, a towering giant of a man, was poised in the bows, preparing to leap down onto the quarterdeck of the stricken *Sea Pig*.

But Old Elijah stood there, upright and unafraid, with one hand upraised in admonishment. "Stop this madness!" he cried. "'Tis not the living we should be fighting, but the undead!"

"You smell fit to wake them! Bath time, Granddad!"

The collector stooped, seized Old Elijah by the throat, and tossed him neatly over the side. And as he did so there was another crash. The crew of the *Unbeatable* had finished their makeshift gangplank, and now they dropped it down onto the *Sea Pig*'s deck, shattering her guardrails and sending her listing and lurching under the impact. And for the *Sea Pig* this was the final blow. She had been worm-eaten and unseaworthy at the start of their voyage, but now, after the sequence of shocks she had suffered, she was mortally wounded.

Silo looked down into her open hatches and saw that all was chaos down below. The sea was gushing in, sweeping her from stem to stern, and carrying with it a tangled mass of ship's stores, the furnishings of Black Tom's cabin, and a flotilla of empty booze bottles. And above decks things were no better, for now the combined forces from the *Unbeatable* and the *Unsinkable* were storming aboard. Black Tom and his crew were retreating and Silo, swinging helplessly above the deck at a rope's end, had a ringside view of their desperate last stand. The first mate was dueling with a toasting fork, the ship's cook was laying about him with his frying pan, and Black Tom wielded his club with the strength of ten men, roaring words of encouragement to his crew. But no man, however powerful, could withstand the overwhelming odds pitted against him, and as Silo watched, the gallant band of defenders was beaten back, and back, and back, until finally they stood at bay in the *Sea Pig*'s bows and Mrs. Morgan's voice, shrill and exultant, rose over the clamor of battle.

"Kill them!" she cried. "Kill them all!"

And then Silo heard the sound of laughter from high above him. Mystified, he stared up at the soaring frontage of St. Paul's—and to his astonishment he saw a great bearded figure staring back down at him. It was the statue of the man who stood atop the portico, but now he was tilted out at an impossible angle. He had a chain around his chest and seemed to hover suspended for a moment, his stone beard rippling in an invisible wind, and then a woman's voice rang out: "Bombs away!"

The statue fell. Silo had a confused impression of its stern features glowering at him as it plummeted past, and then it crashed headfirst onto the bows of the *Unsinkable*. It must have been massively heavy, for its progress was unchecked and it vanished, with a flash of almighty stone feet and a rending of timbers, into the gaping hole it had torn there. The ships rocked under the impact, the fighting stopped dead, and there was a moment of stunned silence. A crowd of collectors gathered around the hole and stared into it in amazement, as though barely able to credit its existence. And then, with a delightful and surprising suddenness, the *Unsinkable* began to sink.

A chorus of cheers rang out overhead and Silo looked up to see a head peering over the parapet of St. Paul's, and then another, and then a whole row of them. And then a multitude of hands were casting ropes over the edge, a great mass of them snaking down from the skies and splashing into the water all around. A woman in a purple coat sprang onto the pediment where the statue had once stood. She raised a sword aloft and cried out in a mighty voice: "Death to the Division! Long live the Raiders!"

Fearlessly she leaped out into space and slid down the centermost rope, her belt stuffed with weapons and her dreadlocks flying in the wind.

Orlando, watching from the balcony, fairly swelled with pride. "That's my sister!" he cried. "It's Val!"

It was Valeria the Violent, and behind her followed her Raider band. Suddenly the air around and above them was full of flying figures. The façade of St. Paul's was alive with Raiders, score upon score of them, all rappelling down with their weapons at the ready and the light of battle in their eyes. The collectors on the decks of the *Sea Pig*, the *Unsinkable*, and the *Unbeatable* stared up in amazement, and many took a boot full in the face as the Raiders hurtled down from the skies. And then the fight was on again—but now the odds had changed drastically, for astonishingly the deserted city of the Ancients was populated, and populated with friends.

Silo saw figures appearing in the windows of the buildings all around them, and there was a rattling and a clanking as they hoisted heavy lengths of dripping chain from beneath the waves, blocking off the streets on either side of St. Paul's. Now there could be no escape. The fleet had sailed into the very heart of the Raiders' secret base, and into an inescapable trap. The tables had been turned with astonishing speed, and now the enemy found themselves hopelessly outnumbered. There were, Silo saw, figures climbing on the rooftops, their dark silhouettes forming a long line along Ludgate Hill: hundreds of Raiders wearing horned helmets or bright bandanas. And they were hurling missiles down on the enemy ships. The collectors aboard the *Undefeatable* and the *Unavoidable* were cowering under showers of roof tiles. The *Unwelcome* was under bombardment from bits of balustrade, the *Unstoppable* was struck by a flying chimney, and the *Unvanquished*, bringing up the rear, was particularly unlucky. A group of Raiders had dislodged a tall spire, and when they tipped it over the parapet it flew through the air like a javelin, impaling the vessel neatly amidships.

In a matter of moments the once-proud fleet was reduced to a state of chaos, and the unwilling seamen who had been press-ganged at Parris Port were abandoning their posts. They leaped over the sides and swam to safety and the ships of the fleet were left adrift, colliding with buildings and each other. And now yet more Raiders rained down from the rooftops, rappelling from buildings the length of Ludgate Hill, leaping from windows and swinging from ropes, whooping and cheering as they boarded the Division's fleet and fell upon the hapless collectors.

Dizzy with relief, Silo pulled himself back into the rigging and enjoyed a panoramic view of the battle as it unfolded before him. Valeria the Violent and Black Tom were fighting side by side, sending the enemy reeling before their combined assault. Growler, wild with excitement, leaped from the balcony to aid his master. The valiant dog dropped like a little hairy bomb and sank his teeth deep into the neck of an astonished collector. Ruby and Drusilla followed him into the fray, shinning down a rope onto the deck of the *Sea Pig*. Old Elijah climbed back aboard, only to be felled by a flying marlinspike. Mrs. Morgan, almost beside herself with fury, was screaming orders from the *Unbeatable*'s quarterdeck until a flying frying pan struck her neatly between the shoulder blades and knocked her clean over the side. And she had company, for scores of panic-stricken collectors were jumping overboard and the waters of Ludgate Hill were thick with bobbing Bucket Heads. Raider reinforcements were launching dinghies out of the windows of Ancient buildings and rowing to board the enemy ships, cheered as they went by the Parris Port seamen. The tide of the battle had turned, and Silo suddenly remembered Maximillian. He set off back up to the crow's nest. The confused sounds of battle drifted up from below: the clash of steel on steel and club on head, the howls of the collectors, the cheers of the Raiders, bangs and splashes, the crash of falling spars, the triumphant barking of Growler and, faint but unmistakable, "Huurugh! Huurugh! Huuur-ugh!"

And in the blue sky overhead, Daisy's rainbow faded and vanished as the sun shone forth, flooding the sparkling waters of Ludgate Hill with a golden late-afternoon light.

Silo experienced a rare glow of satisfaction, for it was his gift of the seeing that had set this tangled chain of events into motion. In seeking to warn the Islanders of their impending doom, he had brought about the destruction of the very expedition that had threatened them, and now the Island would remain festering quietly amid the marshes as the wide world passed it by, its inhabitants free to pursue their lives untroubled by the madness of Mrs. Morgan. The battle was won and he had changed the course of history: a small and muddy corner of history admittedly, but he thought—no, he *knew*, and knew for certain—that greater glories lay ahead. For was he not a seer? Suddenly he saw his gift in a new light: as a blessing conferred on a lucky few. He and Maximillian were members of an elite brotherhood. They were young yet and on the small side, but they possessed the power to influence events as yet undreamed of, and Silo vowed that their gift should be used to further the cause of freedom and justice in the Kingdom Isles. He was eager to share his revelation, but when he arrived at the crow's nest he thought better of it, for Maximillian looked very small and woebegone as he crouched in its shattered remains.

"Is it safe now, Silo?" he said.

"Yeah," said Silo. "Everything's fine. And by the way— nice work with the vomit."

17

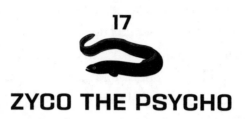

ZYCO THE PSYCHO

The stretch of water in front of St. Paul's was a mass of wreckage, and ships' boats plied to and fro among it. The enemy had surrendered, and what remained of their fleet was scattered the length of Ludgate Hill—or Ludgate Canal, as the Raiders more accurately called it. The Parris Port seamen were watching from the windows of the surrounding buildings as the Raiders rowed hordes of defeated collectors across to the *Undefeatable* and the *Unavoidable*, there to be battened down beneath the hatches until some means could be devised of disposing of them. All now flew the flag of the Raiders, and a small raft, ingeniously constructed from barrels and a hatch cover, was weaving its way among them. It was Silo's handiwork and he stood in the stern, paddle in hand, proudly surveying the battered ships of the enemy fleet and savoring the joys of victory.

Maximillian sat in the bows. "Orlando's waving to us," he said. "I think he wants a lift."

Orlando was standing on the deck of the *Unbeatable*, and he grinned down at them as they approached. His pockets were bulging, he wore a splendid new waistcoat, and a fat gold chain was slung around his neck.

"Just been doing a spot of looting," he explained as Silo brought his raft skimming alongside. "The spoils of victory and all that." He sprang aboard, rocking the raft violently, and managed to catch Maximillian neatly by the collar just before he toppled over the side. "I got you some presents." He handed Silo a telescope and Maximillian a pot of strawberry jam, then observed the scene of chaos all around with a look of benign satisfaction. "Well, that worked out well, didn't it? When you stop and think about it, this is the logical place to have a secret base. Weird we never thought of it really. And apparently there's a pretty good restaurant in Paternoster Dock—it's through that gap in the arch there. I don't know about you, but I'm starving."

Silo paddled the little raft out from under the looming façade of St. Paul's, and as he did so the Raiders' secret base was revealed in all its glory. The surrounding streets were packed with shipping, and Valeria's flagship, the *Beast of Bedlam*, loomed high over a ragtag armada of coasters and fishing boats. The Raider crews were beginning to gather in Paternoster Dock, and when Silo paddled through the broken arch it was easy to see why. It had evidently been a square in Ancient times, and the buildings that surrounded it were flooded to the depth of two or three stories. Wooden pontoons, floating at a convenient level just below the windows, were moored alongside, all bearing a cargo of tables and benches. Canvas awnings and a host of signs advertising inns and restaurants hung overhead: the Octopus, the Raiders' Rest, the Boat and Barrel, the Plaice to Go, and the Plaice to Eat. Scores of small boats were tied up alongside and firelight glowed in the Ancient buildings. Cooks and waiters were at work there, and the hiss and sizzle of frying fish could be heard from within, together with singing, laughter, and the clink of drinking pots.

Silo brought the raft to rest outside the Octopus, where a beautiful and imposing figure stood among a crowd of celebrating mariners. It was Valeria the Violent. She wore her coal-black hair in a magnificent set of dreadlocks, a full-skirted purple coat, and a peaked cap—and a huge smile, for she had just spotted her brother.

"Orlando? My, you've grown! You were just a tiny little snotty thing when I saw you last. I see you're still nicking stuff, though." She prodded his new finery. "Serves me right for leaving you with that thieving scumbag of an uncle! If I'd known you were going to grow up to fight the Division, I'd have taken you with me, but you were such a lazy little slob back then. Anyway"—she engulfed Orlando in a bone-crunching hug—"I'm glad I was wrong."

"It seems that Orlando takes after his valiant sister."

Black Tom and his crew came alongside on a raft. Black Tom was wearing the coat previously occupied by the admiral of the Division's fleet, and although it strained mightily at the seams it sported an impressive quantity of gold braid. He had combed his beard and bristling monobrow and looked almost smart, although Growler, leaning lovingly against his sea boots, let him down a little.

Valeria grinned at him. "Congratulations, Tom!" she said, and then turned to the assembled Raiders. "It looks like we owe Black Tom an apology. To think we reckoned he was too thick to join the Raiders—and then he comes up with a plan like this! How did you manage it?"

All eyes were upon him, but Black Tom remained uncharacteristically silent.

Silo saw that he would have to help him out. "We told him that the Division was desperate to capture Maximillian at all costs," he said, "and straight away he saw his chance to set a trap for them. Obviously it was risky because the *Sea Pig* would be the bait."

Orlando, master of misinformation, took up the story. "But danger means nothing to Black Tom! He set sail the moment the Division's fleet reached the Gutfleet Sound, knowing that with Maximillian aboard they were bound to give chase. He and his crew knew they were running a fearful risk but they didn't hesitate for a minute. The Division's ships were faster, but they trusted to their superior seamanship to stay one step ahead, and of course they knew that they were leading the enemy straight into the heart of Raider territory."

Enlightenment was dawning on Black Tom's face. He uttered a soft "Huurgh! Huurgh!" His scruffy crew looked rather pleased with themselves, and Growler cast his eyes modestly to the ground and began to wag his tail.

"Too right!" said Orlando. "You wouldn't want to visit the Trafalgar household, would you? Not with that thing creeping around behind the sofa. But then I always thought the Ancients were a bunch of nutters."

He pushed aside a plate heaped with empty lobster shells and uttered a sigh of contentment, followed by a modest belch. "Well, I don't know about you, but I'm stuffed. That was what I call a feast."

It seemed that the assembled company had arrived at a similar conclusion, and everyone had reached the stage in the evening where they were comfortably shoving back their stools, picking their teeth, and refilling their drinking pots. There was the occasional splash as Raiders pushed their stools back too far and fell off the edge of their rafts, but that only added to the general merriment.

Valeria took her feet off the tabletop and climbed onto it. A silence fell as she paced up and down, and the only sound was the crunch of oyster shells and plates beneath her sea boots. She was evidently deep in thought. Finally she spoke.

"We've won a great victory here today, and Black Tom and his crew have played a brave part in it. They've proved themselves worthy, and from now on they'll sail with our Raider band!"

Black Tom's face lit up with joy. He beamed like a happy child, albeit a very large one with metal teeth.

"Now that we've captured the enemy fleet we can start making a right nuisance of ourselves," said Valeria. "Black

"That's what we thought," said Valeria. "We keep a look-out up on the dome there." She nodded to the vast bulk of St. Paul's. "We spotted the *Sea Pig* with the fleet hot on her tail, and we guessed you were aiming to draw them into an ambush. We sent scouts up onto the rooftops to track your route—surprised you used Whitefriars, though, on account of the giant squid."

Black Tom seemed affronted. "No tentacled terror of the deep can daunt my valiant crew!"

"Yeah, well, I tend to avoid it myself. Anyway, we guessed you'd make your stand here in the heart of our base, and sure enough you headed straight for the Ludgate Canal. We just had time to sling the chains and get everyone into position for the ambush. But it went off pretty well. How did you know where our base was, though?"

Black Tom winked. "Mum's the word!" he said.

Valeria nodded. "The Code of Silence—fair enough."

Old Elijah sidled up to her, eyeing the buildings around them with fretful eyes. He was none the worse for his ducking—in fact, rather the better, for a bath had been long overdue. "Are you never troubled here," he said, "by the ghosts of the Ancient dead?"

Valeria snorted. "Nah! There aren't any. We spread all those rumors. This place is perfect for a secret base, and we didn't want fishermen or anyone stumbling across it."

Old Elijah seemed almost disappointed. "But there's lights been seen across the water," he persisted, "and the sound of howling."

"That was probably my birthday party," said Valeria. "We

do let our hair down every now and then. And I think to-night should be one of those nights. I vote we hold a victory feast." She turned to the crowded waters of Paternoster Dock. "You lot!" She had the loudest shout that Silo had ever heard. The Raiders froze to attention over their oars, and the very seagulls overhead were silenced in midscreech. "Get a move on! Feast and council of war in St. Paul's—spread the word. And bring some booze!"

"Same old Val," said Orlando.

She took him affectionately by the arm and they walked into the Octopus side by side.

～

The giant squid that lived in Whitefriars Street had had a bad day. Deep down in the watery depths, strange portents had disturbed its slumbers. A ship had passed earlier, a ship that sailed where none should sail, and now other mysterious activities were afoot. The squid could sense some great distur-bance in its watery kingdom; strange echoes and vibrations dimly filtered down to where it lay—mighty, majestic, and multitentacled—in the flooded depths of a basement. Investi-gation was in order. Filled with a dim foreboding, it propelled itself forward with gargantuan grace, out into the seaweed for-est that lay beyond its lair, then glided up toward the world above the sheltering waves. A small boat was advancing toward it, rowed by six sweating collectors, and a bony figure stood in the bows, dressed from head to toe in dripping black. She was urging them on with shrill cries.

"Hurry! Faster! Rebellion is afoot, and the Government must be warned immediately! Put your backs into it! *Hurry*, I said! Why are you stopping?"

For the collectors had paused in their labors and were staring in horror at something that stirred in the dark waters, something big with tentacles.

Mrs. Morgan spun around and regarded the squid with regal contempt. "It's only a squid, you fools!"

She seized a boat hook and hurled it, harpoonlike, at the majestic monster of the deep. It instantly vanished beneath the waves in a churning mass of white water. But not for long. It was only a squid, but it was a very large one, and now it was angry.

The she-creature had invaded its territory. She had insulted and assaulted it, and she would pay dearly for her audacity. It reared up from the depths, eyes blazing with fury, and advanced in a whirlwind of lashing tentacles.

That evening flaming torches burned bright in St. Paul's, throwing dancing reflections across the flooded interior. Beneath the great dome a mass of rafts had been roped together to provide a banqueting area, each one bearing tables, stools, and a selection of cheerful sailors. The Raiders, the seamen who had been press-ganged in Parris Port, and the crew of the *Sea Pig* were all gathered. Vast pillars towered above them, their carved capitals supporting span after span of soaring arches, and the ceiling was so high that it faded into the shadows above. All around the walls the monuments of the

Ancients looked down on the living, and Silo stared about him in awe, for nothing in his life had prepared him for the sight of so much grandeur.

Maximillian followed his gaze. "Do you like it, Silo?"

"Yes. But it's really strange. It makes you wonder what kind of people the Ancients were."

"Well, that one there was a sailor." Black Tom was cheerfully drunk, and he gestured to a nearby statue with his drinking pot. "The one-armed bloke. He's got an anchor alongside him."

And so he had. His single hand rested on the anchor, and below him stood a solemn lady wearing a helmet and what appeared to be a bedspread, her arm around two small stone boys. The plinth upon which he stood was crumbling, but one word remained visible: TRAFALGAR.

"That must be his name," said Ruby. "And I suppose they must be his family."

"And look!" cried Orlando delightedly. "He's got a zoo animal!"

A noble stone beast, a bit like a gigantic cat with a wig on, arose roaring from the dark waters that lapped below the sailor's feet.

"It's true, then! They did keep them as pets!"

"I wonder if that was wise . . . ," said Old Elijah. He looked down to where Growler lay eyeing the legs that surrounded him with an alert, speculative air. "'Tis a lion, and if so large a creature should have some quirk of temperament, a tendency to bite maybe, the consequences could be unpleasant."

Tom can have the pick of the Government's ships to replace the *Sea Pig*, but we need crews for the others. Any volunteers?"

There was a chorus of assent from the Parris Port seamen, and a spokesman rose from among them. He was a bald man, but the wild extravagance of his beard more than made up for the stark nudity of his pate.

"We'll sail with you, and gladly! Parris Port's no place for a sailor these days: the hand of the Government lies heavy there—'tis the third time we've been press-ganged this year. From henceforth we'll sail with you beneath the flag of freedom!"

"So will we!"

It was Ruby. She gestured to the little band of children who sat around her. "Some of us are already experienced sailors"—the Bolton brothers looked smug—"and the rest of us can learn. There is one thing, though. . . ." She hesitated, and Valeria paused in her pacing and looked kindly down upon her.

"Don't be afraid to speak your mind," she said.

"It's just that our parents have been shipped out," said Ruby, "and it would be nice to have them back."

"You and I think alike," said Valeria. "They say that the silver mines in the Northern Isles are worked by those who've been shipped out. Maybe we could mount an attack and free them. Seems to me they're our kind of people. They've all fallen foul of the Government in one way or another—refused to pay taxes or taken arms against the Bucket Heads."

"And we could nick the silver while we're at it," said Orlando.

Valeria frowned at him. "Silver's always handy," she said, "but what we really need is a new secret base. Some of the Division's people are bound to have slipped through our net, and word of what goes on here will soon get back to the Government. This Island they were headed for, though—it's nice and remote, right in the middle of a marsh. I doubt they see government folk from one year's end to the next—could be useful, that. Maybe we could interest them in setting up as a secret trading post where we could take on supplies every now and then. I'd like a word with the headman to see if he's up for it."

Silo thought of Allman Bean and sighed. But at least it meant he could get a lift home. The immediate danger to the Island was past, but he wouldn't rest easy until he had explained to its inhabitants the dangers inherent in digging up power stations.

Valerie continued. "Now we have to decide what to do with all the Bucket Heads we captured today."

"Can't we just kill them?" Drusilla had spoken. A great pile of fish bones lay on the table before her, and her club was propped conveniently nearby.

Valeria shook her head. "It's not the Raider way to kill a man in cold blood. I say we maroon them: dump them on the beach at Normandy."

There was a chorus of approval from the Raiders, but Old Elijah was disappointed.

"Is that all?" he cried. "'Tis too soft on the vermin!"

"You've not met the Normans," said Valerie. "They're the people that live in those parts, and they don't like visitors. They're vicious fighters too," she added approvingly. "We tried to recruit them to our cause, but they speak a strange language that no man can comprehend—caused a lot of misunderstandings, that." She fingered a scar on her forehead. "So Normandy it is, then! The *Unavoidable* and the *Undefeatable* can set sail in the morning.

"And finally!" Valeria raised her drinking pot. "We owe our victory here today to the courage, foresight, and ingenuity of one person. Let's drink to him!"

Silo cast his eyes around the room to find this paragon of virtue and then realized, to his astonishment, that she was looking at him.

"Silo's the one who brought us all together," said Valeria, "and as a result we've dealt a serious blow to the Division. He's a seer, and he could have gone for an easy life as a government-approved one, but when he found out what a bunch of bandits they were, he chose to come home to warn his countrymen and to fight for the cause of freedom. He escaped from the Unicorn Tower, he's kept Maximillian out of the clutches of the Division, and thanks to him Black Tom was able to mount an ambush. So the boy's done good. Only ten years old, but with a price on his head already—nice going! I vote we make him an honorary Raider."

Black Tom lurched to his feet and brandished his drinking pot. "A toast to Silo Zyco! But from henceforth let him be known by the name his enemies call him! We drink to Zyco the Psycho!"

"No, really . . ." Silo hated being called Zyco the Psycho, but his protests went unheeded, for all around, people were raising their drinking pots and toasting him. "To Zyco the Psycho!"

He supposed he would just have to live with it.

18

THE HOMECOMING

The next morning Silo, Orlando, Maximillian, Ruby, and Valeria were standing on the deck of the *Unstoppable*. She had been renamed the *Sea Pig* and was under Black Tom's command, and no longer looked quite the proud ship that had sailed under the flag of the red hand. Growler was meditatively scratching his fleas on the foredeck and Old Elijah, reclining in a hammock, was similarly engaged. The little merpig had been salvaged and now sat proudly on the prow, its snout upraised and its tail lashing as of old.

The waters about them were swarming with sailors and ships and scurrying tenders, for preparations were under way to evacuate the not-so-secret Raiders' base. Shouted commands and the splash of oars arose all around them, and loud over all was a cacophony of hammering and sawing as shipwrights set to work repairing the damage to the Government's old fleet.

The new captains, drawn from the ranks of the Raiders, were busy recruiting crews, and the children who had escaped from the Unicorn Tower were among them. Silo could see their familiar figures at work on neighboring ships—scrubbing decks, coiling ropes, getting entangled in rigging, and, in one case, falling overboard. They had embraced the nautical life with a will, but it might take them a little while to get the hang of it.

The *Unavoidable* and the *Undefeatable* had just set sail, following the old river down to the open sea and Normandy, there to dispose of their unwanted cargo. Silo dearly hoped that Elgarth would be part of it, but he had his doubts. Elgarth seemed to have a gift for getting others into trouble while sliding out of it himself, and Silo had seen no sign of either him or Rankly since the gratifying incident with the vomit. It would have been easy enough for them to slip away amid the chaos of battle, and Sentral Lundun provided hiding places aplenty. His gloomy thoughts were broken by a mighty roar from Black Tom: "Cast off fore and aft! Man the rigging!"

Tom was eager to try out his new ship and had insisted on taking them all to the Island, although as he steered an erratic course through a mass of shipping Silo rather wished that Valeria were at the helm.

"The *Sea Pig* lives to fight again!" cried Black Tom. "Henceforth government folk will tremble when they see her sails on the horizon!"

Innkeepers too might fear her approach, but Silo kept his thoughts to himself.

Later that day the *Sea Pig* was sailing before a fair wind. The long low line of the marsh was visible on their starboard bow and Silo eyed it through his new telescope, prey to strange and mixed emotions. He remembered the distant dreams he had nursed when the Island was his home—of working for the Government and being acknowledged as a great seer. If he ever returned, it was to have been in glory, rich and respected. In his fantasies the Islanders had been deeply apologetic for ever having doubted his worth, and for never having spotted greatness when it walked among them. But the fates had decreed otherwise, and instead he was back after only a few months, a hunted fugitive with a price on his head. He scowled darkly at the featureless coastline, and as he did so his reverie was broken by a mournful lowing: *Moooo-OOH! Moooo-OOH! Moooo-OOH!* The horn on the lookout tower was sounding to signal their approach, and at its familiar note Silo raised his telescope and scanned the distant contours of his old home.

But it was not as he remembered it. The Island had changed, and strangely. The little alleys that ran down to the water had been blocked off with mud walls that bristled with spikes, and behind them he could see rows of figures clutching eel spears. Archers stood on the roof of the meeting hall with their bows at the ready, and a small crowd was standing atop the lookout tower. Then a hostile voice came drifting across the water: "Bog off, gitfaces!"

Orlando grinned. "Glad to be home, Silo?" he said.

"Looks like they've fortified the place," said Black Tom.

"Yeah," said Valeria approvingly. "Seems like they've been expecting company, and planning to put up a fight."

Then an excited voice rang out from the lookout. "It's Silo!" It was Ben Mudford, and evidently his eyesight was as sharp as ever. "It's all right, it's Silo—he's come home!"

Silo ran his telescope over the waiting crowd. Ben was waving enthusiastically, so too were Lula and Lily, but he saw no signs of universal joy. The majority of the Islanders were muttering to one another, and Silo could guess exactly what about: bad luck, unnatural powers, thieving Zycos, ill-gotten Eel Rights, and all the usual. As the stretch of water between him and his old home grew narrower, he found his mood growing blacker by the minute and wished he had never come. But it was too late now. It was high tide and Black Tom was able to bring the *Sea Pig* right up alongside the quay, striking it with a thud that shook it to its foundations, and a moment later Ben was pushing through the crowd to greet them.

"Hello, Silo! Hello, Silo's friends! You're very welcome! It's been a long time since we had a ship in harbor. Why, not since . . ."

He paused, his brow creased in thought, but Silo remembered the Chronicles by heart and was able to help him out.

"Twenty-fifth of November 302. The *Minotaur* dropped by. There was a big fight and Clive Zyco impaled the captain with an eel spear."

"Yeah, well, we come in peace." Valeria stepped ashore

and the Islanders shrank back a little, staring at her in wonder. She cut a striking figure among the muddy, sack-wearing masses: fierce, as exotic as a unicorn, and almost impossibly clean.

"We brought you some presents," she said. And so she had—a random collection of items that had been found floating in Ludgate Canal: a barrel of tea, six cases of corned beef, and Mrs. Morgan's luggage. "And I'd like to talk to your headman. Any chance of a meeting?"

"Of course!" Ben beamed. "Meeting in the big hall, everyone!"

He led the way, Valeria at his side and the Islanders streaming up the alley behind them, whispering and muttering among themselves. Silo felt their eyes upon him, but when he returned their gaze they turned hastily away. They were deliberately avoiding him, that much was obvious, and he dropped scowling to the back of the crowd. But when he reached the top of the alley and the Chronicle Keeper's hut he paused. It had been the scene of the happiest times he could remember on the Island, his home after Ryker had taken him under his wing, but even so he had still been pretty miserable. It had been a mistake to come back, he realized. It brought back a flood of unhappy memories. The Islanders distrusted him as much as ever, and as for his warning about the Division, Valeria could have delivered that just as easily. As he stood brooding, Lily and Lula dashed out of the crowd that was shoving its way into the meeting hall.

"Welcome back, Silo!" they chorused.

"Aren't you going to the meeting?" said Lily.

"No."

"Come and help me make an entry in the Chronicles, then," she said. "I want to record . . ."

". . . all your adventures in the Uplands," said Lula. "And I'll go to the meeting . . ."

". . . so we can report that too," said Lily.

Lula scurried up the steps of the meeting hall.

"We decided to share the Chronicle keeping," said Lily. "That way we can cope if two exciting things happen at once."

"Does that happen often?" asked Silo sarcastically, staring back at the bleak expanse of marsh.

"No! This is the very first time! Come in—we changed the hut about a bit."

It was almost unrecognizable: clean, neatly furnished, and really rather cozy.

"Here . . ." Silo produced a handsome leather-bound volume from beneath his jacket and handed it to Lily. It was the ship's log of the *Unwelcome* and still had many blank pages left. Encouraged by Orlando's example, he too had done a spot of looting.

"Oh thanks, Silo! This is brilliant! We're on the very last page of the old Chronicle—there's so much happened recently!"

"Like what?"

"Well, first the letters came, from something called the State Archaeological Division, and they were full of really, really mad stuff—they said the Island wasn't an island, it was an Ancient power thing. Every family got one, and they said they owned the place—everyone's houses and Eel Rights and everything—and they were going to dig it all up. Well, Allman Bean said we should let them because they were government people, but Mum and Dad and loads of others said they could go to hell. So we held an emergency meeting, and Ben Mudford was voted in as new headman. Even some of the Beans voted for him! Ben's been brilliant. He said we should fight the Division—that's why we fortified the Island. We expect them any day now, but it's a bit of a worry because there aren't that many of us. That woman you came with, though—what lovely clothes she has!—she's a Raider, isn't she? Do you think she'll help us?"

"She already did," said Silo. "Look, why don't you go to the meeting? We'll talk later."

Silo made his way to the top of the lookout tower. A solitary figure stood on the quay, shaking its fist at the dark waters below. Mrs. Mudford was still pursuing her lonely war against mudfish, but otherwise the narrow alleyways of the Island were deserted; nothing stirred in the glittering network of creeks, for all were in the meeting hall, and the great marsh extended flat and featureless under a dull sky. Silo stared out over the familiar landscape with unseeing eyes: he was lost in a tangle of thoughts, and dark and dismal ones at that. He turned his face to the sea as his mother had done so long ago, and as he did so he was swept by a sense of almost unbearable sadness and longing. His mother was long dead, and so was Ryker, and with them had died the bonds of affection that tied him to the Island. He had no place here now, or anywhere else for that matter. Orlando had found his long-lost sister, and perhaps Ruby and the others would soon be reunited with their parents. They would have homes again, and families, but it seemed that he was fated never to share their good fortune. He thought longingly of his father, and then of the unimaginable expanse of lands and seas that lay beyond the Kingdom Isles, and he doubted his chances of ever finding him in so wide a world—if he was even alive. Then something small and bullet-headed bumped against him. It was Maximillian.

"Don't worry, Silo," he said. "He looks very happy."

"Who?"

"Your dad—at least, I think he's your dad. He looks like you—a little man with mad blue eyes."

"You've had a seeing?" Silo gripped Maximillian by the shoulders. "Tell me! Where was he?"

"I don't know. A great flat plain all covered in grass. He's galloping across it on a horse, and thousands and thousands of hairy brown animals are thundering along after him."

"What kind of animals?"

"A bit like cows, only very big and fierce."

"So he's in danger?"

"I don't think so. He's singing a song about a goat."

"And then what happened?"

"I saw a man stealing gardening tools, but that was a different seeing."

"The one about my father, though—when did it happen? In the past? In the future? When?"

"Right now, I think," said Maximillian.

Silo stared wildly to the west, where lay the legendary Us of Ay. And his father. He was out there; he and his horse and a herd of thundering zoo cows. Hope flamed in Silo's heart. He was alive, then; he swore to himself there and then that he would one day find him, however long or difficult the quest might be.

"There's Valeria and that Ben man," said Maximillian.

Silo looked down, his mind in turmoil. Valeria and Ben were clattering down the steps of the meeting hut. The meeting was at an end, and the Islanders came bursting out behind them, chattering and shouting and laughing. The mood seemed euphoric. And friendly, for someone looked up and cried: "There's Silo!" and suddenly he was looking down into a sea of smiling upturned faces. People were waving to him, and there were shouts of "Welcome home!" and Ben was calling to him: "Come down, Silo! Valeria's told us all about the fleet being defeated—seems like a celebration's in order."

The crowd was streaming down the alley to congregate on the quay. Silo descended from the lookout tower, dazed at the strange turn events had taken, and pondering over why his father kept company with cows. But such thoughts would have to wait, for Mudfords and Pattles and even Beans were approaching to shake him by the hand, slap him on the back, and—to his intense annoyance—pat him on the head. The crew of the *Sea Pig* was carrying barrels and trunks ashore, and Silo was relieved that Valeria chose this moment to present the gifts. Corned beef was a novelty on the Island and every-one gathered around to try it; he was thankful that their attention had turned to preserved meat products, for popularity was new to him and he wasn't sure he liked it. It seemed that his whole world had turned upside down in a matter of minutes and he sidled gratefully up to Orlando, a tried and trusted friend who could be relied on not to change—although given his thieving propensities this was perhaps a pity.

Orlando was having an animated conversation with Myles Pattle, father to Lily and Lula.

"Welcome home, Silo!" said Myles. He reached out to pat Silo on the head but decided against it when Silo fixed him with his most powerful stare. "Orlando's been telling me about goatball," he went on. "I wish we had a team! It's a pity we don't keep goats."

Silo remembered the strange picture he had found among the Ancient documents.

"The Ancients played another game as well—one without goats. It's a bit similar but they used a ball instead. They had upright nets at either end of the field and had to kick it into them."

"Maybe we should give it a try," said Myles. "We've got a ball, and Great Goose Flat is big enough for a field. What are the rules?"

"You can't use clubs," said Silo, "but apart from that I'm not sure."

"Well, I dare say we can work them out," said Myles. "What's it called?"

Silo hazarded a wild guess. "Football."

"Anyone for football?" shouted Myles.

Ruby and Drusilla sprang ashore from the *Sea Pig*, followed by a random assortment of Raiders, and within minutes a mixed crew of Mudfords and Pattles were climbing aboard the big raft, ready to ferry the teams over to Great Goose Flat.

The Beans were otherwise occupied. A group of them were rooting through Mrs. Morgan's luggage. It contained a quantity of long black dresses and they were proving to be popular items, especially among the menfolk.

"Sacks with sleeves!" cried Allman's younger brother, Arnott. "How smart is that?"

Silo was about to tell them that on Mainland only women wore dresses, but then he saw his old enemy Boris Bean trying one on and decided against it. He never had liked the Beans.

Ben appeared at his side. "Glad to be home, Silo?" he said.

Silo hadn't made up his mind yet, so he changed the subject.

"Lily told me you're the headman now. Congratulations."

"Yeah—who'd've thought it?" said Ben, his face brightening. "But there's loads of folk as voted for me. It's a real honor, and I mean to make the Island a better place while I'm in charge. We're on the lookout for a new schoolteacher, and we're thinking of putting a seagoing fishing fleet together so we won't be so reliant on eels. And we're making a new harbor to attract a bit of shipping too. Funny, Valeria and Black Tom turning up when they did—they say they and their friends will put in here from time to time, and hopefully other ships will follow. Seems to me we've been cut off for too long. We could do with a bit of a shake-up—new faces and new ideas and so on. Some of the Beans have moaned a bit, but most folk are agreeable to the idea."

Here was a radical change of direction for the Islanders, one that Silo thoroughly approved of. "I think you'll be a brilliant headman," he said.

"It's good of you to say so," said Ben. He looked at Silo, his face full of concern. "I hope you weren't too upset by the poor reception when you arrived, but you know how it is—all those old stories about bad luck and dark powers and so on. But I reckon the record's been put straight now. We know now how much we owe to you and your gift of the seeing. You've your friend Orlando to thank for that."

Silo was struck by sudden misgivings. "What did he say exactly?"

"Why, he told us about your seeing, and how you planned your escape from the Unicorn Tower, and how you rallied your fellow captives. He repeated your speech almost word for word—stirring stuff, that! And he told us about your fighting off the watchman to steal a raft, and your smart plan to recruit the Raiders and set a trap for the fleet. He said you played a brave part in the battle of Ludgate Canal too; told us about you climbing the mast of the *Unsinkable*, arrows whizzing all around you, and setting fire to their flag. It's a wild life you've been leading, Silo—I only wish I'd had adventures like that!"

So did Silo. Indignantly he looked around for Orlando, only to see him drifting across Goose Creek on the big raft. When Silo caught his eye, Orlando grinned and gave him a conspiratorial wink. Truly the boy was incorrigible, and when Silo spoke, his words were a masterpiece of understatement. "Orlando exaggerates a bit sometimes," he said.

And then he related his version of events since he left the Island: the true, chaotic version of their escape and flight, capped with their extraordinary stroke of luck in stumbling upon the Raiders' secret base.

When he had finished Ben was silent for a while, then said: "Seems like your friend talked things up a touch, but the fact is, you had a seeing and you came back to warn us. Not everyone would've done that, not after the way you were treated by some folk here. And you did escape from the Unicorn Tower, and you did find the Raiders and lead the fleet into a trap. You say that things weren't planned out that way, and that luck was on your side—so what? It's still down to you that the Division were defeated—and just as well. If they'd come here, we'd've fought them, but we'd not have beaten them. So you did save the Island, Silo, and I think we'll stick with Orlando's version. It's a fine story for one thing, and besides, most folk here have thought the worst of you for way too long. It seems only fair they should think the best of you for a change. And now"—he smiled down at Silo—"what do you say to watching a bit of football?"

The game on Great Goose Flat was getting along splendidly—the Islanders versus the Sea Pigs. The latter wore horned helmets, so the two teams were easy to distinguish, and a cheering crowd lined the sides of the pitch, urging on their players. A large fishing net supported by spars stood at each end, each manned by a goalkeeper—Myles Pattle and Ruby. Silo and Ben arrived just in time to see Drusilla kicking Lula high into the air, only to be sternly admonished by the referee.

A breathless Orlando hurled himself down at their feet. "I'm spent!" he said. "I've just been substituted. Good game, though, and I think we've sorted the rules. You can't kick other players, only the ball. You can't punch them either, or gore them if you're wearing a horned helmet—might have to ban horned helmets, actually. We've punctured two balls already."

As Silo watched, little Benjamin Bean made a weaving run, the ball seemingly glued to his feet, then passed it to Mrs. Mudford, who, with an agility surprising for her age, chipped it neatly into the net just beyond Ruby's clutching fingertips. Ruby spread her arms in incredulous appeal, and there were cheers from the Islanders and a chorus of boos and cries of "Offside! Are you blind, ref?" from the away support.

Silo surveyed the scene proudly. It seemed that football was a success.

As evening fell Silo was to be found on the Causeway, looking toward the Uplands as he had last done on that fateful April morning. He had seen and learned much since then; already it seemed like a lifetime away. The sea sighed to his left and the marsh festered to his right, and above him the ragged clouds were tinged gold with the first rays of the setting sun. Flocks of wading birds wheeled all about him, and skeins of honking geese were flying home to their evening quarters on Great Goose Flat.

Maximillian was at his side. "It's nice here, Silo. Are you going to stay?"

Silo shook his head. "I'll sail with the Raiders."

"But why?"

Silo had many reasons. He wanted the Island and all the other little places like it to be safe from the greed of the Government. He wanted vengeance on the State Archaeological Division. He wanted Elgarth to find that he was fighting on the losing side. But most of all he wanted his father to be proud of him. He would meet him one day, of that he was certain, and when he did he needed to give a good account of himself. But to Maximillian he said: "I have to try to restore a just government to the Kingdom Isles. It was my mother's dying wish." He drew himself up to his full height. "It's my destiny. I'm the last of the Zycos."

"No you're not," said Maximillian. "You're going to have eleven children."

"Eleven!" Silo was appalled. "Look, just don't tell me stuff like that. If you have any seeings about me, things that happen way in the future, I don't want to know, OK?"

"Not even about the rampaging warthog?"

"Especially not about the rampaging warthog!"

Maximillian was hurt. "I won't if it makes you cross."

—·—

A small fishing boat was making its way to Parris Port. It contained a cargo of sprats, four fishermen, an evil-smelling dog, Rankly, and Elgarth. The latter two looked rather the worse for wear and were much decorated with lumps and bruises. The last few days had been utterly vile, and Elgarth was thinking longingly of the food, bed, bath, and medical services that awaited them in harbor. His recollections of the Battle of Lundun were distressingly vague: Silo fleeing up the mast, a joyful certainty of victory, and then a sudden, terrifying flight, followed by icy water and oblivion. He had awoken hours later with a splitting headache, only to find himself adrift beneath the stars in a small open boat. He had the faithful Rankly to thank for his escape, but he had awoken feeling anything but grateful, and things had gone steeply downhill from there. Navigating their way out of the Ancient city had been a nightmare. There had been strange currents and whirlpools, an unpleasant interlude with a walrus, and they had run aground on something called a DIY superstore.

But now at last they were safe. They had hailed the fishing boat in the Gutfleet Sound. The fishermen had been unwilling to take them on board at first, fearing that they were the ghosts of the Ancient dead, and it had taken all of Elgarth's persuasive powers, together with the promise of a large sum of money, to overcome their superstitious fears. But sanctuary was in sight now, and Elgarth looked longingly at the clustered buildings of Parris Port. He had gone off seafaring in a big way, and everything to do with ships and the sea. And dry land looked especially attractive today: the streets were bustling, colored flags were strung around the harbor, and a band was playing on the quay.

"What's all that in aid of?" he asked one of the fishermen.

"I expect the governor's arrived. They were making an almighty fuss about it when we left. He's a very important bloke, they say, and he's come in person to welcome the fleet home."

Elgarth was struck by a truly dreadful thought. "What's he called?" he asked.

"Governor Early."

Elgarth was overcome with horror. He remembered the optimistic letter he had tossed off before he left Parris Port, but never in his wildest dreams had he thought it would produce such awful consequences.

Rapidly he took stock of the situation, and his conclusions were as grim as could be. Acting on information provided by him, Elgarth Early, the Government's fleet had followed the *Sea Pig* into a well-planned and ruthlessly efficient ambush, and a catastrophic defeat had ensued. Seven ships and their attendant crews had set sail, together with a whole army of collectors, but of that great armada only he and Rankly had arrived back safely, and in a stinking fishing boat at that. The whole fiasco was going to take a huge amount of explaining, and it was he who was to be the bearer of the calamitous news. He thought of his father's volatile and violent temperament and his heart quailed within him. Already he could see his hulking figure among the crowds, for his father was a conspicuous man, big in both size and personality. A small crowd of dignitaries observed him from a safe distance as he strode impatiently up and down the quay.

Rankly stated the obvious. "Looks like your dad's in one of his moods."

Elgarth shuddered. He and Silo shared two things—a mutual hatred and the gift of the seeing—but there the resemblance ended. Silo longed above all things to see his father; Elgarth, at that moment in time, would have given almost anything to see his magically transported to some place far, far distant—to the Us of Ay or beyond.

The *Sea Pig* was making ready to sail. The preparations to evacuate the secret base would be almost complete by now, and Valeria was eager to rejoin her fleet. Silo was leaving the Island again, and the contrast between this and his last departure was overwhelming. This time the entire population had come to see him off, and he looked across at a sea of smiling faces. Except one. Boris Bean was scowling at him from the fringes of the crowd, and Silo felt perversely cheered. Old Elijah was among the well-wishers on the quay, for Black Tom had finally realized his wish and gotten rid of his malodorous shipmate. Ben had persuaded him to stay on at the Island as the new schoolteacher. He was, as he had told them back on the Gutfleet Sound, an old, old man who'd seen and heard much, and learned many strange things in his long years on Earth. Now he could impart these strange things to a new generation and also, by force of negative example, teach them the importance of good personal hygiene.

Ruby was unfurling the sails up aloft, and she swung through the rigging with the easy grace of a gibbon. She seemed to have taken naturally to the seafaring life. Orlando, who had not, lay dozing in a hammock on the foredeck amid the bustle of departure.

Ben scooped up a wandering Maximillian and lifted him aboard the *Sea Pig*. "Yours, I believe." He smiled at Silo. "Well, I wish you a safe journey. I hope things go well for you—and remember: the Island will always be your home. There's always a welcome waiting for you here."

Now Black Tom stood ready at the helm and his crew was casting off fore and aft. The *Sea Pig* was drifting out into Goose Creek, turning with the tide.

"Good-bye, Silo!" cried the Islanders. "Good luck!"

They were waving to him, and then suddenly they were singing to him:

Silo Zyco is a seer, the Island is his home!
He left it for adventure, the Kingdom Isles to roam!
Don't make of him an enemy, for though he's only young
He'll pay you back with an attack that buries you in—

Silo was astonished. "How do they know that song?"

Orlando stirred in his hammock and grinned at him. "It seems to have caught on—Lily and Lula said some eel traders from the Uplands were singing it. You're getting to be quite famous, you know."

And Silo had a sudden vision. A little dark-haired man was pausing midstride in the streets of a sunlit seaport, standing stock-still for a moment, his ears straining to catch the words of a distant song—and then he smiled and his eyes, as blue and intense as Silo's own, flashed with pride. The thought of it made Silo almost dizzy with joy.

His hair is black, he wears a sack, some say he is a psycho,
But if you care for freedom, give three cheers for Silo Zyco!

And the Islanders did—three cheers so loud that they startled the geese into flight, sending them wheeling and honking over the marsh with a great clamor of wings. Silo smiled a rare smile as he waved farewell, watching as the *Sea Pig's* shimmering wake lengthened between him and his childhood home. He would return someday, that much he knew, but when and in what circumstances he could not say. Seer he might be, but the seeing was, as ever, a mysterious and imperfect gift.

Beside him, Maximillian heaved a great sigh. "I hate sailing, Silo. I think I might be sick."

"No!" Silo desperately cast around for something that might take Maximillian's mind off his stomach. "Tell me about the rampaging warthog."

Thus did he sail forth to fulfill his destiny: Silo Zyco, also known as Zyco the Psycho, son of Zenda, son of Aquinus the Accursed, Seer, Sole Survivor, Coffee-Maker, Raft-Taker, Sewage-Shaker, Enemy of Elgarth, Victor by Vomit, Beater of Bucket Heads, and the last of the Zycos—for the time being, at least.

ABOUT THE AUTHOR

Veronica Peyton was raised in an obscure British village and moved to London as soon as was possible. She was a graphic designer for a while, then taught English in a variety of unglamorous foreign locations, mostly in Asia. She turned to writing after a five-year stint in Holloway Prison (as a librarian, not an inmate).